The

CONFUSION

of LANGUAGES

The

CONFUSION

of LANGUAGES

SIOBHAN FALLON

G. P. PUTNAM'S SONS

NEW YORK

G. P. Putnam's Sons
Publishers Since 1838
An imprint of Penguin Random House LLC
375 Hudson Street
New York, New York 10014

Copyright © 2017 by Siobhan Fallon

The Woman in Islam courtesy of Dr. Muhammad Ali Alkhuli, Dar Alfalah
Publishing, P.O. Box 818, Swaileh 11910, Jordan

Library of Congress Cataloging-in-Publication Data

Names: Fallon, Siobhan, author.
Title: The confusion of languages / Siobhan Fallon.
Description: New York : G. P. Putnam's Sons [2017]
Identifiers: LCCN 2016043160 (print) | LCCN 2016050163 (ebook) |
ISBN 9780399158926 (hardback) | ISBN 9780735215566 (Ebook)
Subjects: | BISAC: FICTION / Contemporary Women. | FICTION / Literary. |
FICTION / Family Life.
Classification: LCC PS3606.A45 C66 2017 (print) |
LCC PS3606.A45 (ebook) |
DDC 813/.6—dc23
LC record available at https://lccn.loc.gov/2016043160
p.   cm.

Printed in the United States of America
1   3   5   7   9   10   8   6   4   2

BOOK DESIGN BY AMANDA DEWEY

To Maeve & Evelyn,
You are my shining hope.

Injustice and desperation make men
combustible, like dry wood

From the poem "What Is to Give Light"
by Yahia Lababidi

PART
ONE

May 13, 2011

3:00 P.M.

※

We are close, so close, to Margaret's apartment, and I feel myself sink deeper into the passenger seat, relieved that I have succeeded in my small mission of getting Margaret out of her home, if only for a few hours. The day is a success. Sure, I had to let her drive, something I usually avoid. Margaret is always too nervous, too chatty, looking around at the pedestrians, forgetting to put on her signal, stomping on the brakes too late. But today I actually managed to snap her out of her sadness. I have done everything a good friend should.

It's not until we reach the intersection at Horreyya and Hashimeyeen that I realize my mistake. I've misjudged the time, something I never do. Friday prayers have already let out. We'd stopped by the ceramics house to pick up a box of pottery I'd ordered and Margaret, being Margaret, sat down for too long with the *hijab*-ed women at their worktable, letting them touch Mather, pinching his cheeks and thighs, rubbing silica dust all over his tender baby skin. Now the intersection ahead is congested, chaotic. I see men strolling from the mosques, climbing into the cars they triple-parked along the main road.

I sit up straight, the seat belt pressing against my chest.

The traffic light turns yellow as we approach and cars alongside us speed by. Margaret could step on the gas and easily make the light but both of us see a man on the sidewalk, waving his entire arm in the air.

"Just go—" I urge, but Margaret shakes her head, slowing the car, the corner of her mouth turning up.

"It's uncanny how he always sees me." She says something like this every single time and I usually reply, *The man's livelihood depends on his ability to spot the softhearted suckers.* But today I am silent. Mather shouts from his car seat but she ignores him too.

Her window is down before we've come to a complete stop. The man reaches into the cluster of dented white buckets at his corner-side stand, pulls free a few dripping-wet bouquets, then dodges traffic until he's at Margaret's side.

He leans through the window, wearing a red and white checked *kaffiyeh* around his throat. Margaret's wallet is on her lap, ready.

"Hello, baby!" the man shouts at Mather, avoiding looking at both of us women with our loose hair and bared elbows. His flowers are spread perfectly across his arm, inches from the very face he will not peer into. The car fills with the scent of crushed rose petals, exhaust, and his sweat, a faint mix of onions and soil. I do not point out that most of his offerings are wilted, tinged with brown. I notice the cluster of pristine white blossoms at the same time Margaret does, fragile, lacy blooms on very green stems, and she nods toward them, holding up her money. It takes only seconds.

As he passes the chosen bouquet to Margaret through the window, Mather yells again from the backseat, wanting something; that child is always wanting something. The man turns to the baby but he doesn't stop there; he lifts his face and stares behind our car, his brown eyes widening with fear as he stumbles backward. Before I can look around, there is a ripping scream of brakes and our car leaps forward with a thud of crushed metal. Our heads rock on our spines and there are flowers in flight across the dashboard, white blossoms spread open like tiny, reaching hands.

May 13, 2011

3:33 P.M.

M argaret, this happens all the time." We stand outside her apartment, her baby on my hip. I know I am too chipper for the occasion, that I am still on uncertain ground, but I am glad to be here. It's been weeks since she's invited me in, weeks since I have held her child close. I continue directing words at her as she digs through her massive handbag: "You haven't really lived in the Middle East until you've been in a car accident." She glances up and I see my attempt at humor has failed. Her blue eyes are so red she looks like a white lab mouse, worn and wary from too many experiments. Her gaze is naked, injured, disturbing.

"I should go to the police station with you," I say. "It'll be easier to find with the two of us."

She shakes her head, lifting a fist of keys from her purse; loose Cheerios fall out on the floor. "No, the baby's hungry, he needs a nap." She watches her son for a moment before training those red eyes back on me. "I mean, if you don't mind, I'd rather you stay here with him."

I nod. Mather reaches for the large black garbage bag slumped at the side of the welcome mat and I swing him away, press a kiss on his sweaty little head. I want to ask Margaret why no one has cleared her trash away—that lazy *boab* of hers is always hovering about trying to get a glimpse down her T-shirts; where is he when she needs him?—but I notice her hands are shaking so badly she can't get the key in the lock. I give her the baby, remove the key from her grip.

"I've got it," I say as I twist the lock and then push the apartment door open.

"Thanks, Cass." She doesn't seem grateful. Instead she's even more crestfallen, as if I've taken something from her I shouldn't have. The ability to open her door? I'm confused and I step aside to let her scurry past into the blacked-out foyer. I watch her flick a few lights on. She usually keeps the windows wide and full of sun. It's disorienting to leave the afternoon behind us and face something so dark, all the shades drawn. Her apartment also smells funny, not quite rank, but stale, used diapers and food that has sat out too long. I hesitate in the doorway, then kick off my shoes and follow her.

"Margaret, you should print out directions to the police station—it's a mess down there," I say as she heads into the master bedroom. She closes the door behind her, a solid click, a sudden *Do not enter* between us. I stop and wait for her to emerge, wait for her to shout to me, wait for anything, but there is only silence. Usually Margaret breast-feeds Mather wherever the inclination takes her, never bothering to cover up or hide the act, sitting on the couch, at the kitchen table, on the linoleum floor with her knees up and the baby on her thighs, kicking his feet. Not today.

After a moment, I head toward the kitchen, turning on more lights as I go.

The sink is a disaster, withered tea bags left curled around spoons, baby bowls caked with dried oatmeal and smears of yogurt. I begin to tidy up, stacking the dishes and peeling balled-up dishtowels from the countertops. We should have gone directly to the police station the way we were supposed to. The embassy fixer had come out to the scene of the accident, explained Margaret would need to file a report at the main headquarters in downtown Amman, sign a few forms. He even offered to lead us there in his embassy vehicle and act as a translator.

"Yes," I'd agreed. "It won't take long."

"And the guilt fee is not so expensive," the guard had said amicably. "Perhaps it is less than fifteen American dollars."

That's when Margaret lost it. She said she was taking her baby home, she was *innocent, damn it, innocent! Didn't he know what that meant? How could the price matter?* The man stood there, baffled beneath his mustache.

Though I shouldn't have been surprised. Margaret never actually does what she's *supposed* to do here in Jordan, does she? Why, we could have already been finishing up now, this could have already been transformed into nothing more than an anecdote to tell at the next cocktail party. Another expat found guilty in a fender bender, it's the cross we all bear, trial by traffic accident. But no, Margaret never listens. Margaret never takes my advice or anyone else's, Margaret has to do everything her own way.

I slam a dirty-rimmed coffee cup into the sink. There are few dishwashers, even in the ritzy, newer neighborhoods like this near the US embassy. I don't feel like rolling up my sleeves and washing dishes for her today. When she comes out from behind her closed door, disobedient Margaret can do it herself.

I dry my hands and walk into the living room. The lamps throw off a brittle light. It's late afternoon but might as well be midnight. I go to the window, feel around behind the curtain for the cord. There's not much that Jordan does better than America, but it does do blackout. The shutters here are built right into the window, between two layers of glass, and when you close them you have effectively put up a wall between you and the outside world. I tug the shutters open and sun spills in.

"Oh, wait, don't!" Margaret cries from behind me. I turn. She stands with her hands up, fingers spread, covering her face. I can see in the sunlight how blotchy her skin is. She must have gone into that bedroom with the baby and continued to cry; she must not have wanted me to see. Her white blouse is askew on her collarbones, her blond, nearly translucent hair dangling around her face. Her lips are so chapped I can see peeling bits glow in the light.

She looks awful.

Everything I have been warning her about, everything she has ignored, all of it is unfolding just the way I knew it would.

"Margaret," I start softly, trying to stop the words *I told you so* from rising to the surface of my throat.

She comes toward me quickly, unsteady on her feet, almost falling. She catches herself on the wall with her right hand and straightens. Then she tugs on the cord, narrows the shutters, angling them in a way that lets in light but doesn't allow anyone on the outside to see in.

"Is that all right?" she asks, apology in her voice.

I stare. Does she not want people to know she is home? Does she have a Peeping Tom she's never mentioned? "Why keep them down?"

"I need to thank you, Cassie," she says, evasive. "Really, really thank you." She touches the glass of the window with her fingertips, then faces me. "I've been meaning to for so long. Thank you. You've been the only person I could depend on."

These are the very words I've been waiting to hear since January.

"Don't be silly," I say, embarrassed. It's as if she's read my mind and realized exactly how to soothe me. "That's what friends are for." She moves closer and I lift my hands and begin to straighten her shirt, but really I want to make sure we are reconciled. As an answer, she places her palms on top of my fingers, trapping them on her shoulders. Her bones feel light and sharp.

I look into her swollen eyes. "It's going to be fine, Margaret."

"Is it?" She slides her hands down and slips away from my grip. "Are you sure you don't mind watching Mather?"

"No problem." Five minutes ago I wanted to smash her dishes. Now, after a simple show of gratitude, I'd do anything for her. This is a lesson my husband, Dan, ought to learn.

"I put the baby in his crib. He'll nap for an hour or so. I left my bag in the bedroom in case you want to take him for a walk." Her eyes blink around the room as if there is something she's forgotten and she wants to retrieve it.

I hesitate. "I bet the police station is open all night. We could let the baby sleep and then all go together. I've been there before. They found me guilty too, Margaret. I know I told you the story, how I was waiting for someone to pull out of a parking space, had my blinker on, and this taxi just plowed into me. The worst part was that I was eating an ice-cream cone. I always thought that was the reason I was found guilty. How could anyone take me seriously with vanilla Häagen-Dazs down the front of my shirt?"

She shakes her head vaguely, not listening to a word. "If I leave now I might make it back before Mather wakes up."

"Then just get in and get out. No more arguing. Sign the paperwork, pay the money, the embassy will figure it all out next week."

She looks into my eyes. "Tell me again it'll be OK."

"It'll be OK," I repeat. "Call me if you have any trouble."

She nods, tucks her keys carefully into the canvas purse she uses as a wallet. She looks odd without the baby in one arm and her overflowing diaper bag in the other, like she has been stripped of half herself. I can see flecks of salt dried into her lashes.

"Margaret?"

Her head snaps up and her eyes widen at my voice. "Cass, if Crick calls, don't tell him about the accident, OK?"

I feel myself blush. So we might be reconciled, but she still doesn't entirely trust me. "All right."

"And if Saleh knocks, don't let him in."

"What are you talking about? Why would he even come to your door?"

She pulls her hair behind her ears and glances up at the mural on her living room ceiling. When she speaks, I'm not sure if she is talking to me or to the angels painted there. "Please tell Mather I'll be home soon."

"You know what, let's do this tomorrow—" I say, moving toward her, but she turns and walks out the door without another word.

It's only after I've heard the elevator ding shut in the hallway that I realize I forgot to ask if she printed directions.

May 13, 2011

4:00 P.M.

I fasten every lock on Margaret's front door. She has left me feeling unsettled. I check my phone to make sure I haven't missed any embassy alert texts. Nothing. Jordan is quiet today. The only unread messages I have on my phone are from Dan, and I'm not ready to talk to him yet.

I return to the living room, stand in the center, try to recapture the pleasure I felt earlier about being welcome here again. This particular room is my favorite. The husbands have been gone for six weeks but this space is still Crick's and only Crick's. His bottles of hard-to-find scotch on the bar, his framed vintage maps on the walls, his books about Middle Eastern history and diplomacy on the bookshelves. There aren't any family or wedding photos, just an especially newborn and unattractive one of Mather on an end table in the corner. This picture is blurry enough to make me think it was taken on Margaret's cell phone and then blown up a size larger than its resolution allowed, although Crick has an expensive camera and knows how to use it.

Margaret once told me he prefers to be behind the camera rather than in front of it, which is clear from the photos he has chosen to hang. He isn't in any of them but they are stamped by his presence nonetheless, the ponderous heads of Mount Rushmore, the Grand Canyon with the sun tossing long and strange shadows against the multihued rock, and the Yellowstone geysers going off in a way I'm sure he hopes will remind the viewer of his rampant virility. Even his maps feel like masculine challenges: mountain ranges of Paktika Province, Afghanistan; a topographical survey of Yemen; an antique map of Arabia before Western powers divvied it up. All those grand and dangerous places pinned behind glass and tamed by velvet matting, places where only a man like Crick could triumph.

It was Dan who signed us up to "sponsor" the Brickshaws. This was a few months ago, when everyone was first seized with the possibility of the Arab Spring, or, to those more romantically inclined, the Jasmine Revolution. Those sudden bids for freedom made everyone feel more social than usual, slapping one another on the back, exuding brotherly love. It's incredible that one man setting himself on fire could ignite so much. *Arab Spring* was of course coined by a Westerner, such an unassuming title, so gentle, like a song from the sixties. And we accuse the media of focusing on the negative! How those eager journalists showed their hands, their optimism, with such a disarming moniker. We at the embassy were no different. *See! See!* thought both the State Department and the members of the military. *See! We actually did something right over here! Democracy is taking hold!*

Enter Dan, caught up in the communal spirit, signing us up to sponsor a family without even bothering to ask my approval.

"Major and Mrs. Brickshaw, plus one child aged eleven months."
I was not happy. Of all the incoming embassy employees, Dan
had chosen a family with a baby. He should have known better.
We've been trying to have a child ever since we got married nine
years ago, but these past two years in Jordan have been our most
difficult. There is only so much scrutiny two people can take,
their attention turned on each other morning and night, never
distracted by a small being throwing a tantrum, no talk of school
or Disney films or playground scuffles, just an unenthusiastic
How was your day, dear? Even sex stopped being an act of love and
became an act of failure. Each month I'd start banging things
around and Dan would watch me for a moment, understanding
that this was not my usual ill temper but the frustration of a
menstrual cycle that had disappointed once again, and he'd
glance away so I couldn't see the blame in his eyes.

And yet he expected me to ease the transition of life from
America to Jordan for this woman who had achieved the one
thing I couldn't.

On the day the Brickshaws arrived, Dan and I came to this
very apartment to get it ready. I was immediately aggrieved. This
is a game we American embassy folk abroad play, everyone certain that the next guy has better housing or that the grass is
always greener in another villa's yard. But the Brickshaw apartment is truly spectacular. It came fully furnished from the
landlord rather than outfitted with the shabby offerings of the
embassy warehouse. Red and gold velvet couches stuffed to
bursting. Granite countertops. Marble floors. Tremendous windows blooming with sky and light. Cathedral ceilings. My apartment looks like the set of a cable comedy poking fun at the 1970s.

I tried to temper my fury with action and went over to inspect the furniture the cleaners had inexplicably pushed against the living room window.

Dan took in the lush and glossy space, let loose a low whistle, and gave me a concerned look. The man can read me like a billboard.

"Baby death trap," I muttered to deflect him as I tried to move a bookcase—a toddler's scaling dream—away from the window. Dan waited a moment, perhaps to see if I could do it on my own, perhaps to think about a rejoinder to my comment. I looked at him. If he in any way twisted *baby death trap* around so it was aimed at me, nothing could save us.

We've gotten to the point where I'd skirt around the topic of infertility rather than risk launching into a gouging fight. Always lingering in the back of my mind are the things that can never be unsaid, like *I hate you* or *I want a divorce*. I assume they are always on the tip of Dan's tongue. Every day I find myself more and more afraid of what he might say, more and more cautious about provoking him. But that afternoon he just came over and helped me push the bookcase against the far wall. His restraint made me feel tender.

"Don't worry, those cupids will drive them mad," he said. "I don't think that artist ever even laid eyes on a human baby." I glanced up. I hadn't noticed cupids! They were painted in a ceiling mural from one end of the living room to the other, each angel resembling a Chernobyled monkey with wings.

I laughed, loud and sudden, and for a moment Dan leaned against me. I couldn't remember the last time we had laughed together, touched to simply feel each other nearby.

"I should head to the airport to pick them up," he said,

straightening, still smiling. "Can you handle the rest?" I glanced at the large cardboard box full of supplies we'd carried in; he was leaving me with an enormous amount of work.

"Sure," I replied. He put his jacket on quickly, as if afraid I might realize how easily I was letting him off my usually overeager hook.

I watched him leave. Not so long ago, he used to make a point of kissing me at every departure and hello, just a peck, a centering in on me as the one person in the room who belonged to him. But the kiss I miss most is the one he used to bestow on me before we went to sleep. Every night, he'd roll over, press his lips against my shoulder. I assumed his parents had taught him this, like so many of the habits he had learned from them, saying grace before dinner, giving clothes to Goodwill every spring, watching *It's a Wonderful Life* on Christmas Eve. Each of these has fallen away. Now Dan doesn't kiss me hello or good-bye, and he certainly doesn't kiss me good night. I am too proud to let him know I have noticed the omission.

I began to unpack the Brickshaw box of necessities. Oven mitts, plastic water pitcher and spatula, rolls of toilet paper and paper towels, cutting boards and steak knives. I made the beds, hung the towels, put a chicken casserole in the oven. I checked the size of the bedrooms (every one of them larger than mine) and counted the bathrooms (three! three in a four-bedroom apartment! Dan and I had only one!) and almost had a stroke at the fact that there were closets, real closets, in every single bedroom. Dan and I had had to purchase flimsy plywood wardrobes. Even the crisp new smell of the oven and the way the silverware drawers opened smoothly made me seethe.

All this because biology favored the Brickshaws with a child.

As if that's fair. As if lucking out and being able to conceive isn't enough, then the US government gives you extra bedrooms to pat your propagation of the species on the back.

Meanwhile Dan and I live in a cramped and scuffed villa whose fuses explode every time I try to blow-dry my hair.

That was when someone kicked open the front door. I spun, dropping a handful of spoons on the countertop. I left the kitchen to see a tall, broad-shouldered man walking—no, pacing—the perimeter of the living room, looking into the light fixtures as if searching for listening devices. When he saw me, he dropped his suitcases and clapped as if to get the blood circulating, all the while looking me up and down with a nonchalance that was both disturbing and complimentary. He crossed the floor to me with the certainty and effortlessness of an athlete.

When he took my hand and squeezed, I felt the pressure all the way to my scalp.

"I'm Crick," he said.

There was something odd about his features, a puzzle that didn't exactly fit together, the eyebrows too thick, the brown eyes a millimeter too close, the neck too wide. It made me look at his face longer than I should have, trying to figure it out. I realized I was staring but couldn't think of anything to say, not even my own name. He held on, assessing me as much as I was him, and there was a savagery in his touch, in the way he managed to press his fingers into the soft flesh of my palm, as if signaling to me he knew his way around a woman's body, or sports equipment. Perhaps there is very little difference. Soccer ball and goal, basketball and hoop, golf ball and green; he seemed like someone who knew how to coax the ball into the hole.

"Welcome," I finally managed to say.

That's when a woman peeked into the doorway. I saw a blond head, thin arms wrapped around an enormous baby, and I pulled free from Crick.

"Oh, you must be Cassandra?" she asked.

Crick lifted an eyebrow. "Cassandra," he repeated, dragging out the S's. Before I could nod my head he had turned and walked back out into the hallway. I wiped my sweaty hands on my khakis. Why had I worn these pants that looked so much better on me five pounds ago?

"I'm Margaret," the woman said. Her voice annoyed me, too gaspy, like someone doing a bad Marilyn Monroe impression. I put on my mildly interested smile. The rest of her didn't make me feel any better. She was blond and Brahmin thin, the sort of body that denotes an entire class system in America, its own regal title regardless of bank account or upbringing, *Mayflower* ancestors or cabbage soup diet. As long as the thinness comes with a decent set of teeth, the bearer of such luck has it made.

"Hello, Margaret. I hope your flight wasn't too terrible?"

She shook her head. "Oh, we had a whole row of seats to ourselves—"

Crick was suddenly next to her again, dropping two more suitcases at her feet. She jumped.

"Jeez, Mar, they only moved us there after Mather screamed for six straight hours and then puked all over anyone within a five-foot blast radius." He was directing his words at me. I now detected the vague odor of vomit emanating from his polo shirt. "The stewardess stuck us in the back to keep the little monster away from everyone. But she also gave me a few complimentary shots of Jameson, so maybe not so bad after all."

Margaret didn't reply, just stood straighter, drawing her eyebrows together as if she much preferred her version of events. I noticed how tiny she was, only as high as Crick's shoulder. One minute after meeting them and it was clear she was his opposite in every way: small to his hulk, pale to his dark, shy to his confident.

That's when Dan walked in, also loaded down with Brickshaw luggage, the exertion showing on his face. Dan is five nine, I am five five. If I wear high heels, he refuses to stand next to me. Beside Crick, he looked almost delicate, like a prematurely aged child.

My husband placed what could only be Margaret's suitcase (beige with big turquoise flowers) next to the couch, sure to put it in her line of vision. I had a feeling she would turn and utter a little starlet gasp of appreciation, and that was exactly what she did. Dan grinned bashfully. He's always had a thing for blondes. Who doesn't? Especially blondes with enormous blue eyes and fine wrists who make no attempt whatsoever to carry their own baggage. Margaret held her precious baby as if that was her only role in life, looking fresh and sweet after twenty-four hours of travel, just the slightest smear of mascara under her eyes, smiling as if complete strangers always went out of their way for her.

"Have the introductions already been made?" Dan asked.

Margaret jiggled the ball of baby flesh on her hip. "Mather was just about to meet Cassandra." She preened, turning the baby toward me. He was as washed out as his mother, whitish hair sticking up in startled-looking tufts, the rolls under his chin giving him the look of goiter rather than health. The baby was busy shoving a rubber dinosaur halfway down his throat, gagging, giggling, and doing it again.

"Mather?" I repeated, stalling for the right note of under-enthusiastic praise. "That's an interesting name."

"Old English for *conquering army*," Margaret replied. She held Mather's fist to stop him from putting the disgusting thing inside his mouth again. The little bulimic began to shriek.

"Or it's a pre-seventh-century Old English surname of occupational origins," Crick said, ignoring the baby's yells. "Meaning *mower*, as in *one who mows grass*, depending on what Google search you read."

Margaret cut her eyes at him, a brief flutter of annoyed blue. She let go of the baby's hand and the object flew back into his mouth, stoppering the noise. She turned to me. "I didn't name him after a Google search. He's named after a campsite in California." She hesitated. "The only vacation my family ever took." Crick seemed to have never heard this detail before. His eyebrows reached new heights.

She suddenly held her unbidden child out to me. "Cassandra, you wouldn't mind holding him for a sec, would you?" I backed away unsuccessfully as she shoved the baby into my arms. Why would she give him to me with her husband standing right there, and who names a child after a campsite?

"See, he likes you!" she said, which was clearly not the case since the child immediately started screaming and made a grab for her, getting a fist around one of her ears. He was awfully fast for such a fat thing. She winced, and rather than peel back his fingers, she unclipped the feathered earring he was clutching and let the child bat me in the face with its hook.

Then she ran down the hallway, I assume to one of her many bathrooms. The baby stopped yelling and began to cry in earnest, his face instantly covered in a slime of tears and mucus. I stood, unsure, then looked over my shoulder at the men, who both ignored me, Crick probably afraid I'd give him his son, Dan because he did not want to see me holding a baby, knowing there would be a scene later, there was always a scene after someone with a splendidly working womb handed me its product. The men raised their voices above the din, Dan asking Crick if he'd heard that President Ben Ali had fled Tunisia just yesterday, and Crick, even though he must have been on an airplane when it happened, said that of course he had. Then he nimbly changed the conversation to the recent upheavals in Algeria, how a mayor there had told a group of protesters to prove their courage by setting themselves on fire, and, unfortunately, the men did. Suddenly, as if testosterone lent them a moment of male telepathy, they turned in unison and walked into the kitchen. When Mather quieted to take a shuddering breath, I heard the fridge door and the hiss and snap of beer bottles opening.

I rocked the baby, mostly so anyone looking in my direction would assume I was trying to soothe him, but in reality I hoped he'd continue being a hateful, unpleasant little thing and I could give him back to his mother with genuine relief rather than any longing. Instead, as soon as we were alone, he quieted. He swiveled his large skull around to look at my face, sniveling, and lifted his fists as if contemplating which object he ought to shove in my mouth, earring or saliva-slick dinosaur? He smelled of coconut sunblock, bruised bananas, the sweetness balanced out with an edge of sour milk. There was comfort in his weight somehow, and I seemed to intrinsically know how to balance him on my hip just right. Then he put his head on my shoulder.

I stood absolutely still; I could feel him breathing on my neck, hear a soft catch in his throat.

This is everything I want, I thought, *everything*.

Then Margaret was standing in front of me, hands out. Mather lurched for her and I almost lost hold of him. He didn't even glance at me; I was forgotten, his head on his mother's shoulder now as if it had never been on mine. Margaret smoothly retrieved her earring from his sticky fist and slid it back in her ear.

I noticed she'd put on a bit of lipstick in the bathroom, wiped the smudged mascara from under her eyes, pinched her cheeks, put a comb through her hair.

She made a show of sniffing the air. "You didn't make us dinner, did you?"

I nodded, trying to not feel hurt over Mather's total dismissal. "I thought you'd appreciate a home-cooked meal." I saw Dan stick his head out of the kitchen doorway, eavesdropping and trying not to choke on his beer. I knew exactly what he wanted to say, that I hadn't cooked since I set foot in Jordan. Of course I hadn't. I also hadn't scrubbed out a toilet. That's why we American wives allow our husbands to take us to the Middle East, for goodness' sake, so we can have household help for the first time in our lives. The silver lining of no longer living in the West. I followed Margaret into the kitchen and glared at Dan before he could out me with some quip.

Crick straightened from where he was leaning against the counter, went to Margaret, offered her his beer. She shook her head quickly, *no*. He shrugged, draped an arm around her waist. I looked to Dan, wanting him to come up and do that same thing, pull me close, prove his ownership, but Dan remained out of reach.

"Campbell's cream of chicken soup casserole. It should be ready in fifteen minutes," I said, too loudly perhaps. She had it all, I kept thinking, it wasn't fair for one person to have so very much—the affectionate husband, the fat and happy baby, the pleasure with which she gazed around the room, as if she deserved every bright and shiny new appliance. I glanced warningly at Dan as he continued to shake his head in disbelief at my ownership of the dish. Yes, I had left the recipe out for my helper, Tharushi. But I had bought all of the ingredients. I had reheated it.

Then I noticed Crick watching Margaret, and Margaret refusing to meet his gaze. "What?" I asked.

"Margaret's a vegetarian," he said.

"Crick!" she gasped, looking miserable. "It's so kind of you, Cassandra, really! Don't worry, I'll pick out the chicken."

We all stood there for a moment, avoiding one another's eyes. A vegetarian? Then I remembered the Chardonnay with enormous relief, opening up the fridge and grabbing at the cold bottle inside. "How about some of this?"

Margaret again looked away.

Dan glanced at me and raised his shoulders slightly in confusion.

"That's super nice, Cassandra," Margaret said. "Actually, I can't drink while I'm nursing. Maybe I'll have a glass after I put Mather to bed?"

"Go ahead, Mar," Crick said. He was no longer touching her. "You are so much more fun after a few drinks."

"One is fine," I said, opening the cabinets. There aren't any wineglasses in an apartment furnished by a Muslim landlord, but the tall, etched tea glasses would do nicely. I quickly poured and slid one to Margaret over that glorious granite. "And please call me Cassie. If Dan told you my name was Cassandra, he's trying to get me riled; only my mother calls me that and I hate it."

Margaret placed Mather on the floor, stood, and tapped her fingers on the countertop. "My mom only called me Margaret, too." She didn't touch the wine.

I pushed her tea glass closer toward her, itching to drink my own but not wanting to be the first to sip. "My mother says she gave me a name, not an abbreviation. That nicknames are insulting." When she didn't budge, I gave in and tasted my wine; it was cold, tart, a hint of oak and formaldehyde. Just what I needed. I continued, "Now, to her horror, I call her *Mommy Dearest*. But she has never in my life called me anything other than Cassandra."

Margaret looked at me with those big, mournful eyes. "My mom died a few months ago," she said. "She suffered from lupus. I'd give anything for her to call me whatever she liked."

I put my glass down. I wanted to catapult over the countertop between us, straddle this woman, and pour the rest of the Chardonnay bottle down her throat just to stop this excruciating conversation. I glanced at the men, hoping this was a sick joke, but Crick was staring down at his hiking boots and biting the side of his cheek.

"Shit, I'm so sorry," I said.

She lifted her head. "I like your idea though." I blinked; I wasn't sure what she was talking about. She continued, hesitantly, like she was thinking through some epiphany as she spoke. "I'd like to think we have the power to rename ourselves.

Maybe . . . you'll help me come up with a name that's all mine? A name that fits this new place?"

I waited. She was a little off, no? Throwing her dead mother into the room and then suddenly making nice before anyone had a chance to acknowledge the corpse?

I picked my glass up. "I'll try to think of something." I felt Crick watching me. "In the meantime, let's toast to new places." I was poking fun. "To peace in the region, and to a fresh start for everyone."

Margaret looked at me like I had touched her with a lit match. I inhaled, waiting to find out how I'd managed to put my foot in it this time. But then she smiled and reached for her Chardonnay. Crick lifted an eyebrow in amazement. "Yes," she sang out. "To a fresh start!" She raised her glass. "To new places, new friends, and new names!"

Her enthusiasm embarrassed me; maybe it embarrassed everyone in the room except Margaret. I clinked my glass against hers. I'd filled them too high and both sloshed liquid down to our elbows, but Margaret didn't wipe hers so I didn't either. A moment earlier I'd expected her to sputter into tears and instead she was smiling her face off. She took a sip, her eyes never leaving mine, and I sipped too.

Now, almost four months later to the day, here I am, once more tidying up Margaret's life. I go to my purse, take out my cell phone, and check the time. I find *Margaret Brickshaw* in my list of contacts. How is it that after all this time, I never called her anything other than Margaret? There are so many possibilities, it feels like a failure on my part that I never arrived at the perfect choice: Mags, Peggy, Meg, Maggie.

There are no messages from her. On a Friday late afternoon it could take anywhere from twenty minutes to an hour to get to the heart of downtown Amman, depending on traffic, road construction, protests. So many Friday protests. I hope Margaret has enough sense not to drive by the King Hussein Mosque. On a good day, the car GPS system Margaret has can only get her so far with all the random streets shut down for constant construction. And even when she knows exactly where she ought to be, she still manages to get herself hideously lost. I resist the impulse to call her. She doesn't need to be reaching for a ringing cell phone on top of everything else.

Surely she'll be fine, I think. *Surely she's learned something from me after all.*

May 13, 2011

4:25 P.M.

I check the bookshelves for a newspaper, something to occupy my time while the baby naps. Margaret always has stacks of them, usually in Arabic as well as English, even though she can't actually read Arabic. She's incapable of saying no to the scabby teenage boys who sell them on the corner. But the only thing I find today on the shelves is Crick's collection of academic tomes about conflict in the Middle East.

She probably has something to read in her room, I think. I walk down the hallway. For all of Margaret's apparent openness, she always keeps her bedroom door closed. It's the only room I haven't seen since I set up her apartment. I'm curious. There's plenty of time before she comes back, what harm can it do?

I nudge the door open with my foot, peer inside. There's one bedside lamp on; it has a blue and green lampshade and fills the room with an ethereal aquarium light, enough to show me clothes strewn over every surface, alphabet blocks and stuffed animals and soft toys piled up on the floor.

I flip on the overhead light.

The room is nothing like the living room. There is no master here. It reeks of the feminine, from the lavender bedsheets to the women's clothing strewn about, the frilly lamp and the scent of shampoo. The more I look, the more I realize the room is not as decimated as it seems. There is order to the chaos; it's messy in the way Margaret is messy, not unclean as much as untidy, careless. What I first assume are dirty clothes are really gauzy scarves piled and drifting over the mirrors, creating a sensual mash-up of colors.

I pause at Margaret's bureau. Here are all the photos that are missing from the living area. Strange they are collected here for Margaret's own private viewing. Plenty of a baby Mather, a few of what must be a young Margaret, then lots of a woman who could only be her dead mother. I study them. The newer and crisper the photos, the sicker and more formless the woman becomes—waterlogged, weighed down, her eyes sinking deeper and deeper, her light brown hair getting thinner as her lupus ravages on. There's only one small photo of Margaret's father, a rangy, slightly stooped man wearing eyeglasses, who Margaret told me remarried when she was a teenager. In a particularly overexposed picture, her mother sits in a hospital bed holding a birthday cake while an adolescent Margaret, lit up by the flash, blows the candles out. But the most arresting photo of all is one with a small tear in the corner, discolored in that early 1980s way of Polaroids. It's a close-up, and the enormous blue eyes that stare out are nearly identical to Margaret's and Mather's own. Despite permed hair and thick eyeliner, the resemblance is eerie—her mother is even wearing the obnoxious feathered earrings that double as Mather's favorite weapon.

Then I find a picture of Crick off to the side. It's jarring to see his healthy face next to these faded pictures taken inside Margaret's pill bottle–filled home. He is in full battle rattle, uniform and Kevlar, helmet and gun, and surrounded by children. Such shoulders on this man. I reflexively lift the frame, run my thumb over Crick's chest. I imagine trying to span those shoulders with my arms. It gives me a chill, imagining that rough camouflage moving against my tender skin.

I glance up quickly, as if Margaret might be standing in the doorway watching me, and then hide Crick's photo behind all the rest.

I walk over to her bedside lamp. The satin has seen better days but small glass butterflies still glint and sway prettily from the bottom. I notice Margaret's massive hobo-style bag of fake teal crocodile skin on the floor next to her bed, toppled over. I get down on my knees and pick up the contents: a small Tupperware container of pacifiers in differing states of filth, a burp cloth "cover-up" she uses while breast-feeding in public—which does not in fact cover anything since Mather always kicks it aside—countless pens and dirty tissues and candy wrappers. Every time Margaret sets this bag down it vomits out its innards, ensuring she will leave something precious under park benches, next to Dumpsters, or in the backseats of taxis.

I feel a shudder of guilt. Like Mather's dinosaur. I found it in my bedroom one evening after Margaret had nursed the baby there. And I kept it. I told myself a teething child should absolutely not have it in his mouth, let alone down his throat.

Right now it's in my scarf drawer at the bottom of my bedside table, deep down amid the silks and wools, with other discarded toys Mather should never have had to begin with. A rattle with part of its handle chewed off, a teddy bear the size of my palm, a red ball the exact size of the opening of a child-sized esophagus.

I took these things because I thought Margaret had everything and I had nothing. They seemed so small, a token, a lucky charm. She would never miss them, I thought.

I am about to stand when I notice a few books under her bed: *Middle East for Dummies* and *Lonely Planet: Jordan*, as well as *Women in Islam*, the small paperback I gave her. I pull out *Women in Islam*, flip through it to see if she ever bothered to read it, and am glad to see her penciled check-marked passages.

I notice a few more books on the ground, stuck behind her bedside table, spines up, pages limp and wounded.

Curious, I reach back and try to tug them free. The one on top is an old hardcover of *The Pied Piper*. The character on the cover is disturbing, stretched and leering, with large black eyes. The next book is Margaret's pocket dictionary. I remember the first time I saw this, soon after she arrived. I had come to her apartment for lunch after giving her a driving tour of Amman. When she threw her bag on the kitchen table, the book fell out.

"I'd like to see the so-called 'pocket' that thing fits into," I said.

Margaret lifted the dictionary over her head as if it was a dumbbell. "I can feel the burn, Cass!"

"Are you a writer?"

"Oh, gosh, no way." She brought it down and flipped through it. "I wouldn't talk in school, like not at all, until I was eight. Everyone thought I had a learning disability? Maybe dyslexia?" She dropped it back into her bag and started to clean up the other detritus that had fallen out. "One of the aides had me write out dictionaries. I think she was testing to see if I mixed up my letters, or maybe she just wanted me to keep busy since I wouldn't read aloud with everyone else. But I loved it." She glanced at me. "It was genius, really. I mean, I was just super shy, and the kids made fun of me and called me all sorts of names, Helen Keller, Margaret the Mute. The usual kid stuff. But learning those big words, it felt like a power. Knowing words other kids didn't know. It became a hobby."

"When I was eight my hobby was collecting scratch-and-sniff stickers."

"I was a total freak show, no doubt about it!" She made that terrible honk of a laugh. "But kids believe in magic spells, right? *Abracadabra. Hocus pocus. Once upon a time.* Mysterious doors and treasure chests open up. You say the right combination of words and wondrous things happen. That's what I thought. I'd learn the words and everything else would fall into place."

Now I push the bedside table aside to get at these supposed treasure chests Margaret has treated so shabbily: *Elmo's ABC Book. Anzeh al-Azeeza Cleans Up Petra.*

ENGLISH/ARABIC Dictionary.

The English-Arabic dictionary makes me pause. It is definitely something that would have come in handy at a Jordanian police station. I can't imagine why she would have left this. I lean in to pick it up.

That's when I spot the final book behind her bedside table.

I sit back on my heels in surprise.

Margaret's journal.

It's one of those foil-embossed notebooks you find near the registers of upscale bookstores, next to high-end chocolates and bejeweled ballpoint pens, things so unnecessary they can only be purchased when you are holding an open wallet and suddenly feeling reckless with those shiny credit cards. It's too pretty. Green with a filigree of gold along the edges.

This is something she always keeps with her. Always.

Her first or second week, I took her to the Park of the Martyrs, and she sat with the baby in the sandbox (a glorified kitty litter pit for all the neighborhood strays, if you ask me) and reached deep into her bag to pull this book out. Then she started scribbling into its pages, hunched over, biting her bottom lip, her hair falling in her eyes.

"What are you working on, Margaret?" I asked.

"Nothing." She smiled. "And everything." She ran one of her ragged fingernails across the page as if it was sacred. "I wanted to keep notes for Mather, so he could look back and read about all the things he did in Jordan before his memory kicked in. You've heard that, right? Kids don't actually remember anything before the age of four?"

I nodded. I thought she was rude, writing her entries as if I wasn't even there.

"But now it's more for me, to keep track of all these days, to make *me* remember them. Maybe I can figure things out later that I can't understand now." She slipped the diary back in her bag. "In the end, that's really all there is to life, right? What you remember? And what other people remember? The forgotten moments are totally gone, no matter how good or important they might have been."

I had never had any desire to record those moments other people seem to keep track of as pathetic validation that their lives are less boring than everyone else's. I have a keen memory; just ask Dan, he tells me I never forget a thing. But sitting there at the park, watching Mather lift an old Styrofoam cup up out of the sand and proceed to pour it over his mother's shoulder, I was curious to know if I would make it into Margaret's little book, if I would someday be worth her ink and paper, worth trapping on a page.

Now I am afraid to see what she may have written about me.

I get up and walk out of the room, leaving the journal stuck behind the bedside table, untouched.

May 13, 2011

5:04 P.M.

❧

I pause to listen outside Mather's nursery.

If the baby sleeps too long now, will he have trouble sleeping tonight? Do I need to change his diaper? Feed him? What will I feed him? All of these questions buzz in my head, though I know Margaret is fairly lax. She lets Mather sleep wherever and whenever he likes. I have seen the child stretched out on the kitchen floor while Margaret stepped over him to get the pasta pot, the Parmesan, the jar of marinara, just lifting her feet as if he was a neighbor's old dog dozing in the sun.

Do I hear choking? I convince myself he's managed to wind something around his throat and I crack the door open the tiniest bit. The room is dark, cool, quiet. I tread carefully to the edge of his crib and watch the little guy in his downy cocoon. As I feared, he has blankets all around him—clearly Margaret is not up on her SIDS awareness. But he is alive and well. As I turn to go, the baby's hand shoots out from underneath his chin and flails along the sheet next to him. He must be looking for a pacifier and I quickly pat the blankets within reach, hoping to find one that I can jam in his mouth before he is completely conscious. His eyes open and his face wrinkles up in horror upon seeing me instead of his mother, and though I find three pacifiers and try to fit them into his mouth in quick succession, none of them shut him up.

I bring him and the failed pacifiers out into the living room. He grudgingly takes each and, one at a time, sucks savagely, until he has decided on a favorite and tosses the other two on the ground. He is crying less now, more of an occasional wail of "Mama!" interrupted by some violent pacifier masticating, as if he wants to let me know he is woefully disappointed by the sight of me. I'd love to know if anyone has ever done a study on the links between pacifier use in early childhood and cigarette use in adulthood. I used to bite my nails when I was a child. My mother dissuaded me from that despicable habit by putting lighter fluid on my fingertips, then threatening to set them on fire if she caught me biting again. That did the trick. When I told Margaret that story, hinting it was time to break Mather's own addiction, her eyes widened as if she wanted to cry. But I know that sometimes the most unpleasant things are necessary. Love must sometimes wear a frightening face.

I strap the little beast into his high chair, which cheers him, and when he stops yelling I start liking him again. I root around for his dinner. Surprisingly, there is an exceptional amount of baby food stacked up in Tupperware cubes in both the fridge and the freezer. I take out what I assume is carrot and pea, microwave it, and feed the very hungry fifteen-month-old. When I'm not looking, he runs the bright orange and green paste through his hair.

I check my phone. It's been well over an hour since Margaret left. Between spoonfuls, I text:

Did you find the police station? Everything OK?

You never know how these things will work. Sometimes an American ID will move you to the front of the line, sometimes it will move you to the back. And Margaret was uncharacteristically indignant earlier.

And then, as we drove home, she had cried.

I wish she hadn't cried.

I get a glass of mint lemonade out of the fridge. Mather tries to swipe it from me so I pour a bit into his sippy cup. He winces at the tartness, then drinks it all down and wants more. I try to divert his attention with a spoonful of peas; he promptly knocks it out of my hand and starts screaming, "*JUUUUUUUUUUS!*" Though his translucence and blue eyes might fool you into believing he is like Margaret, this child is pure Crick. *Give it to me, I want it, and if you don't give it to me I will take it.*

I sip my lemonade, remembering Margaret's hands on mine. *You've been the only person I could depend on.*

Not so true a few days ago, when she called me in the middle of the night. *Cass, was it you?* I cannot shake the rough, raw quality of her voice over the telephone, the tears and the seeping doubt that have been filling me ever since. *Did you tell?*

I pick up my glass, pour the rest down the sink. It has turned sour on my tongue.

I only meant to help her. At least that's what I intended in the beginning. In the beginning, when things were so perfect between us.

Like her first full day in Jordan. She called me. *Me*. It was so early, not even nine. I was going to let her sleep, thinking she would want to get settled a bit before I checked in, but then my phone began to ring and it was her unmistakably breathy voice on the other end.

"Hey, Cass! I think I slept maybe eleven minutes total last night, but how could I sleep! I was walking Mather around at three a.m. and I noticed my floors are *heated*! I mean, like, they're warm for my cold little feet. Can you imagine that?"

My floors are definitely not heated. "Hmmm, how very nice for you."

"Anyway, Crick went to work. Your husband, Danny, he's a real sweetheart, isn't he? He picked Crick up super early. But Crick left me your number and a loaner cell phone, and since you're the only person I know in this whole country, I thought I'd call!"

She was like that with me from the very first, effusive, rambling, chummy. Already shortening my short name even further. "Cass!" A whispered, thrilled gasp, as if my very name is exciting. Every sentence out of her mouth is either a question or an exclamation, she somehow manages to be both too uncertain and too enthusiastic about everything. I'm usually rather reserved—it takes me a while to warm to a person—but not Margaret. As soon as I pulled up in front of her apartment building that day she came running over, bouncing that child at her side and dragging his car seat. "You came!" She swung Mather around and pressed his snotty face to my surprised cheek. "Kiss Miss Cass, Mather, she will be our savior here."

I took her to the embassy. She seemed disappointed that this was the first destination, but as soon as we stopped at the front gate she perked up, gazing intently at the armed vehicles and traffic barriers.

Two guards came sauntering over to check our IDs. The guard at the passenger side ignored Margaret; instead of checking the passport she held out he began tapping on the glass to get the baby's attention, making grotesque faces that destroyed any credibility that there was serious security. He called to another guard, who called to another. Margaret asked me to roll down the baby's window and within moments there were four grown men leaning in and poking Mather's belly, pinching his cheeks, handing him gum and hard candies, choking hazards every one. "*Masha'allah!*" they said. The phrase means *Allah has willed it* and I couldn't help but wonder what exactly they meant, that Allah had willed the child to be alarmingly overweight? Margaret twisted around, introducing herself, asking the men their names, acting as if they were a social welcoming committee rather than professionals tasked with checking automobiles for explosive devices.

The men began to say, "Chai, chai!" and motion toward the guard shack. "Tea!"

"Oh, yes!" Margaret replied.

"I don't think we can today," I said. I leaned toward Margaret and said under my breath, "They aren't *actually* asking us, it's just a tradition left over from a Bedouin culture of welcoming guests in the desert."

"It seems like an *actual* invitation to me." She put her hand on the door as if she would debark right there, at the embassy front gate, with all those cars waiting impatiently behind us, her child strapped into my backseat.

I reached for her right wrist, startled by the heat of her, how frail her arm felt in my grasp. I squeezed. "Trust me. Have tea another time."

She looked at my hand, lifted her face, narrowed her eyes.

Then Hassan, an older guard who has been at the embassy for many years, leaned into my open window to check the badge at my throat. I released Margaret. Hassan once told me he'd lived in New York for a few years, working with Royal Jordanian Airlines, and you could tell, he had an easy way around us Americans. He glanced at Margaret, then at a large white truck behind us. The windows of the truck were completely opaque, which was technically illegal; our USA cars can only ship to Jordan if there is zero tint on the windows. It had to be a Jordanian government vehicle or a local with a hell of a lot of clout, or *wasta*. The truck honked a quick *toot*, a nudge for us to hurry. At the sound, the other guards stepped away from Mather and moved back toward the gate.

"Perhaps the next time you will join us?" Though Hassan's English wasn't perfect, the stiffness of his syllables made him sound impeccable.

Margaret let go of the door handle. "Yes, please!"

He smiled, the teeth beneath his silver mustache startlingly white for a country that has more cell phones than toothbrushes. "It is now a promise. *Inshallah*." He tapped my door twice with his palm, then stepped back and waved to one of the men ahead, who began to lift the heavy metal security pole. But Margaret wouldn't let it go that easily. She leaned across before I managed to get my foot on the gas pedal, pinning her sharp little elbow into my side.

"I'm Margaret, Margaret Brickshaw!" she called to Hassan. He tilted his head, confused, and returned to my car.

The white truck behind us honked longer.

"Nice to meet you!" Margaret said loudly. She reached for him. Hassan looked at her outstretched palm, looked at me, looked back at Margaret. He lifted an eyebrow, amused.

"Yes, very pleased, you are very welcome," he said. "I am Hassan Mahmoud." He gave her his hand. She held it just a second too long, as if she wanted me to notice.

I smiled tightly, and immediately drove on when she let go of the poor man. I told myself she did not yet realize that such an ordinary American gesture was exactly the wrong thing to do. One of the first things they tell you during the embassy security brief is to abstain from physical contact with the opposite sex in order not to make anyone feel uncomfortable. If a man is a devout Muslim, he will not touch a woman outside of his family. I told myself that Margaret was ignorant of all of these rules, but she'd learn them the way we all do, over time, and of course with my help. I would guide her. Obviously I had a lot of work to do.

I hadn't yet realized Margaret would cling to her ignorance. Delight in it.

I hadn't realized that handshake was just the beginning of things to come.

May 13, 2011

5:37 P.M.

❧

The baby escapes while I am cleaning up after his meal, an astounding amount of which has ended up on the floor. I find him in the hallway outside of Margaret's room, writing on the wall with a ballpoint pen that appears to be from my pocketbook.

He has earned his most apt nickname, *the Destroyer*. Margaret never calls him that; it's all Crick's doing. Other than providing the original spurt of DNA, making up nicknames for Mather seems to be the only part of parenting Crick enjoys. He has a glib, deadpan Army knack for coming up with disturbing monikers. I have heard him refer to his son as: Booger Eater, BCB (for Broken Condom Baby), and My Little EFFP (for Example of Failed Family Planning, but of course he is playing on the Army acronym EFP—explosively formed penetrator—for Iranian-made roadside bombs that wreak havoc in Iraq). Crick uses *the Destroyer* the most, making Margaret wince every time. "C'mere, Destroyer, get your mitts off your father's computer," and Crick would snatch the laptop just as Mather was knocking it off the table. But Margaret never seemed to notice that Crick actually respects his son's special skill set, looking on with a bit of pride. He's a man who knows how to break things himself. What man in the Army isn't?

She also always misses the inevitable glance that Crick gives me, accompanied by one of his winks, as if to say, *You understand me, Cassie, you and you alone.* And each time I try to swallow the smile he draws out of me, try to look away and pretend I need to fetch something in the kitchen. On occasion I have had to open the freezer to feel the cold air on my flushed cheeks.

I pull the pen from Mather's hand, certain I put my bag on top of a bookshelf. How did he get at it? The baby, screeching, throws himself around my legs. I bend over and start to tickle him, which makes him go limp and fall to the ground with peals of laughter. I drop to my knees. "Damn it, you are cute, aren't you?" I whisper. There is something wonderful in having no one judge me as I play with him, no one feeling sorry for me. Just tickling a baby; who could have known there could be so much pleasure in this? "Oh, you love the ladies, do you? Just like your daddy." The baby, delighted, rolls around the floor, but as soon as he escapes, he rolls back into my grasp, inviting more.

I manage to get Mather into the bath. I call Margaret but it just rings and rings. I know how she is with her phone, all those times she's forgotten to charge it or left it in her car.

As Mather tries to fit bath toys up his nose, I imagine a protest downtown, the streets clogged, barricaded, Margaret lost as furious young *shababs* wave signs, standing in the way of her car, not letting her pass. I consider turning on the TV but I know what I will find: news clip after news clip of police dressed in

Kevlar, helmeted and shielded so that little of the human is left of them as they rush into a crowd of young men with *kaffiyehs* tied tight across their mouths. Footage from Libya, Tunisia, Egypt, Yemen, Syria. The same story playing in a loop, scrawny youths armed with nothing but Facebook and cell phones facing a wall of might. But I would have gotten an embassy text alert if anything potentially violent was going on here in Jordan, and my phone has remained silent all day, unbothered.

This is Margaret, I think. She is a woman of tangents. She can't stick to the topic at hand; there are diversions and asides and roads not taken she must immediately run down without looking both ways. I tell myself not to worry, knowing her penchant for wrong turns and roadside fruit stands. She'll taste whatever is thrust her way and buy more produce than she could eat in weeks. Today's fender bender is the perfect example. If only she had sped up and gone through the yellow light, all would have been well. But no, not Margaret, Margaret whose car cup holders are overflowing with Chiclets chewing gum, Chiclets, of course, being the hawking merchandise of choice for anyone disfigured or old. Whenever Margaret is driving, it seems like every traffic light turns red just so all the beggars and shysters can rap on her window with dirty knuckles, holding up their fingers, *Ten dinars, five dinars, three dinars*, and she can buy things she doesn't need, lighters for cigarettes she doesn't smoke, kites that Mather is too young to fly, cheap polyester socks Crick would never wear.

Today, Friday, is also the day for alms, and fallen women and widows often stand outside of mosques, carrying tightly swaddled children as if they are stones. Damaged women. Missing teeth. Their loose robes, or *abayas*, dusty, their flesh pungent. They come too close to the moving cars, as if nothing more can hurt them. They go from car window to car window. Margaret tosses her coins, coos at the stoic babies wrapped in polyester blankets. Margaret in her breathable, no-wrinkle cotton blouses, her three-hundred-dollar car seat in the back. Can't she feel how much they hate her?

Margaret doesn't recognize that the line between *us* and *them* is real. She's infected with our great American hubris of assuming that deep down every single person wants the same thing: autonomy, freedom, democracy, independence. I try to tell Margaret things here are different, that our American tolerance, even veneration, of the rule-breaker is not shared in a place where the literal translation of the name of the faith, *Islam*, means *"submission."*

The longer Margaret has lived here, the less willing she has been to submit to anything.

May 13, 2011

6:01 P.M.

***

I park Mather on the couch in front of the Arabic TV children's programming with every pacifier I can find as well as a bowl of Oreo cookies. I watch the baby stare at the screen, take a bite of cookie, chew a couple of times, stick the pacifier in his mouth, and suck. The combination produces a black paste that seeps out the sides of his mouth.

It will be dark soon. I look at my phone; Margaret has been gone for two hours. Sure, the only plan I had for the evening was to watch a Netflix DVD that took nearly a month to arrive at my embassy mailbox, but Margaret doesn't know that. I can feel the familiar burn starting in my stomach, an empty feeling that will slowly, slowly fill and squeeze. This is how she treats me. Walks off and doesn't even bother calling, taking me for granted. Again.

I restart my phone. Still nothing but the four text messages from my husband over the past five days, all some derivation of *What is going on?* I delete them; I'll call him later, I tell myself, when Margaret is back, when I have fewer things to worry about. I don't need a lecture from him right now. I check the bars on my screen, the battery, almost hoping it is broken, that Mather managed to drop it in the toilet when I wasn't looking. No, it's fine. I tap her name on the screen for what seems the hundredth time, put the phone against my ear, hear it ring and ring and ring until it clicks and the recording, in Arabic, says, "Please try again." It drives me crazy that you can't leave phone messages here; this seems like such a simple innovation, a voice mailbox for a cell phone, and deliberately tiresome that Jordan's cell phone providers do not, inexplicably, offer this service. I text: WHERE THE HELL ARE YOU???!!!

Mather is passed out in his Oreos, facedown on the couch, muddy drool smeared across the gold velvet. I lift him up and bring him to his crib, carefully wiping off his dirty little cookie mouth. The night-light is tinkling and twinkling shards of colored light across his ceiling. The baby mutters incoherently as I shut the nursery door behind me.

I do a loop of her home, half expecting to find Margaret opening up an oil-stained paper bag full of Lebanese takeout, spilling hot pitas and small containers of delicious meze across the dining room table. But there is no one.

Back in the kitchen, I start to run the hot water and then wash the very dishes I swore not to earlier. When I run out of dishes, I search through her pantry until I find half a bottle of red wine in the back. I pour a splash into a coffee mug and smell it; it's not yet gone to vinegar. I take a cautious sip. Drinkable. Barely. But it will do.

Mug of wine in hand, I return to her room. I walk directly to her bedside table and, using my hip, shove it completely out from the wall. Her lamp teeters dangerously but remains standing. I kneel and reach until the journal is in my fist.

I sit on her bed, placing the journal, closed and prim, under the blue-tinted light of the lamp. I look at my cell phone. It would take just one text, one hastily written On my way!, and I would go back to the living room, turn on the television, wait for her, and never open these pages.

This is her last chance, I tell myself as I dial her number, and this time it doesn't even ring, this time it goes directly to the message that says the owner of the phone is not available.

So I place my cell phone on the table under the lamp. I take a steadying breath and lift the journal, turning it over in my hands before opening it up and flipping through. I am amazed at how lovely her writing is, how small and deliberate, as if she is conserving both paper and energy. I'm also surprised at the length of her entries, how she goes on! When did she possibly find the time? Pages and pages of her tiny script, broken up by the occasional coffee ring or smear of avocado, a sketch—could that be a drawing of a goat in a bowtie?—phone numbers (I am pleased that mine is listed first), and then rambling blocks of her dense writing. There are also lists of Arabic vocabulary in a different hand: *haada=this, hawn=here, hunaak=there, Allah ysalmik=God keep you*, phrases of thanks, compliments, pleasantries she never quite got right. It looks like Mather grabbed the notebook more than once, scribbled ruthlessly, ripping through a few pages. There are grocery lists. Recipes. Cat names and descriptions: *Tiger: gray striped male; Zara: calico, skittish; Frankie: my girl, adoptable?* A list of places I never brought her to: *Madaba, Jerash, John the Baptist site, Nebo, Umm Qais, Ajloun, Petra.*

Petra. I feel a tiny, uncomfortable tightening in my chest. I should have taken her. She asked me more than once. But it was the last place I wanted to go with her, all those cliff faces and gorges, knowing how often Margaret strayed from marked paths, how she let Mather touch and climb everything he shouldn't.

I very slowly open to the back of the book, to what I assume will be her most recent entry. I brace myself for what I might find. I expect to read my name, I expect an angry indictment, accusations blaming me for the fact that things have been strained between us. I expect an entry I will wish I never read.

I find today.

May 13
I MUST FIND HIM.
I MUST MAKE IT RIGHT.

I hear the sharp intake of my breath, unsure if this is a relief or somehow all the more crushing. I close the book.

No mention of me. But there is a man.

I was right.

My heart is throbbing; it feels as if it has changed shape and no longer fits its cavity. I hold the book between my palms, the spine of it touching my nose and forehead, almost as if I am praying.

I'll just read a little bit, I tell myself. And really, why shouldn't I? I was with her so much of the time. Wasn't I the one who eased her into life here, and didn't I pick up her pieces and try to put them back together again when she started to fall apart?

Unless there has been someone else all along.

January 15

NEW HOME!

At least I think it's the fifteenth, or is it the sixteenth? I don't even know! OK, it's almost midnight according to my sleeping husband's wristwatch. Crazy that I can roll over, lift his arm, read the time, and he doesn't even twitch. 11:59 p.m. here is 1:59 p.m. in San Jose. No wonder I can't sleep. At midnight, my old life will be yesterday.

I can already tell everything will be different here.

When we landed, Danny Hugo stood beyond the arrival gates with a handwritten sign: *The Brickshaw Family*, and that's exactly what we are, aren't we? FAMILY. The three of us, Mather with little bits of vomit still trapped in the folds of his neck, Crick walking in front stubbornly dragging the luggage as if our biggest suitcase hadn't lost a wheel in transit, and me, stopping every few steps to pick up the sippy cup Mather kept flinging on the floor.

I wanted to hug Danny before I even knew his name, just to

see someone waiting for us, holding that sign, letting me know that this is our new beginning.

We walked out of the airport and into his SUV and the whole place blazed in its own unique way. People parking wherever they pleased, pulling up crooked to the curb and throwing suitcases in or throwing suitcases out, traffic police in pointy little hats and too-fitted uniforms whistling and waving and no one paying any attention. As he drove, Danny tried to point things out but Crick kept leaning into him, questioning, low voiced, as if I couldn't hear *protests on the rise* and *military action* and *Who can tell terrorists from freedom fighters these days?* I played with Mather, glad we'd brought his car seat all the way from Monterey, no matter how many people I'd hit in the head with it as I lugged it on and off the plane (*Sorry! Excuse me! Oh my, oh gosh, sir? Are you OK? So sorry!* Crick's arms too full with our baby and carry-on bags to do much but avert his eyes and pretend I didn't belong to him).

Danny drove down a highway with sand drifting in from both sides, every once in a while with random speed bumps right in the middle. A van passed us and I could see sheep peeking out the back windows.

Then Amman rose in the distance, the sun setting the whole city on fire, all those windows, all the golden sandstone, buildings stacked like Mather's wooden blocks, square windows of glass erupting with light. It seemed to go on forever, an Escher painting. Once your eyes got used to the uniformity, other images would surface. I could pick out mosque after mosque, some with high domed roofs and shining minarets while others were nothing but small, square concrete buildings with a loudspeaker next to a rusting tin cutout of a crescent moon. I saw a boy on a donkey, two pinkies holding the reins while his thumbs texted madly on his phone. Businesses had signs in Arabic and occasionally in English, like TITANIC TRAVEL AND TOURISM AGENCY or GENTLE MANS SALOON. The "saloon" was definitely not a Wild West hangout. I glimpsed a white-haired barber standing behind a man who seemed to be wearing a black plastic bag over his chest. A sign on an apartment building advertised LUXURIOUS PARTIES, which may have been a bad translation, but with its rusted air-conditioning units, perhaps closer to the truth than any claim of *luxury apartments*. Kids sat at the side of the road trying to sell eggs, eggs! arranged in a little pyramid on a handkerchief. Long-haired goats grazed on narrow swaths of green between ritzy housing complexes, while canvas tents were pitched in the distance with knock-kneed camels tied up out front.

We passed a park and I saw two girls swinging, *hijabs* fluttering over their heads, sneakered feet kicking at the sky.

Incredible, all of it, I can hardly bear it, so untamed, an overflowing quality to everything. America is the land of plenty but it's a different kind of plenty, strip malls spreading on and on, parking lots with rows of cars pointing in the same bleak direction, skyscrapers reaching, but there's always a sense of, I don't know, zoning? Not here. People ignore the sidewalks and walk along the busy roads, fruit carts are pitched at random corners with pomegranates and bananas spilling out, windows of shops are so full I can't tell what they're selling, all to a soundtrack of honking and brakes and squealing tires. There's *more* here. It's so alive. At the red lights people came running up to the window of Danny's SUV with newspapers and boxes of tomatoes, Dora helium balloons and plastic-wrapped sunglasses.

Even our apartment is thrillingly alien. The water runs through the taps like a heartbeat. I turn the faucet on and water comes out *thick, thin, thick, thin*, and the toilet seems sort of animal too, gasping every time I flush. But we have a Western toilet! As we were getting ready to de-board the plane, Crick leaned over and stage-whispered into my shoulder in a way I knew was not going to be nice, "Mar, you better learn fast how to pee into a trough in the floor, 'cause that's how the public restrooms roll here, no toilet paper, just a big jug of water to pour over your private parts." He really said *private parts*—he can be adorable like that, but I didn't appreciate how he thought his adorableness ought to be shared with anyone in a three-row circumference, so that the two teenage boys behind us started staring at the parts of my body that definitely ought to be private.

Crick made up for it all later; he always does. He put on his big-boy macho routine for Cassie and Danny: *Oh yeah, I'm the man, hey hey look at me, suitcases bend to my strength, women swoon at my squeeze.* But when they left he washed all the dishes, from Mather's sippy cup that had hit the ground from one end of the planet to the other, to the Pyrex dish Cassie had baked dinner in.

"Really, Campbell's cream of chicken soup casserole is quite the delicacy here," Crick said in a high-pitched, nasally voice, then walked from one end of the kitchen to the other on tippy-toes with his butt in the air, wearing the oven mitts. Cassie was such a dear to make us dinner, to put eggs and milk and butter in the empty fridge, that's kindness, pure and simple. I watched Crick, startled by his mincing, and then I laughed until I was wiping away tears. Oh, how he nailed her walk! But more than that, he was trying to make me laugh. We'd come halfway across the world together and I wanted him to see, yes, I'm happy! You make me happy! This is a good place! He seemed surprised at my reaction, or maybe at his ability to mince like a pro, but he did that rare, wide smile of his he does only when he's thinking it's not so bad to be married to me after all. He threw off the oven mitts, picked me up, swung me to the master bedroom.

And you know what we did in the aforementioned bedroom?

We flossed. We were too traveled out to make love. Washed our faces, brushed our teeth, changed into pajamas. Like real married couples everywhere. And then he fell asleep. So maybe Crick and I didn't have a chance to plan much before Mather came along, to consider our options, write lists of pros and cons, match hobbies and moviegoing tastes, scrutinize each other's parents to see what the other might look like in thirty years. We didn't create memories of a life together without a child, years of premarriage dates and trips and fights and reconciliations. We never made those memories worth remembering when things get rough.

But we're going to make them now.

Look at him. My bedside lamp doesn't faze him. He's a carved knight on a tomb. On his back, profile up, hands crossed on his chest. *Sarkophagos*, Greek for "flesh-eating stone." That's how still and solid he is, my husband. Maybe it's from sleeping in one too many narrow cots, but he stays like that all night long, tightly wound inside himself the way he is when he's awake, no sprawling of legs and arms, no snoring, just closes his eyes and sleeps through Mather's midnight screaming the same way he claims he once used to sleep through mortar attacks. He's proud of this ability to sleep and I don't blame him; he has levels of perfection he needs to maintain, like how he never gets a cold or food poisoning, sunburn or mosquito bites. If I can just exist in the same sphere as Crick for long enough he'll fix me, I know he will.

Good-bye, Margaret Gearney of the constant blush, I'm Mrs. Creighton Brickshaw with a ring on my finger and a healthy baby in my arms, a world of time zones, latitude, and longitude piled up at my feet. This is old news for my brave and jaded man; he's been to Iraq, Afghanistan, Iraq again. His infantry soul laughs in the face of peaceful Jordan. But for me, this is the beginning of my life.

Mom. Wish I could tell her everything I've seen. She'd listen like every word could transport her out of her swollen limbs. I understand why cats bring home mice and lay them at their mistresses' feet. It didn't matter what my stories were. The lady wearing her bra over her tank top at the 7-Eleven. A photo exhibit—forty pictures of the creased bottoms of feet. A new word: *fenestrate*, from the Latin for *window*: "*having windows,*" or "*having translucent spots, like the wings of certain butterflies.*"

Writing feels a little like talking to her. The habit. Reviewing my life, catching moments I missed the first time I lived them.

Though when I told her stories, I sometimes made things up as I went along. Exaggerated. Said things I thought she'd like to hear.

But now I'm only going to write down *true* things. Because the lady wasn't actually wearing her bra over her T-shirt, it was two sports bras doubled up. And not all the photos were feet, some were palms, and some were footprints, and there were even a few close-ups of ears thrown in. But *fenestrate*, well, that's really the definition. Because words are beautiful and weird enough all by themselves.

Unlike me, Crick cannot tell a lie. For him, there is only one truth, and he tells it.

I'm learning from him. Small steps. Tiny truths add up. *Transparency*. Here it is: *transparent: capable of transmitting light so that objects or images can be seen as if there were no intervening material*. Isn't that beautiful? Being so honest you're flooded with light. Like those fenestrate butterfly wings.

Everything else is behind us, and I'll try to make everything right. I can do anything with Crick beside me. You know when it's quiet and dark and still and you can't help but squint your eyes and look at the stars? Well that was me, sitting for so long, looking up, waiting for something to shoot across my night sky. And along came Crick, drawing me into his mighty constellation, and now there are three of us here with too many wondrous stars above for me to even begin to count.

May 13, 2011

6:30 P.M.

❧

I close her book.

My spine is rigid with mortification. Crick pranced around, mocking *me*? Well, Campbell's soup chicken casserole is actually a delicacy here. It's difficult to find Campbell's cream of chicken soup! I have to order it off of Amazon! One of the components flew more than five thousand miles just to be taken for granted by their digestive tracts. If that's not a delicacy then I don't know what is.

I take a deep breath. I tell myself this was the first night, we had just met, Crick and I had only exchanged a few words. Maybe it was natural for them to poke fun. Didn't Dan and I do the same thing, more or less, driving home from the Brickshaw apartment that very evening?

"What'd you think?" Dan asked, yawning as he pulled out into the night.

"How many beers did you have?" I asked. "Are you sure you ought to be driving?"

"Two, Cassie. Two light beers."

I'd seen an empty six-pack on the floor of the tiny balcony where the men had retreated so Crick could sneak a cigarette, but I decided to let it slide. Dan always said I never let anything slide, but that was because if I was indeed *letting something slide* I couldn't very well point it out to him, could I? So he had no idea how often I let things go.

"They're slightly ridiculous," I began. "Gushing Goldilocks and her big bear of a husband. With a baby resembling a bowl of porridge." Dan made a phlegmy-sounding noise in his throat when I said the word *baby* and I watched the side of his face with terror, noticed the tick in his right eye starting up. I was certain he was about to launch into a conversation I didn't want to have.

I quickly leaned forward, looking for a new topic, and noticed a celebration or a protest ahead. "What's that?" I almost shouted in my desperation to stop whatever my husband was trying to enunciate.

There were men sitting in the back of pickups waving Jordanian flags, horns honking, clogging up the traffic circle. It was nearly impossible for us Westerners to tell the difference, rage and joy looking so similar to us with all the noise and gesticulating. When Ben Ali had left Tunisia the day before, protests had been sparked across Jordan, across the whole Middle East. I'd been getting alert text messages from the US embassy all day warning US citizens to stay away from large gatherings of people.

One of the young men in the back of a Toyota Hilux had a massive Jordanian flag pinned to his shoulders like a cape. A blue SUV pulled up alongside and a man leaned out the window, arms outstretched, and began yelling at the caped youth. I rolled my window up. "Pro-king or anti-?"

Dan watched the argument unfold as he waited for the chance to ease our car into the traffic circle. He, like Crick, like all the Army foreign area officers stationed at the US embassy, spoke Arabic.

"Pro." He glanced at the cars to our left and right; we were hemmed in. "Maybe. But we don't know what's around the corner." He kicked the gas, sped past the pickup, took the first exit off the circle, and didn't slow down until we reached a less congested street ahead.

It reminded me that there was a time when he'd been deployed, when he had led men and feared improvised explosive devices. I thought of that younger Dan, in his camouflage, a Velcro American flag patch on his shoulder, our wedding photo taped to the inside of his helmet, and I scooted closer, put my hand on his. I needed to make sure I didn't mention ovulation and maybe, just maybe, in bed together tonight we'd rub these edges of ours smooth. It always happened; every few months we would get to where our only communication was cutting little spats, my demand for procreational rather than recreational sex certainly not helping, and then something would remind us there was a bit of unplanned excitement left. Like the laugh we had shared that afternoon looking at the heinous Brickshaw ceiling mural. *These small reprieves might just keep us going*, I thought.

But he moved his hand away from mine to brush something nonexistent from his face. I let my own drop into my lap. Spurned.

I couldn't help but think of Crick, how, when he shook my hand, he had so deliberately pressed his fingers into the lifeline in my palm. I bet that man never turned down sex.

Dan said, "I have to brief the defense attaché tomorrow. Early. There's a lot going on in the Middle East right now."

I shrugged, slightly relieved he was thinking of work, not marital discord. There was a lot going on, but we all knew Jordan was the safest place to be. Just look at all the billboards of handsome and solidly built King Abdullah, his framed photo in every business and living room in the country. Even the cars around us had photocopied pictures of him taped to their back windows.

I looked around at the families who were out at nine o'clock at night, as if this was a holiday rather than just an ordinary, and nearly freezing, January night. Boys in hooded sweatshirts sat on a low wall, the blue neon of cell phones illuminating their faces and setting their cloudy breath aglow, while a group of teenage girls in bright lipstick and eyeliner pretended they weren't watching them, whispering, covering their mouths with the ends of their headscarves. Children played on a sidewalk a couple of feet from the main drag with no parental supervision, just a stumble or shove from being mangled by an automobile.

Then I noticed the way Dan was watching me, too carefully. I sat up straight. "Wait. The unrest in Algeria and Tunisia can't reach us here, can it?" When he hesitated, I continued. "What were you and Crick talking about on the porch, so secretive?"

He looked away. "Things are changing, Cassie, changing fast. Jordan is right smack-dab in the middle of it. There's a reason why this is one of the biggest embassies in the region. And why so many of us who work here are military."

I kept my eyes on him, hoping he would say more, but he shook his head as if to silence himself and didn't say anything for the rest of our ride home. I thought of Margaret and her baby, of how hard it is to adapt to a new place in the best of times, and wondered what changes might come.

I didn't have a clue.

January 16
HOME

Earlier this morning, a noise ripped me out of my sleep. Mather? I sat straight up, afraid, confused, no idea where and when I was in the world.

There was Crick next to me, stretched out, eyebrow raised in amusement. "It's the good old deployment alarm clock," he said, yawning and nodding toward the shuttered windows.

I realized the reverberation was coming from outside our apartment building; it was slowly coalescing into words, song, music: the call to prayer! *Allahuakbar. Allahuakbar.*

Crick rubbed a palm roughly over his chin and then began to sign along, *"Ash-haduan la ilahailla Allah."*

In the two years I've known him, I've never heard him sing, not in the shower, not driving his old Jeep along the Pacific Coast Highway with the top down. I gasped. His singing voice was sweet, more boy band than heavy metal, which is probably why he's never let me hear it before.

He slipped an arm under my waist, still murmuring the

prayer. I felt his stubble against my neck. I wanted him to keep singing and I nuzzled close. Instead he said, "Wake up, wife. As they say, 'prayer is better than sleep.'"

"*Deployment alarm clock?* What's that?"

His lips moved down my shoulder and the outside of my arm. I could feel him pressed against me, his legs becoming tangled up in mine.

"Wait." I said. "Tell me—"

He hesitated like he just might say something real, then his hands slipped off my pajama bottoms and there was no more talk. He can push a fragile and precious piece of himself inside a fragile and precious piece of me, and yet he thinks my asking about his childhood or deployments is too invasive. If I say *I love you*, he gets nervous, glances away. He's a man of action, and sex is action, he's OK with that, without realizing it's the moment we are most open to each other, literally, the most opened up you can possibly be with another human being.

This is what I was thinking as I ran fingers over the ab muscles Crick's not-so-secretly proud of, doing his sit-ups every night before bed. This is what I thought when I watched his face, the way he concentrated on how my breasts bounced to his beat.

This is what I was thinking when he put his hand over my forehead, wiped his palm across my eyes to shut them, and said, "Your eyes are too big for your head."

I froze. I know I want too much. But when I look at Crick it's only because I want him and only him.

He collapsed on top of me. I held on, not letting him pull away at first, not wanting my skin bared to the air conditioner and the new day, wanting instead this closeness, his breath loud on the curve of my neck, a wind in his mouth, his fingers in my hair, my legs tight around his hips. He propped himself up on his elbows, and it felt like he was sheltering me, a tent of strength, almost like his body was saying the very words that make him so awkward. My heart was pounding and I dug my nails into the small of his back, anything to keep him longer, because I never feel as real as I do when I am holding on to him.

Then he peeled himself free and took a shower while I rolled over, seeking whatever warmth he'd left in the blankets. I pulled the comforter over my head and thought of our first time: the one moment in my life when I did things right, when I was certain, really truly certain. Before that, I thought there might be someone else, all those times he walked out of earshot to talk on his cell, the weekends he couldn't meet me and didn't give an excuse, some distance in his eyes that made me feel like he was comparing my actions to another's, and I was coming up short. But that day in his loft in Pacific Grove, no curtains on those big windows, Post-it notes covered with Arabic script sticking out from every piece of furniture, Green Day playing on his stereo, that day was perfect. He was rooted entirely in me. The yellow Post-it notes fluttered down on us, coming loose from the headboard, the ceiling fan, the windowsill. I picked them up, pressed them into a sticky little bouquet, and put them into my purse when he wasn't looking. I couldn't read the words but I was determined to read him, learn him. *This man will take me places,* I thought.

And he has.

This morning, after his shower, he came back in with his towel knotted low on his waist. He leaned against the door frame and watched me the way I hoped he would, noticing the way I held the sheet to my body with one hand, covering my breasts, my stretching legs peeking out and bare. He looked like he wanted to hop right back into me. Wouldn't that have been the best first day in Jordan? Crick unable to leave.

"What should we do first?" I asked. I broke the spell; I could tell in the way he straightened, turned, went to the suitcase on the floor. I wrapped my sheet tighter, scooted to the edge of the bed. "There's the citadel, or the Roman amphitheater, or maybe we have a taxi drive us all around the city?"

"I have to work." He glanced over his shoulder in my direction, drawing his blue suit from his bag. "Snooze you lose, babe."

"You've got to be kidding," I said in a jokey voice. He had to be kidding, right? "We've been here, like, I don't know, less than thirteen hours. You can't *work*."

"Welcome to the Army, buttercup. Dan's picking me up in ten minutes. I have to get badged and briefed. I left Cassie's number for you on the kitchen counter. She'll help you out." He started to slap the wool of his suit with his palm as if he could beat the wrinkles out of it.

Should I have unpacked and hung up all his clothes last night instead of writing in my journal? Is that what good wives do? Should I have complained about his leaving me, forcing me to depend on the kindness of strangers? Was there a chance complaining might have made him stick around, or would it have pissed him off, made him more eager to leave?

He dressed, checking his tie in the mirror, not needing any help from me. He came over to the bed. I was halfway between pouting and putting on a happy face.

"Call Cassie," he said, and made a kissing noise by my forehead, which I took as an apology. "I'll try not to be home late. You'll be OK?"

"I'll be OK," I said, and really that was the best way to describe how I felt in that moment. OK. Its origins baffling. Just look at it. OK? More hieroglyphic than word, a stick person lying on her back, like she's been run over by a train: big head, arms out, legs stuck at an angle. West African, Choctaw Native American Indian, or Boston American slang from the mid-1800s; no one knows.

Crick left.

But then, a minute later, the doorbell rang.

I hopped out of bed, tossed on my pajamas, and ran, thinking, *Ha! He forgot his keys! Here's another chance to lure my love back to my siren depths!* I opened the door without realizing my spaghetti-strapped top was the only thing between my nipples and the outside world, the bottoms low on my hips, revealing stretch-marked skin.

Definitely not my husband. But a man.

"Saleh, Saleh," the guy said, nervously tapping his collarbones. He had unexpectedly green eyes, was clean shaven, full lipped. Sort of Bollywood, his clothes tight, wearing eyeliner? Or maybe his lashes really are that dark and thick.

"Oh . . . hi. I mean, good morning!" I stepped sideways to get most of my body behind the door. "I'm Margaret Brickshaw."

"I *boab*. The one to helps," the stranger said. "Yes?"

I smiled and he slowly smiled in return and we stood like that for too long, to the point when you are no longer actually smiling but just creepily aware of showing your teeth. Then, thank goodness, his cell phone started to ring.

He checked the number. "This landlord." He lifted the phone in my direction as if making introductions. "I tell you here."

"Nice to meet you!" I said. "So sweet of you to stop by!"

Then I started to close the door very slowly so as not to hurt Saleh's feelings. I wondered if I should lock the door, or would that hurt his feelings too, implying I was scared? White woman overreacting to brown man? But how long should I wait before locking the door? Should I *not* lock the door at all to imply how safe I felt thanks to Saleh's being there in the hallway protecting me? I started to slide the chain across the door one loud link at a time, then stopped, not wanting him to hear. Oh the mental anguish of trying to be nice! *Kindness*, I reminded myself. *Just be kind*. Right and wrong can be tricky, but kindness, well, I'm hoping kindness is simple enough that even I can't screw it up.

May 13, 2011

6:45 P.M.

I stand up from the bed, disgusted that a scene of such heat occurred under these very sheets. It's also discomfiting to think
of anyone having great sex when you are not, even more so when
they are people you spend so much time with. Not that I want
their sex to be *unpleasant*, mind you, but Crick always seems
vaguely dissatisfied with Margaret, giving me glances that seem
to be the assessment of a man who is *not* being serviced properly
by his young wife.

The *boab*. I should have mentioned him. Of course he waited
until Crick left before making his introductions, wanting to
catch Margaret all alone, nearly undressed, defenseless, and suc-
ceeding. I have run into that man countless times and he always
seems to be hovering around Margaret's door or her parking
spot in the basement garage. Lurking. Unlike so many of the
unwashed migrant masses here from God knows where, this
fellow smells like hairspray and baby oil. His cleanliness, fitted
yellow T-shirt, and tight jeans all make me suspicious. He must

have some sort of familial relationship to the landlord, other-wise who would hire a maintenance man who doesn't seem like he would ever get his hands dirty?

I turn to the next page of Margaret's journal. *EMBASSY BRIEF.*

I feel a warm flush surge through me. It was my idea she at-tend this. I prepare myself, wondering what she will write about me this time.

That morning, after she had glad-handed the entire security force at the front gate, I took her to the embassy park, that rare place in Jordan with real grass.

"Is it too cold for the baby?" I asked.

"No! It's . . . perfectly brisk!" The child had managed not to choke on the Mentos that had been shoved down his greedy baby gullet, but drool dripped down his chin, uncollected by his mother. He grunted toward the swings and Margaret merrily carried him over and plopped him inside a bucket seat.

I was pleased with myself. My new charges were happy, the day was crisp and sunny, all was well in our world. "I know it's awfully soon, but Dan and I want to throw you a party, so you can meet the people who work with Crick—"

"Please don't," Margaret said, dropping her arms to her sides and looking at me. Mather, when he realized she'd stopped push-ing him, began to grunt louder and kick. She bit her lip. "It's really good of you, but you won't believe how socially retarded I am at parties. Ask Crick. I'm better like this"—she waved her fingers between us—"one on one, you know? Raising my hand in a classroom, really any public speaking, that sort of stuff makes my heart stampede. I almost threw up during our wed-ding when I had to say the vows, and there were only four people there! Crick said it was morning sickness, but trust me, I know a panic attack."

"Morning sickness?"

She covered her mouth with her hand. I have never seen a face so easy to read, every small, flickering emotion blazing. "You got me!" She snorted and I stood there, hoping no one would walk by and hear this woman barking at me like a German shepherd. "Mather was our Cupid!"

I struggled to find a reply. I hardly knew this woman but I wanted to despise her, her perky body, her dashing husband, and now this revelation that her ovaries were so fertile, and Crick's sperm so potent, they had managed to make a life out of a mistake. All while Dan and I had been trying desperately, willfully, every ounce longing, for years and years.

"Well." I floundered. "You and Crick seem happy."

She stopped laughing. "Do we?"

I saw her vulnerability then, how she actually thought my answer somehow mattered, having known me for all of sixteen hours. As if I could say she and Crick looked miserable and it would be so. "Better than most," I replied, picking my phone out of my purse. "We'll have a party at some point. I'll keep it small." I had to admit it was gratifying that she wasn't eager to make more friends, that she might be content with me and only me. The embassy community in Jordan is a very social one: Tuesday taco nights, wine tastings, Easter egg hunts on the ambassador's lawn. But lately I've seen how the lives of married couples bend and narrow around the social lives of their children. As the children begin school, parents adjust accordingly: age-appropriate children pair off for playdates and their parents have no choice but to do the same. This has had a serious impact on my ability to make friends. To be honest, there was not one person currently in Amman that I could call to meet me for coffee or a manicure. But Margaret—maybe Margaret would fill that empty place.

"How about we let Mather play, then I'll show you the mail room, the souvenir shop, and the mini grocery store with all the American goodies, including booze. Later we'll hit the cafeteria. I'll call Dan; maybe he and Crick can join us for lunch."

"Oh, no." Margaret concentrated on pushing Mather again. "I mean, Crick has a briefing?" She shrugged. "It seemed important."

I waited a beat. "The security brief? But you need to go with him! It's a requirement, and it's always better if spouses attend together. Didn't Crick tell you?"

She tilted her head at me. "Can I bring the baby?"

"No." I examined her face, searching for guile; was she trying to get me to volunteer? Was she more manipulative than she looked? "I can watch him."

"Can't I go another time?"

Technically, she could. There were security briefs for newcomers every two weeks. But one look at Margaret and it was obvious she needed that brief immediately. Didn't she know Jordan's borders—Iraq, Syria, Saudi Arabia, and Israel—were all beset with turmoil? There were areas of Jordan we weren't supposed to visit. Why, even here at the American embassy, we were only fifteen miles from the Jordanian city of Zarqa, birthplace of Zarqawi, the al-Qaeda leader in Iraq and the mastermind behind the hotel bombings in Amman that killed sixty people in 2005. His first wife and sons live in Zarqa still. Of course Zarqawi had been blown to deserved smithereens in Iraq and nothing horrible had happened to Americans in Jordan lately—no one had been kidnapped on their way to a pirated-DVD shop or found a car bomb nestled under the hood of their Honda. That might have been because, unlike Margaret, we were all so *aware* and therefore mentally armed. But Margaret, Margaret exuded absolute naïveté. She might as well have been wearing a big bull's-eye reading, *Shoot here.*

"You need to go today," I said. "I'll watch Mather."

"You don't mind?"

"We'll stay here. If it gets too cold, we'll be in the cafeteria."

She didn't hesitate. Didn't make me a cautious list of things to do, didn't try to explain how to change his diaper or when to give him a snack or a bottle.

"That'd be super." Her smile was tremendous. I looked away, not wanting her to know how touched I was she was giving me this responsibility, trusting me already.

I called Dan, who was able to find Crick, who came to the park ten minutes later. He barely acknowledged me, perhaps realizing what an idiot he'd been by not thinking of this himself. He put a hand on Margaret's back and steered her out of the park. I watched them leave. But at the gate, Crick hesitated, letting Margaret walk ahead. He turned, seemed to be seeking me out. I lifted my chin, curious, watching him over the swinging baby body hurdling toward me. I was afraid he was going to shake his head with a quick, scornful motion, letting me know he was angry I had thrust his wife into his day.

Instead, he winked.

I felt a constriction in my throat and pelvis, some cross between being turned on and being electrocuted, and before I could stop myself, my mouth pulled wide into a smile.

January 16 continued!

Some Advice on Social Interaction in Jordan:

Conservative dress is best. Jordan is a primarily Muslim country and most Jordanians favor traditional values. For men, wearing shorts in public is not encouraged but they can be worn within the embassy athletic facilities. For women, shorts are not acceptable except inside a gym or camping/hiking in remote regions (but this is still discouraged). Tank or halter tops are considered provocative and offensive by many. When in doubt, covering from wrist to ankle is always a safe bet. Women do not need to cover their heads, except at religious sites.

We're in the back row because we came late. Crick hates to be late. I tried to tell him it was Cassie's idea, I wanted to go another time, but he shushed and pushed me all the way from the swing set to this conference room. We walked past Mr. Robert Riding, who stood in front next to his PowerPoint slides and paused, staring at the clock over his head as if wanting every single person in the room to know we were exactly eleven minutes tardy.

In public, women should not touch a member of the opposite sex outside their immediate family. This includes shaking hands. This also includes the male cashier's hand at a store. When you give him money, either bills or change, drop it into his palm and be sure he does the same to you.

Crick is watching me as each new slide comes up, nodding his head and arching those eyebrows . . . I point at my journal, then shake my pen as if I'm writing so much it hurts.

Don't indulge in public displays of affection with members of the opposite sex. But don't be surprised if you see members of the same sex holding hands, especially young men; this is normal.

Don't use your left hand to touch, eat, or give gifts. The left is used for toilet matters and therefore is considered unclean.

I'd rather be in the park. Do other babies grunt? When is Mather due for his next checkup? I need to check my Dr. Sears. Also his poop was orange this morning, must look that up.

Women, it is best to avoid making direct eye contact with men, especially strangers. This can be misconstrued as flirting. In turn, when men don't look you in the eye and when they avoid talking to you, don't think they are being rude, they are being respectful of your modesty.

There are two couples in the front row, the women maybe older than me but not so much, in their thirties? When we walked (ran) past in our lateness, I smiled apologetically, but they were leaning toward each other, as if they're already buddies and I'm the rude late girl they don't want to know. Two men sitting off to our right look a lot like Crick, tall, fit, with military-short hair, bristling with annoyance about having to listen to an embassy security brief when they're probably used to leading missions into war zones.

The embassy has fielded quite a few complaints of sexual harassment occurring in cabs and we recommend the embassy community only use the yellow and white officially marked taxis. All women are advised NOT to sit in the front seat, which can be misconstrued as a sexual advance.

Crick knowingly looks my way, as if I am in the habit of crawling into taxi drivers' laps every chance I get.

SECURITY ISSUES:
MAIL
ABDUCTION
BOMBINGS

Really? Jumping from cab drivers to abductions? Why won't anyone look at me? No one else mildly amused that mail and bombings are in the same category? Nope. Only Crick watching me. And clearly not amused that I'm amused.

MAIL:
Embassy employees must open all mail in the secure area outside of the embassy mail room. If white powder is found inside, slowly place the package on the ground while shouting, "WHITE

POWDER, WHITE POWDER," then calmly exit and wait
for security.

ABDUCTION:
Every embassy residence is equipped with a panic room with
bulletproof door. If you fear you are in danger, lock yourself in
your panic room and radio the embassy immediately.

My mom lived in a panic room of her own making my entire
life. I do not intend on having one of my own.

Things to keep in your panic room:
Enough nonperishable food and water to last a week
All important documents (wedding and birth certificates, pass-
    ports, etc.)
Travel bag packed and ready for immediate departure
Cash in both Jordanian and American currencies

Then, tada! BOMBINGS!!
Everyone leans forward the tiniest bit; finally something exciting! Even Mr. Robert Riding grins for the first time. He goes
to the desk and lifts up an iPod with a little portable dock and
two tiny speakers. He proudly rubs a thumb over the corner of
one of the speakers, the way a man checks the keenness of a
pocketknife. He has an adorably narrow little feral face, Mr. Riding does. Like a goat.
    Hmmm. He's not actually playing music but all the different
alarms.
    When we believe a bomb is about to go off in the embassy (seriously,
did he really just say that?), *we will hear this alarm:*

"Duck and cover, stay away from windows" (this in calm, British-accented voice). *De dah, de dah!!!*

If we have warning of a dangerous situation and the time to act accordingly, we will hear this one:

"Secure all classified documents and evacuate building immediately!" (in a stressed-out American female voice. Do Americans move faster when an American accent tells them to hurry up?). *Whoowhoowhoowhoo!!*

Now Mr. Riding is saying we must remember to check under vehicles for explosives and mix up driving routines so we can't be followed.

Here's a head. Now a stick body. Now a stick body wearing a necktie and name tag. Here's another. One stick-man Mr. Robert Riding and one stick-man Crick. Because all this shock and awe, doom and gloom, is getting me a little sad. *Abductions?* How about this slide: *Welcome to Jordan! You will have the time of your life here, young woman who has been waiting much too long for her life to begin. Emergency action: weekend getaway to Petra, because clearly you, Major and Mrs. Brickshaw, are newlyweds who never had time for a honeymoon.*

How about I give you a daisy, Mr. Riding? A daisy with a smiley face seems to be just what you need right now, here, right below your sweet little goat face!

Uh-oh.

Mr. Riding just came over, stood at my shoulder, and inspected my doodle.

Yikes.

Why, oh why, did I have to give my goat-man a *Mr. Robert Riding* name tag?

January 16 continued yet again

Today was not my best day.

After Mr. Robert Riding saw my drawings, he said, "I assure you, Mrs. Brickshaw, this information is of the utmost importance."

The people in the front row, the people who were on time and hadn't been squirming or smiling or had notes checked by Robert Riding, all turned around and stared. Mr. Riding looked at Crick as if he thought my husband ought to punish me. Where's Crick's sense of humor? For all his swagger, his smoking, his poetic use of the F-word and every obscene bit of Army humor, he's very keen on rules. The "right" thing. Crick leaned over and looked at my sketch before I could finish scratching out the one I'd done of him with briar-patch eyebrows. I felt awful. Does Robert Riding *like* looking like a goat? No way. Does Crick *like* his Amazon eyebrows? No. As a matter of fact he once asked me really nicely if I could trim them for him and I giggled, just a tiny giggle, but he never asked again, and sometimes I catch him looking into the bathroom mirror, smoothing his eyebrows down with wet fingertips, and if he sees me watching him he gets all angry as if I've caught him trying on my lip gloss. I know I missed an opportunity for true intimacy between us, and I imagine the way I could have hovered over him with scissors in one hand, a palm cupped gently to his chin, how he would have looked up at me, exposed.

I felt bad enough, then Crick made it worse at the end when we were packing up our stuff to leave. "You're a real mixed bag, Mar, you know that?"

I nodded. "I'm sorry," I said loud enough so Mr. Robert Riding, who was carefully putting away his miniature speaker set and definitely not making eye contact with us, could hear if he wanted to.

Crick's called me a "mixed bag" before. It used to make me think of grocery store deals on fruit that's about to go bad, a brown banana, a smashed kiwi, apples with leprous bumps, all cellophaned together on a flat piece of Styrofoam, *Sale!* But I looked it up and it originally referred to a bag of game brought home after a day of hunting. Now I think of crushed and bloody birds that just a little while ago were flying, and he can't possibly mean that, so I pretend he means *mixed blessing* and just leave it be.

The best part of the day was when we returned to the park and found Cassie still pushing Mather on a swing. I wondered if she'd been doing that for the whole hour we'd been at our brief. The baby was shrieking with joy, so maybe he won't have whiplash or frostbite, and I didn't want to seem critical by asking her. I want her to like me but I can't tell if she does. She keeps her forehead crinkled when I speak, as if my voice doesn't sound quite human. But she's interesting, I think. Handsome, the way they used to describe big-boned women in the 1800s. She ought to have her hair in a bun at the back of her neck and be sawing off gangrenous legs on a battlefield. Someone who knows how to get things done. A description that has never been used for me. She wears ironed clothes! I can't imagine ironing. Every time I try to tuck in my shirt Mather knocks over a potted plant or poops himself up to the nape of his neck.

As we drew closer, Crick leaned over and in his typically savage way whispered, "That woman looks like a gargoyle." I kept walking; it was not a nice thing to say, I know that, and yet the fact that he was speaking to me after the brief debacle was a relief. And, though Cassie is arresting, curvy and tall, with dark brown hair and nicely shaped hazel eyes, Crick's right, there is also something *stony* about her. Hard. The way she sets her chin to let you know she's thinking harsh thoughts. I remembered the moms in my Monterey prenatal yoga class who were sinewy and tan, smiled all the time, spoke with singsong voices, how they frightened me when they ferociously ate their salads, *stab stab stab*, such vast and duplicitous anger under that too-groomed surface. But with Cassie, I can tell she speaks her mind. It makes me want to hear what she'll say next.

I didn't reply to Crick; I'd already done enough karmic damage with my doodles, and I'm trying to ignore him when he's mean, same way I try not to give Mather positive reinforcement when he bites. Crick, for all his confidence, needs women to smile and admire him, I know he does, and in this small way I think I can prune his behavior, the strain of cruelty he confuses with humor. I shouldn't have laughed so hard when he made fun of Cassie's casserole.

"You're really good with the baby," I said to her at the swing. "Do you and Danny plan on having kids?"

"We're trying," she mumbled. "It's not so easy for everyone."

I nodded. If she meant that as a barb, I ignored it. She really was good with the baby. Any woman who can get my son to yell with such glee is a woman destined to be my friend.

May 13, 2011

⚜

G argoyle.

I stand up and throw the journal across the room. It smacks the wall, then falls in a flutter on a pile of her cheap and tawdry scarves.

Gargoyle?!

I almost rip the pages from Margaret's pocket dictionary to look up the exact definition: *gargoyle: a spout, terminating in a grotesque representation of a human or animal figure with open mouth, projecting from the gutter for throwing rainwater clear of a building.*

That bastard.

Sure, I am plain. I am unthreatening. Safe. Not pretty enough to turn the heads of strangers, but certainly not hideous in a way that would scare away pigeons. Greenish eyes, shoulder-length hair, square face, a strong chin that I believe gives the impression I can keep my mouth shut. Childbearing hips that have not done their job, but my breasts have withstood the ravages of gravity: the bright side of never having to nurse a baby. In Jordan I too often have to cover up those charms with matronly tops and cardigans, but, compared to Margaret's meatless chest, I am proud of what Dan used to call my *great rack*.

My looks were certainly good enough the night of their belated welcome party. As if I could ever forget the feel of Crick's palms sliding up my back, the way he pulled me in tight. And then his hot whiskey breath in my ear as he murmured, "Sometimes you end up with the wrong woman."

Margaret is right about her husband's needing the admiration of the opposite sex.

Thinking about his hands sends a thrill through me now, a thrill that even the word *gargoyle* does not erase.

I shouldn't be reading this. I should go into the living room, watch the news, drink Crick's scotch.

But instead I sit on the floor and poke the journal as if it might wound me. These are all the things you just don't ever want to know. What a person, what a *friend*, really thinks of you. This truth that Margaret praises so much is a cruel thing indeed.

And impossible to resist.

I pick the book up, smooth the injured pages down. Start where I left off.

—a woman destined to be my friend—

And I hear something in the living room.

I lift my head.

Yes, there it is again, an electronic sound; could it be the doorbell? I quickly get up and put the journal on the bedside table. It must be Margaret; maybe someone stole her purse with her cell phone and keys inside, that's why she hasn't answered my calls, and she has returned home and will be asking me to pay the taxi driver in his car below.

I run my fingers through my hair, try to rub the guilt from my eyes. I am pretty sure she will know as soon as she sees my face that I have been reading her journal.

"Margaret?" I shout, heedless of sleeping Mather; let him welcome her home with a wail, I don't care. "Is it finally you?"

I stand in the doorway of the living room, looking around, getting spooked because there is no knocking, no doorbell ringing. Then I realize the sound is coming from her computer. It's the sound of Skype. I walk over. Could this be Margaret? Has she lost her phone but somehow is managing to contact me, letting me know she will be home soon?

The computer screen, under the blank icon for a man's head, reads CRICK.

Shit. I consider ignoring the call, but what if he knows something? I pinch my cheeks to get the blood up and hope I am presentable.

"Hello?" I say as the screen fills with color.

Crick is leaning forward too far into the camera; I can only see the right plane of his face, as if he is urging himself through cyberspace and into his living room. Just from that angle I can tell the man is furious.

"Where is she?" he asks, no smile, no wink, no *Well, hello there, Cassie, how you doing today? Funny to find you in my living room.*

I wait to see something in his face that tells me he is at least a little glad to see me.

He is not.

"I don't know," I reply, deliberately sullen.

"For fuck's sake, put her on!"

For a moment I hate him with the familiar loathing I have only ever felt for Dan. "Margaret's not here."

He shakes his head. "Someone told me she went to see the regional security officer after I told her not to."

"Is that where she is right now?" I ask, confused.

He sits back in his chair. "No." Watching me closely. "She went yesterday, or maybe a couple days ago. How the fuck would I know? I'm on a different continent and she doesn't tell me a damn thing. I figured if anyone knew, it'd be you." I look away. Margaret never said anything about going to see Robert Riding. It seems like every moment I find out something new she's been keeping from me. Crick snaps his fingers in front of the screen to regain my attention. "Cassie? She's really not home?"

I move close to the computer's camera. I want him to see the sincerity and anxiety on my face. "Don't worry, I have Mather."

His eyes widen with amazement. "She hasn't gotten herself into enough trouble since I've been gone?" But his words are all wrong for his face. His face is betraying him and starting to look afraid. "Tell me where she is."

I hesitate. What should I tell him? Where does my loyalty lie? "She ran out for a minute. She should be home soon."

"How long has she been gone?"

I glance at the time at the corner of the screen and feel my shoulders sink. "About three hours."

"*Three hours?* Three hours and you don't know where she is? What the hell?"

How easily I break. "We were in a little accident this afternoon. Your Land Rover is fine, everybody is fine. Margaret had to go to the police station to pay the fine. But I haven't heard from her since she left. What should I do?"

He stares at me for five long seconds. "I don't know." Coming from Crick, those words are terrifying. He is not the kind of man who ever admits ignorance. He continues to stare as if I am keeping something from him. I could tell him more, it's true, I could tell him about her scrawled words: *I MUST FIND HIM.* Instead I think of Margaret's wet and bleary voice, more sad than accusatory, *Did you tell?*

"You know how she is with her cell phone," I say weakly.

I can see Crick's mind working behind his dark eyes. He finally says, "Let me call around, see if anyone has heard anything. It hasn't been long enough to constitute much of anything, let alone an emergency. We don't want to blow this out of proportion." Am I being paranoid or did he say those words with more emphasis than necessary? He continues. "It's possible she got a flat tire and her phone's dead. OK, Cassie? I'm serious, don't call anyone, don't do *anything* until you hear from me again. Promise me you won't make any calls."

I nod, wondering if he is testing me. He says he will call back soon. "Do not do anything," he says again, as if I am unreliable, as if I have the ability to wreak havoc, me, the woman stuck in his apartment, left to care for his only child. It's insulting, our entire exchange, his abrupt manner, but again I nod my head, and, as Dan has taught me, "let it slide."

When he disconnects, I move away from the computer screen and back to the bedroom, rubbing my neck, releasing the tension, wondering if we were hit harder than we thought this afternoon. Could something have happened to Margaret? Could she have slammed her head on the steering wheel and now be curled up somewhere, suffering from the delayed effects of a concussion?

But I'll listen to Crick. This time I'll let him decide what to do next. This time he can be the one to get the embassy involved.

May 13, 2011

7:07 P.M.

Talking with Crick has left me restless. I skim Margaret's entries, impatient, read a paragraph here, a paragraph there. Her journal-writing steam tapers off in February, when more days pass between entries. Crick, Saleh, Mather, Mather, Mather; occasionally there is a brief mention of me.

Margaret is an odd duck indeed. She thinks all the chickens on a spit in the window of a rotisserie shop in Abdoun look like headless, naked, impaled babies. No wonder she is a vegetarian. She's discovered that *labneh*, a yogurt cheese ubiquitous in the Middle East, can substitute for both hard-to-come-by sour cream and even-harder-to-find ricotta. I could have told her that. She is very disappointed that her neighbors, three Iraqi teenagers who wear voluminous *hijabs* but skintight leggings, do not speak a word of English, but she is optimistic she will learn enough Arabic to be able to converse with them soon. Ha.

I stare at the time. Mather and I should have gone with her. When Margaret holds Mather she proves she has sworn her fealty to a man, given him an heir. She is "mother" rather than "woman." He is her shield, her victory. I should have made Margaret wake the baby from his nap, I should have driven her to the station. As unpleasant as it may have been to bring a toddler, if we had all gone together I'd know exactly what she was up to right now.

February 11

HOME

F riday is the first full day of the weekend in the Arab world. Like America's Saturday.

But we didn't take advantage of Crick's day off. Instead, he paced in front of the television blasting Al Jazeera English, his BlackBerry never out of his hand. Newspapers spread across the living room table, in Arabic and in English. He scanned every paragraph, comparing each story line by line.

The leader of Egypt, Hosni Mubarak, has resigned.

Mather and I played within earshot. Over Crick's shoulders, I watched hundreds of thousands of protestors in Tahrir Square fall on their knees, praying, weeping, chanting, cheering. They waved flags, they hugged soldiers. It seemed glorious. Only eighteen days of protest and now, a new government. So much hope. All those protesters must feel like they worked hard to create this new world, this new life, and now everything will be so much better. All those protesters must feel just like me.

"Seriously?" Crick keeps shouting at the TV. "Seriously? No

one at the American embassy in Cairo saw this coming? What the fuck, Uncle Sam! One point five billion a year in military aid and we got nothing on this?"

He doesn't like it when there are things he doesn't know. He doesn't like it at all.

February 14

HOME

M ather is ONE!

Of course, Crick forgot both his son's birthday AND Valentine's Day.

Regional turmoil, Mar! Realignment of power! Don't give me one of those looks about being late, I told you . . . All said with less and less vigor as he stood in the kitchen, first noticing the Valentine I'd cut out of red construction paper, then the crooked little birthday cake. No protest when I took his BlackBerry from him and put it in the drawer next to the stove, inside an oven mitt.

I made *cusa*, zucchini stuffed with rice with yogurt sauce on top, so yummy, a Jordanian recipe. I actually managed to cook it properly (minus the ground lamb! If Crick knew there was supposed to be meat, he never said a word). For dessert, sugar cookies shaped like hearts with the imprint of Mather's tiny hands. Also a cake with one candle for Mather; we didn't even get a chance to take a picture before the baby attacked it with his face. Crick and I sang "Happy Birthday," looking at each other over the explosion of vanilla frosting and cake chunks, care of our rabid, sugar-high toddler, and I could tell Crick was thinking, *This isn't so bad after all.*

During bathtime, Mather kept neighing like a horse (we've been doing animal sounds), and Crick and I laughed too much the first time, which meant the baby neighed for an hour straight. When he was dry and cozy in his little footed pajamas, Crick got down on the floor and gave him a horsey ride up and down the hallway.

I'm so happy. This has been the most perfect night ever. I knew everything would come together for us in Jordan.

February 20

HOME

Today Cassie said I show too much skin. My sexy wrinkled elbows? My ankle socks and inch of stubbly shin, revealed by daring capris?

Sure, people stare. I'm getting used to it, but I'm always aware. Cassie gets looked at just as much as I do. I think it's curiosity. Most of the time if I give a big smile, the person looks totally shocked to have been caught and will smile back. They go from a sort of blankness to this welling gladness. Women especially blossom into joy and will give really lovely, open smiles in return, with an *ilhamdallah* or *masha'allah* and a pat on the head or a pinched cheek for Mather, maybe a few words for me, *Welcome to Jordan!* They're so surprised and grateful I'm smiling at *them!* Even women who are fully covered, just a tiny window for their eyes peeking from the veil. You can see the uplift in the corners of their eyelids, feel their genuine warmth. Somehow it makes me even more friendly than I was in America, less afraid of making a fool of myself. At home, everyone says *Hi there* or *Have a nice day*, right? But here, since it's not just a *habit* to greet everyone you meet, it feels more genuine, feels more authentic for being hard-won. It's worth the potential embarrassment.

That's something Cassie forgets when she is harping on all the things I *shouldn't* do. She forgets the things we *should* do. At the end of the security brief, after I'd been caught doodling and was too mortified to keep writing, Mr. Robert Riding said we need to remember at all times that we might be the only *real* Americans the Jordanians here will ever know. Just ordinary Americans, removed from Hollywood films or front pages of newspapers or the politics of our nation. We need to represent our country well. We need to behave in a way that shows we are decent human beings. I appreciated Robert Riding's saying that, even if he was sort of looking at me in an injured way, as if he thought I couldn't possibly be a decent human being if I made a caricature of him that looked like a goat.

May 13, 2011

7:14 P.M.

❧

I hear something through the walls and close her journal. It's not Mather, it's not from an adjacent apartment. Maybe the hallway? It's not quite a knock but seems to be coming from her front door, a gentle rap. Could Margaret have lost her keys? I put the journal neatly at the side of her bed, wondering who else it might be. There's the doctor from Topeka who lives on the ground floor, but he is often traveling to the embassies and consulates in the region that don't have a permanent health unit staff. There is also the woman, Deborah Something, she works in Consular, whom Margaret has taken a severe disliking to. When I asked about her once, Margaret said, "It's *Deborah*, as in rhymes with *Gomorrah*, like Sodom and Gomorrah."

"Margaret! What are you talking about?"

She pursed her lips to stop from smiling. "No, really, she corrected my pronunciation when we met. This was the same day she told me I shouldn't feed the stray cats on our street. She lives on the second floor. I see her every once in a while in the elevator."

Now I open Margaret's front door a few inches, keeping the chain lock on. I see it's only Saleh, gathering up the garbage bags. I close the door, unlock the chain, open it again.

"It's about time," I say to him.

He looks at me for a moment and then throws down the bags, as well as his broom and the dustpan, and they all clatter loudly, making me jump. He leaves them there, walks down the hallway.

"Excuse me!" I shout at his back. He ignores me, takes the steps down.

I'm enraged. One of the tossed bags has split open, diapers and coffee grinds oozing everywhere. Injury upon injury, I can't even slam the door closed because I am afraid I will wake the baby.

I close the door quietly, relock every single bolt.

What was Saleh hoping for? Margaret, certainly, instead of me. What would Margaret have done if she was home? Flirt with him as he tidied up the hallway? Welcome him inside? Though she did warn me not to let him in. As if I would in a million years.

I return to the journal. I know exactly what Robert Riding meant about representing America properly. Margaret had it wrong. He was telling us not to look like MTV strumpets.

From the day she arrived, Margaret has ignored the effect she has on men.

Granted, she never wears tight or revealing clothing. But here, the Islamic ideal is that members of the opposite sex do not engage. Jordanians, especially women, are taught to be modest in all ways. People learn to keep their eyes to themselves. It becomes habit. I realize this must be difficult for Margaret. We in the West are used to being greeted and smiled at, viewed and appraised. I remember when I first arrived, how jarring it was to say hello to men in the elevator and have them nervously turn their entire body away from me, how we would stand like that until the elevator spat us out on our respective floors. Once I was introduced to a Jordanian man at an embassy function, someone who worked with Dan. When the din grew too loud and I leaned in to ask a question, placing my hand on his upper arm to get his attention, he flinched. *Flinched.* He recovered, angled his head toward me, answered cheerfully enough. But that instinctual reaction taught me everything. I would obey from then on, I told myself, I would not shake hands or make eye contact or wear clothing that made men flinch. I would be impeccable. I would respect this culture, I would embrace this idea of modesty as much as I could.

Margaret, however, ignored this. Like the time we caught a taxi after shopping at the bakeries in Swefieh. "Where are you from?" she asked, leaning forward to talk to the driver. He replied he was from Kabul. I knocked her knee with mine, tried to shut her up with a cross look. She ignored me.

"Afghanistan! Have you been to the Gardens of Babur? Whenever I hear the word *Kabul*, that's just what I think of. Gardens."

The driver narrowed all of his attention on Margaret and none on the road. I could see his eyes in the rearview mirror, mesmerized by the way her T-shirt pulled tight across her breasts, how she swung her blond ponytail. Her flashing, lascivious teeth and naked collarbones.

They spoke for a bit, Margaret refusing to acknowledge me. She said how long she'd been here, how much she loved this place.

Then the driver said, "I like you much. What is phone number? Tomorrow we meet?"

As I imagined an al-Qaeda kidnapping, Margaret began to write on the back of a grocery store receipt. Of course I snatched the note from her and demanded the driver pull over, "Here, please, yes, this is fine. I understand it's not the address we originally gave you but please stop this taxi immediately."

She burst out laughing as we stood on a strange curb in a neighborhood I had never seen before. A woman sloshed water off a balcony above. A barefoot girl wearing eyeliner and lipstick ran by us shouting, "Hello! Hello! Hello!"

I scanned the road. We were a few long blocks from her home, not far enough to hazard another taxi. It was cold and we hadn't brought Mather's stroller. We each had a bag full of warm pita and rounds of *manakeesh* bread topped with olive oil and thyme, but I figured it would teach her a lesson if I made her walk. "Promise me you won't open your mouth again until we're safely at your apartment."

"Aye, aye, Captain Cassie!" She saluted, no apology, no remorse, then slipped her arm through mine. "You know, I was giving him Crick's work number. I'm not as innocent as you think."

I stopped and looked at her. She was smiling, blinking into the sun. For a moment I couldn't tell which scenario was preferable, her being exactly what she seemed, or her being so adept at lying that I couldn't even tell.

Margaret is a force of minor collisions, setting off small earthquakes, never thinking about what her tremors might rearrange or crack.

You play with the bull, you get the horns, my mother always says.

No pity for the six-year-old who scraped her knee on the side-walk, the thirteen-year-old with the crookedly pierced ear, the thirty-four-year-old whose husband was drifting away.

I turn a couple pages ahead until I find my name again, glance at my cell phone to once more check the time.

Wherever she is, Margaret is playing with the bull right now.

February 25
HOME

C assie brought me to Cozmo's grocery store today. David Gray's "Babylon" was playing. Spices overflowed from barrels, a rainbow of orange, yellow, green, red, and every shade of brown. Barrels were filled to the top with rice, lentils, dates, almonds, dried chickpeas, cardamom pods, wizened lemons and limes.

"There's something . . . *unsettling* about that *boab* of yours," she said, pushing the shopping cart ahead of me, keeping my baby hostage so I had to keep up and couldn't linger.

"Saleh?"

"He wants something."

"Maybe you should try a little harder to find the good in people, Cassie?"

She made that dismissive noise in her throat she thinks I can't hear. Or maybe she thinks if she doesn't look at me while harrumphing like a character out of Dickens, it will somehow be less rude.

She paused in the cool shelter of the meat aisle, her chin set. "It's different here."

"Kindness is the same everywhere—" I started, but just then Mather threw his chew dinosaur at her head. I adored how she didn't even bat an eye, just picked it up without a word and gave it to me.

"You know my villa is on the ground floor, with our little yard?"

I nodded; she talks about her yard all the time, how hard it is to get her gardener to sod and weed, how she's always catching him sleeping or smoking and hiding the butts under her big stone planters.

"I'd only been here in Jordan a month when I caught a teenager standing in my backyard. He must have climbed the fence. He was watching me through the window as I peeled hard-boiled eggs."

"What was he doing?" I asked.

I realized "Babylon" was still playing. Putting it on infinite loop must be a Western manager's idea of a joke. Cassie handed me something wrapped. "Let me just say that I'll never be able to eat egg salad again," she said, pointing at the package. I touched the cellophane in confusion, reading the label in both Arabic and English: *Fresh Lamb Balls.*

"He was masturbating," she hissed in a voice she may have thought was quiet but was actually super loud. A middle-aged woman in a headscarf, previously perusing the packages of hamburger meat nearby, did a double take and quickly walked away. "Right there!" Cassie continued. "Staring at me the whole time. I stood there with a freshly peeled egg in the palm of each hand. I called the embassy, guards came to my apartment, but he was gone."

I was still holding the lamb balls. How do men put these between their teeth and bite down when they're always squealing and protecting their own? I dropped it on a stack of purplish sacks. Oh God, spleens!

"That's really, really disturbing, Cassie. I don't know what I would have done." We walked past kidneys, livers, hearts, all lined up for consumption. I put an arm around her for a moment, some abbreviated hug that only seemed to embarrass her, her body stiffening until I took my arm away. "Danny must have been very upset. Crick would go on a rampage if someone did that to me. He'd land-mine our backyard." I giggled, imagining Crick unspooling barbed wire, then quickly covered my mouth, afraid Cass would think I was laughing at her. It must have been so hard for her to reveal this and there I was not taking it seriously!

She sniffed. Pushed the cart as Mather kept reaching for the packaged carnage. "Yes, Dan was upset," she murmured. "But I am telling you this as a cautionary tale. Saleh, the men at that construction site next door, you need to be careful."

"I'm careful. Really. But don't worry. I'm good at reading people. Like how I knew you and I would be friends immediately."

She glanced at me, softening.

I noticed Mather was clutching a Styrofoam container of whitish gray that looked like brains. I took a closer look. The label read: *Sheep Brains.*

"No, no, sweetie, give that to Mommy," I said calmly, putting out my hand, afraid that if I grabbed it the cellophane would rip and we'd have a cerebrum bouncing on the floor. Cassie looked at the baby, realized he had the brains dangerously close to his mouth, pulled them from his fists without hesitating, and shoved the cart onward, not caring in the least that he was screaming his head off, a little zombie wanting his dinner.

Back at the apartment, of course Saleh was sweeping the front and grinning so big when we pulled up it looked like he'd been waiting for us. Cassie gave me a deadly look, that chin of hers clenched so hard I was afraid she'd crack a molar. He put his broom down, came over as I unloaded grocery bags and Mather. It was totally Cassie's fault I was imagining him with pants down around his ankles. I blushed an incendiary blush. "Oh, it's all right, Saleh, we've got it."

Then I reached into a grocery bag and pulled out a random container of cheese.

I held the cheese, we all stood there wondering what I was going to do with it, and then I handed the cheese to Saleh.

He took it from me, keeping it at arm's length for a moment as if confused, then nodded. "Thank you, madam."

"Christ, Margaret, what did I tell you?" Cassie muttered.

Maybe it *was* passive-aggressive, I don't know, but I'd bought so much and it felt like he had so little, wearing the same yellow T-shirt every day! Cassie's phone buzzed, some sonic vibration mode so every message shakes the whole side of her body. She checked it, lifted her face. "Get inside, Margaret, there's a protest forming. Seven to ten thousand people. Don't leave the apartment again today. I'll call you later."

I was glad Cassie couldn't see Saleh helping me with the bags, how he got into the elevator with us, carried them all to my front door. I couldn't figure out if a tip would be demeaning; is a tip ever demeaning? So I handed him a box of Ritz crackers. He sort of looked at it in the same slightly uncomfortable way he'd looked at the cheese, but he took it.

Now Mather's kicking a tremendous pomegranate across our living room as I write everything down, looking too often at the clock in the kitchen that tells me Crick is still hours from home. Seems a shame to be trapped inside on this sunny, perfect day. I keep finding myself at the window, watching, waiting, writing to kill time. I'm not quite sure what I'm hoping for, but I want to be ready when it comes.

May 13, 2011

7:27 P.M.

I shouldn't have mentioned the boy in my backyard. I was trying to educate Margaret in security, safety, and she only dismissed it the way she dismisses all of my precautions.

And, fine, maybe I exaggerated a little bit. Yes, I had been making egg salad. Yes, I have not eaten it since. I knew exactly what that young man wanted to do. A woman can tell. She can feel a man's eyes on her; she knows. He stared up at my window, didn't seem the least bit bashful when I noticed him, just remained there until I made a show of getting my cell phone out and holding it up to my ear so he could see I was calling for help. Then he walked away, certainly not rushing, just strolling over to the edge of my yard, stepping over the broken piece of fencing I had been nagging our useless gardener to fix. He looked over his shoulder at me knowingly, as if to say someday he'd come back.

That night, when Dan came in, he stood inside the door of our apartment for a long time, weighing his house keys in his hand as if considering turning around and walking out again. "What?" I called from the kitchen. I walked into the foyer, kept my eyes on him as if my look alone could keep him there. I had expected him to rush in early, sweep me up in his arms, offer to install an electric fence himself.

But he blinked up slowly as if I had changed my hair or lipstick and he was trying to figure out what was different, or wrong, about me. "Cassie, I'm sorry, but I need to ask this. This kid, this guy, he was really *masturbating* in front of you?"

Goddamn, my husband knows me. "Yes," I said uncertainly.

He read the indecision on my face and took a step closer. "What exactly did you see?"

"He was in the yard. I could tell he was about to . . . touch himself."

"*About to?* So you didn't actually see him choking the chicken? Buffing the banana? Fishing with his zipper trout?"

"Dan, stop it! I am the victim here."

"You saw a penis?" The tick above his right eye was twitching spasmodically as if someone was holding a cattle prod to his eyebrow.

"Sort of."

"*Sort of.* And yet you felt the need to call the Marines." His voice was quiet; I would have preferred him to have started shouting, to have lost his temper, but the incredulous sadness on his face was too much. "You called the United States Marines, who are the quick-reaction force at the United States embassy in Amman, Jordan. Do you not realize what you bring down on my head every time you do this? Maybe the kid had to take a piss."

"You don't believe me?"

"Remember the Eisenbergs?" he asked.

I stormed back into the kitchen. Rebecca Eisenberg had been my first friend when we arrived in Jordan. My own sponsor had been negligent, to say the least, and it was Becca who walked me through this place. Then her adolescent daughter with the peanut allergy had a severe reaction at the American Community School cafeteria, and Becca decided to homeschool. We had only begun a fledgling friendship but I knew there would be no more days of shopping, no future red wine lunches now that she had her lesson plans and schedules. In an attempt to be helpful, I set up a Google Alert about all the conflict in the region, search words like *violence, honor killings, terrorist attacks, Jordan, Middle East*, and had it sent directly to Becca's inbox. It seemed like a splendid way to help her teach social studies, geography, contemporary conflict. Who knew you would get that many hits every single day? Her husband, not so nicely, told Dan, *Make your f—ing wife stop.* Fortunately they left Jordan a few months later.

"This has nothing to do with the Eisenbergs," I said over my shoulder to Dan, pouring myself a glass of white wine. "And really, with a name like that, why would they even allow themselves to be stationed anywhere in the Middle East outside of Tel Aviv?"

He followed me, put his keys on the kitchen table. I remember being very relieved he'd put them down and had started to loosen his tie, that this wouldn't be the straw that broke our marriage's back. "Cassie, just talk to me first. Why don't you ever talk to me? Tell me these things before you go calling the embassy, before you start searching the Internet, before you start overreacting and stirring things up. Please."

"But you weren't here, Dan, you didn't see the intruder. I could read his intent—"

He shook his head and walked out of the room.

Now I go to Margaret's window. The sun is setting, the night has come. I should have told Dan what was going on with Margaret weeks ago, and with each new text he sends me, each text I ignore, I keep thinking the same. But once things were set into motion, I couldn't tell him anything, couldn't bear the thought of his shouting at me from his hotel room in Italy, his face twitching in apoplexy, asking why I hadn't called him first. He wasn't here; he couldn't understand what I, a woman, could. That Margaret was up to something. That something just wasn't right. But now, reading her life, all of my arguments feel so feeble.

I stare down at the light of random, dangling bare bulbs rising yellow and oily from the construction site. It is so ugly, all the orange wires of random extension cords, the blue tarp of a badly tacked-up tent, dusty men coming and going at all hours of the day and night. I can hear the noise from it as well, a generator, a drill, music buzzing from a hidden radio. How depressing to look down on this each day, I think. No wonder Margaret started shuttering the windows. Then I startle. There is someone down there, looking up, where the Dumpsters for the apartment building squat darkly. I recognize Saleh's yellow T-shirt, the shine of his black and glossy hair. I stand very still staring at him; I don't wave or smile. I go closer to the glass, peer down. I will not be intimidated. I can't tell for sure if he is looking at this window but his face is upward, still aggrieved and glowering, his empty hands clutched into fists at his sides. Then, shaking his head as if he has not seen what he hoped to see, he turns and walks around the side of the building.

When he is out of sight I reach for the cord and pull all the shutters down.

March 15

THE IDES

I thought everything was good. Wonderful even. Between Crick and me.

But then, today happened.

It's night now and Crick's in bed next to me; he has the *Jordan Times* and *Ad-Dustour* newspapers spread out across his thighs, his nightly checks and balances to see what makes it into the English vs. Arabic newspapers. He thinks the truth is in those spaces. He knows an awful lot about how to read what's meant to be hidden.

Yet all this time, I've been reading him wrong.

I'd give anything to be the girl who woke up when Crick's alarm went off this morning. The pinking of the day, luminous beads of light coming through the blinds on the window. I didn't move, hoping to ease back into the pool of sleep. I was thinking about Mom, urging her to visit my dreams. That time we baked gingerbread cookies until two in the morning. When she got me out of bed at sunrise and showed me how to waltz—*Margaret, we don't know if I'll ever be able to dance again, this is a life skill, get up!* Everything had to happen when she wasn't in a flare, whole years squeezed into a month, a week, a day.

I heard Crick opening drawers, the muted zippering and buttoning up. I thought he'd left but then I felt the edge of the mattress shift beneath me. I almost rolled over but felt his warm breath on the back of my arm and then his mouth, the slightest wisp of a kiss, halfway between shoulder and elbow. A benediction. The mattress lifted and there was the sound of shoes sliding away across carpet. I tried not to breathe; I knew if I looked at him he'd be forced to crack a joke, *Just feeling hungry for some elbow* or *Jeez, Mar, you gonna sleep another day away?* He turns mean when I glimpse something soft in his muscle. I pressed my happy face into the pillow. *He loves me! He really does!*

I got up when I was sure he'd left. *See, the things I've done haven't ruined our lives after all. Everything that's happened before will be dimmed by the bright happiness in front of us, everything will be right.*

On my bureau, next to my photos of Mom, I grinned at my favorite picture of Crick, the one from Iraq. He takes lots of photos but despises being the subject. It's like he resents someone telling him to smile or pose, and he gets stiff and angry, refusing to bend to the photographer's will. So I was psyched to find this rare picture of him when we were packing up the apartment in Monterey, in a shoe box full of green Army notebooks, with a few bits of Iraqi currency and postcards of the Euphrates, all coated in fine sand. In it, he's a young lieutenant (*Butter bar,* Crick said scornfully when I asked him about it, as if he's ashamed of the sweetly smiling, inexperienced young man he used to be), a platoon leader, maybe twenty-three, surrounded by Iraqi kids. He's walled into his Kevlar vest and helmet and spiky gun, so tall, his eyes looking directly into the camera, his teeth so American, white and straight. The kids crowd around in torn T-shirts, barefooted. He's strong and they're fragile; different species. I'm like those kids. I too want to stand next to his bulk, his armor. That hopeful, kind young man looks like someone who could build a nation. And a family.

I started tidying the room, picking up things Crick must have left in his hurry. Discarded tie across the chair, workout clothes and a wet towel on the floor. I hung the towel in the bathroom and saw his toiletry kit. He always keeps this packed and ready; somehow he finds imminent travel more comforting than the permanence of leaving his toothbrush in the cup next to mine. Or so I thought. I'd never had a chance to look through it before, so many little pockets, so many small bottles. Where is my husband's Spartan warrior ethos? Expensive shaving cream, cologne, deodorant? Spearmint and rosemary after-shave lotion? I loved him right then as I put his secret creams back into his kit, loved every hair on his chinny chin chin. The floors were warm beneath my feet, the sink breathing, the call to prayer warbling in the distance. Even God is glad, *Allahu akbar. God is great.*

But I needed to know more. Eve in the garden. What else besides nail trimmer, floss, sunblock, tube of mint ChapStick?

So I opened every section, pouch, and pocket, as if it was a game, as if this sort of prying wouldn't lead to repercussions.

Then the final pouch. Size of a condom.

Inside, a photo.

Of Crick. And a woman.

Sitting close together. On a bed. The bedspread boring and blank the way hotel beds are, so people can writhe fantasies across them, leaving sheets crumpled on the floor for someone else to clean up. Crick's clearly the one taking the photo; you can see a bit of his forearm as he holds the camera or phone up, my God, my husband who hates to have his picture taken, smiling and looking directly into the lens? But the woman, I recognize her, a name, KAREN, in my head, yes, Karen, that's right. She's surprised, face tipped forward, mouth open. As if she's saying the word *don't*, as if she's about to scoot out of frame. The look on her face, she must have wanted to know why he'd create evidence. *Evidence.* From the Old French from the Latin *evidens*, *"obvious to the eye or mind."* Has it been obvious from the very beginning, obvious to every eye and mind except mine?

Karen. I'd met her at one of the quarterly cocktail parties at Crick's language school in Monterey. I remember Crick guiding me toward a knot of people near the buffet. He was so beautiful that night, it made me nervous. That itchy feeling of hives on my chest. Crick in tailored charcoal-gray suit and me in half-price maternity dress from Sears. I hesitated and felt his hand go tense, from gentle to insistent, palm suddenly sweaty on the thin cotton at my back. There are so many muscles in the hand, thirty-four muscles to move the fingers and thumbs and seventeen in the palm alone, and those fifty-one muscles were pushing me in a way that said, *Mar, get a fucking move on, now.*

He steered me toward her: dark hair swept up into a relaxed twist, a khaki dress cinched tight at the waist. I got my smile ready; I wanted this woman to like me, the way I want everyone to like me, but I knew she was something special. I thought she was an instructor. Or maybe she was on his coed soccer team, or the wife of a colonel. She turned, her dark eyes filled with light at the sight of Crick, but then they slid to the place where his hand was on my back, and all joy seeped out of her face like water draining from a swimming pool.

"Hey, Karen," he said softly, so softly, which made it strange. "Hey there."

Later, on the way home, I asked, "Who was that woman, Karen?"

He didn't look at me. "Karen? I don't really *know* her."

I waited, unsure. The omission was in the car; it clung to his knuckles on the steering wheel, clutched too rigid, too careful at ten and two o'clock. Instead, he asked me about Mom; he never asked about Mom. In his spirit of total honesty he once said, "Your mother depresses the hell out of me," but there he was making small and indolent talk about vitamin C and aromatherapy, eyes staring ahead. I told myself I was paranoid, he and Karen were acquaintances.

I don't really know her.

Here is a photo that tells me my husband is a liar.

When was it taken? There's no date. Maybe before Crick and I met. Maybe when I was in the hospital, when I fell asleep after nursing Mather for the first time, Crick sitting beside me, and then woke up all alone. Or our last night in Monterey, when he said he was returning his library books and was gone for two hours. When? His hair is Army short, the way it's always been. Same tattoos peeking out from a snug Under Armour T-shirt.

He has kept this. Kept it close. Hidden. Cut down to size, and that makes me ache most, imagining Crick finding scissors and carefully snipping the corners, making them straight, getting it to slide perfectly into this pocket.

I put it back, shoved it in like it scorched me. Maybe he's forgotten about it, maybe Karen gave it to him, maybe she trimmed it down and put it there without his ever knowing. But it changes everything.

Crick came home tonight oddly jubilant, carrying a stack of newspapers. "Operation Odyssey Dawn, baby." Lifting a mass of black and white at me. "We're officially bombing the shit out of Libya."

I stood in the kitchen doorway holding Mather. No dinner. Apartment a wreck. Eyes swollen. "I thought the USA liked Gaddhafi."

He walked past me; either he didn't hear me or my question was beneath him, didn't see my tear-stained face or didn't care. He turned the television on. I made Mather and me toast and put the baby down to sleep. How do I find words that'll make Crick tell me the truth, but also transform that truth into something less terrible than it seems?

When I came out from the nursery, Crick was still rapt in front of the television, still in his suit, watching Al Jazeera, remote in hand. I felt like if I opened my mouth, I'd destroy what we've created together here in Jordan, and I'd break into infinitesimal pieces and disappear.

Now he's watching me write. Maybe he said something? I arc my notebook away from his view and he smirks, turns back to his papers as if thinking, *Mar, you can't possibly be writing anything worth such secrecy.*

Maybe I'm missing something.

Crick's voice when he spoke to her at that cocktail party, so soft.

He keeps glancing at me, annoyed with the way I won't talk

to him, the way I'm furiously scribbling instead of asking about his day.

Glimpses swirl to the surface of my memory.

He introduced me to her and others (Who else was there? How come I can't remember a husband?). I started chatting with someone about . . . olives, I remember olives on my plate, someone telling me about olive oil production in Jordan. I had a rough kalamata olive pit in the side of my mouth and didn't know how to spit it out politely. Then Crick leaned toward Karen, whispered into the hollow of her throat and shoulder. I watched her stretch her neck minutely as if beckoning him to take a bite. There was something intimate about his entering her personal space, her return offer of her pulse. Whatever he said made her smile hugely at him, and he smiled in return, an open, boyish grin. I almost choked; I coughed the olive pit into my napkin and finished my plastic cup of Sprite, and when I looked up again, Karen was gone and Crick was talking to a bald man in a bad suit.

Am I making this up? Did he really smile at her in a way that made me think, *Wow, he can smile like that? Big eyed and glad and no wriggling of his eyebrows?*

How come I can't make him look like that?

He's rustling newspapers again. His BlackBerry vibrates and he lifts it from the blankets, reads the screen, says without looking up, "The Hugos are finally throwing us that very belated welcome party next weekend."

I nod. So Cassie's gotten tired of my excuses and planned it. I think she needs a reason to have a party. And Crick will appreciate a night out with other people instead of coming home to me and my eager, puppyish waiting, my litany of things Mather did all day long when he just wants to sequester himself with his BlackBerry and a cold beer. His office in his pocket. It's his way to block me out, wagging that malignant little technology, implying, *This is so much more important than anything you have to say. I have to get this, this is Work.* Oh, right, Work, capital-W *Work.* Only a man could separate his life into that sort of divide and choose to put Work in the *important* category and family in the *not.* That's why men rule the world.

"Is that an affirmative on the Hugos?"

"I don't care," I say softly. He lifts an eyebrow and studies me. I hold his gaze. I can feel it rise up in me, the flush warming its way up my neck, this prelude to tears. *Please ask me what's the matter,* I think. *Please make me talk to you, make me tell you everything, I'm not strong enough to do it on my own.* I'll finally tell him everything, I promise, I really will.

But instead he puts the BlackBerry on his bedside table, within reach, and slides the papers off the bed into a soft mountain on the floor for me to pick up tomorrow and recycle. I see his black fingerprints on the edge of the duvet as he tugs it to his chin, yawning. "Night, Mar."

He has no idea that everything, everything, is wrong.

He has no idea that a lie always finds its way to the truth.

May 13, 2011
7:38 P.M.

❦

I am stunned. I skim over the last few pages again. Who the hell is this Karen? Margaret found this photo in *March*? And day after day since, she sat across the table from me with those wide, untroubled eyes of hers, whispering and laughing, and never breathed a word?

I wonder. There was that day, yes, that day when Margaret called me even earlier than usual, begging for an "adventure." She wanted to see the citadel. "Please, Cassie. It sits on the highest hill in Amman. Please let's go!" Maybe there had been a bit more hysteria, more pleading in her voice than her usual hyper-enthusiasm.

We took a taxi. Once we got there, Margaret seemed to know exactly what she wanted to see, heading directly to the crumbled pillars of a Roman temple, where she let Mather crawl around and put rocks in his mouth. This being the Middle East, there were no signs that read *Do Not Touch*, nor were there any signs that gave visitors any information about what they were touching. The only thing stopping Mather from careening off the edge was a thin metal-pole perimeter. Margaret kept reading aloud from her guidebook, which is how I knew that the strangely shaped rock Mather was leaping off of was actually the two-thousand-year-old remnants of the fist of a massive statue of Hercules.

She seemed disappointed at the tiny museum, standing for much too long over an empty exhibit that explained in bad English that the Dead Sea Scrolls once housed there had recently been moved. She held her journal, pencil poised, but didn't write anything, just packed it away with a sigh.

Outside again, we could see Amman all around us, as well as a huge Jordanian flag flapping in the distance.

"You can see that flag for twenty kilometers," Margaret whispered, tracing a finger over the words in her guide. "It's the largest freestanding flag in the world!" Then her face fell. "Well, it was, in 2003. Oh, poor thing, now it's the seventh-largest in the world . . ." Her voice trailed off. She pointed away as if she didn't want me to stare too long at the flag in its diminished standing. "Let's walk down to the Roman amphitheater," she suggested. "It looks like a straight shot."

The amphitheater, a large bowl below, didn't seem too far away. "Sure," I said. I helped her shove an unhappy Mather into the canvas sling on her back.

Looks can be deceiving. It was a long and grueling downward haul.

"Are your parents divorced?" she asked out of nowhere, maybe fifteen minutes in. I was distracted. We were lost; clearly tourists were not meant to walk from the highest hill in Amman to the amphitheater in the heart of the city below. Our eyes had tricked us, some optical illusion of light and distance. We found ourselves in winding, narrow streets, switchbacking up and down a warren of stacked apartment buildings. Gray laundry hung from windows, plastic bags drifted in the soupy stream of gutters, empty doorways opened up into the street like toothless mouths. Kids kicked around an electrical-taped-up soccer ball, cars drove much too fast for the sharp turns, and there was not one sign in English. All we knew was that we had to keep walking down.

"Yes." I was wheezing. "Why would you ask that?" The boys stopped their soccer game and watched us. Margaret waved. One of them shouted, "Money, give me money!" and then they all ran away.

"You seem like you don't like conflict. Children of divorce like to play the peacemaker. Like me."

I looked at her; had she never seen Dan and I speak to each other? But it made me pause for a moment; was she telling me that Dan and I were avoiding issues in our relationship? I shook my head uncomfortably. When was the last time Dan and I had had an honest conversation rather than some skirmish over something that didn't actually matter? "I am no stranger to conflict, Margaret. I worked in human resources for years."

She nodded. "You're a good listener." She sipped from her water bottle and gave me a sly glance. "Have you ever heard of anyone getting separated? I mean, here, in the embassy world? Like a *trial separation?*"

I stopped in my tracks. She was sweating too, damp tendrils of blond hair around her face, and Mather's two fists lifted above her shoulders like the nubs of denuded wings. "Margaret, that seems like a very serious question. What's going on?" My own parents had used that expression, and even as a child of eleven, I'd known there was nothing *trial* about it. When a married couple lived in separate places, they were separated, and I didn't know anyone who ever returned from that brink.

"Oh, I'm just curious. Do you think the embassy would send the spouse home or give additional money for housing in Jordan?"

I shook my head. "I can't imagine the State Department or the United States Army would give anyone money for additional housing in a foreign country."

Did I feel the smallest shiver of joy at her question? Perhaps. So often I thought Dan and I were the only couple having problems, the only couple who might not make it back to America intact.

She was about to say more. But we heard a shout from a window and we looked up. Mather grunted from Margaret's back and she handed me a cookie to give him. The street suddenly seemed too quiet and, even though my thighs were screaming, I urged Margaret to hurry.

Then I noticed the little boys were back and following us, minus the soccer ball. When I told Margaret, she looked over her shoulder, waved again. One of them threw something at us.

"They're throwing stones!" I cried. I grabbed at Margaret's arm, wanting to pull her into a run.

She calmly watched them, how they bent to the road, seemed to pick something up, stood, lifted their arms, and threw. "They're pretending," she said. I listened for a moment and knew she was right, I didn't hear any clatter of rocks. She shrugged. "If they were throwing stones we'd feel it. We're easy targets." This seemed like an oddly jaded response from her, but she was right;

we stood there and watched the children, and after a minute or two, they ran off. This did not mean I wasn't petrified. By the time we got to the bottom and were finally spit out into the middle of a busy thoroughfare, we must have walked a total of two miles. It was noisy and I felt safer, seeing the *souk*, the traffic, the crowds of pedestrians on the sidewalks. The King Hussein Mosque on our right caught the first red rays of the sunset.

However, the Roman amphitheater was closed. Her impotent guidebook had the hours wrong. Margaret only smiled slightly, as if she had already been indoctrinated into the whole *inshallah/ If God wills it* mentality that seems to run the country. Everything is *inshallah*. We order a pizza without any sense of when the delivery man might arrive, *inshallah*. We call a plumber hoping he might actually come to fix the overflowing toilet, *inshallah*. It's hard to figure out if this phrase is a nod toward willful ignorance or if concepts like *yes* and *no*, that seem so inexplicably ordinary to Western minds, are really so difficult here. Whatever the truth, putting everything in the hands of God can be awfully convenient. I was as tired of *inshallah* as I was of letting Margaret's will define the outcome of our days. That's when I decided I would not take her to any more historical sites. Shopping, coffee, dinner, the embassy, yes, I would do the things *I* was comfortable doing, the things I understood, but anything that required long distances or uncertain destinations that might put us in danger, absolutely not.

This long night makes me wish I had taken her anywhere and everywhere she wanted.

March 16

HOME

Karen Karen Karen Karen. Her name has been in my head all day, sneaking up and then shivering through me with a sick feeling of dread.

I turn the news on to drown her out. Terrible things happening in southern Syria, in Dara'a, near the border of Jordan, schoolboys arrested and tortured for graffiti, police and security forces shooting protesters in the chest. Dozens, maybe hundreds, killed, no one sure of anything since news out of Syria has been shut down. Crick called to say he was charting it all, his entire office working late again, not to expect him for dinner.

"You marry that man," Mom said. She didn't know a thing about Crick until I was three months pregnant. I'd been telling her, *The animal shelter asked me to volunteer for a few night shifts! The new girl at my temp job invited me to Napa!* Lies lies lies. I didn't want her to know; how could I? From the very beginning Crick was my path away from her.

The night before our wedding, I started doubting everything.

I looked at my bouquet, calla lilies, in their pint glass in the fridge. White flowers, white dress, with my baby bump for all to see. I was about to do something I could never undo. I wondered if maybe it'd be better to start untying the knot now before it caught everything in its tangle.

Mom came in around midnight, stood in the doorway a moment and watched me cry. I'd be blotchy and bloodshot in those photos at Lover's Point the next day.

"You marry that man and you raise your child and that's the way it will be."

I knew how hard it was for her to tell me to leave her. Who would change the sheets, pay the bills, know the morning tea she drank to wake up and the tea that helped her sleep at night? I kept my eyes on her slippers as she moved slowly from the dark hallway and into the kitchen light, thinking, *I have done this to her*. I've always known the only reason Mom had lupus was because I was tenacious; her womb couldn't shake me loose like the others. All those years no one understood why she kept losing babies. Sometimes she called me a miracle, other times she didn't, and when she didn't I knew she was thinking it was my fault. I was the preeclampsia, the fatigue that didn't go away, the rashes on face, arms, and legs, all of it traced to one simple source: me.

That night, I couldn't help but think what I might do to Crick's life next.

"I don't know if he loves me," I whispered. I wanted my mom to convince me. Isn't that what mothers do? Convince us we aren't nearly as bad as we think?

"Didn't stop him from sleeping with you, did it?" She wasn't going to even try. Silence. I wanted to be thirteen, when she'd bake pumpkin scones for me after school, say the boys called me "Mouse Face" because they liked me.

"You have enough love for both of you." She took a step closer and I hoped she'd run her fingers through my hair like she did when I had a fever. She didn't touch me but her voice dipped soft. "I was so sick I could hardly pick you up when you were a newborn, have I ever told you that?"

She glanced at my hands, which were clasped together on the table. I looked at them too. They were naked of jewelry, the nails bitten down. They looked like the hands of a high schooler who was nervous before finals. But tomorrow, they'd be a woman's hands with a smooth gold band for all to see.

"I was a terrible mother," she whispered. "There were days I felt so weak I let you cry in your crib for hours, waiting for your father to get home from work to change you, feed you, clean you up." I kept my eyes on my knuckles, afraid of what she'd say next. That she shouldn't have ever had me. That she had been healthy, happy, normal before I came along.

"But I made you, Margaret. And you're perfect. No matter what else, I managed that. That might be enough." I looked up at her, surprised. "Now you need to think about *your* baby. You marry that man. You and Crick are doing the right thing. End of story."

It wasn't the end of the story, Mom.

You and Crick are doing the right thing.

Karen Karen Karen.

Crick came home tonight when I was putting the baby down to sleep.

I left the nursery and found him in the bedroom, naked in front of the mirror.

He turned toward me and winked. It was the first time ever his wink had no effect.

He stood there with an erection and a smile that seemed to say, *Wife, take care of this.* Maybe he really does know me better than I know myself, maybe he knows I'll pity that poor swollen creature. Wasn't that how I ended up in the arms of Jerry McKay with the world's tiniest penis? Three Bud Lights and Jerry took all his clothes off in his college dorm room, did a pathetic little excited dance, and how could a woman with half a heart not offer that poor soul some semblance of a happy ending?

But not tonight.

"I need to talk to you," I said. Words that drive fear into the heart of every married man. He cupped his penis as if my words might damage it forever.

"Crick, is there someone else?"

He blanked. Stood in front of me with no emotion on his face. I thought, *That's how he looks when he's deployed, when he's in the shit and all the human leaks right out of him so he can do his thing. That's the face of a man who can lie.* I stared and wondered what else he's keeping from me. My throat started to close up, heat in my face, in my eyes. "Did you have an affair?"

He turned away and began to put on boxers. "Jeez, Mar, 'cause I have so much extra time on my hands? All I do is work, work hard and long, and when I come home and want to bed my wife, you go bat-shit crazy on me?"

"I found the photograph." I felt pretty calm, not the least bit bat-shit crazy, but maybe I'm not the best judge.

"Margaret, relax, there is no one else."

"Are you . . . *content* with the life we have?"

He started going through drawers, pulling them out and then

slamming them shut when he couldn't find a T-shirt, suddenly desperate to cover the body he'd wanted to pin to mine just a moment ago. I remembered all his T-shirts were in the washing machine.

He stopped, his head bent. "This life is . . . fine." He turned to me, bare-chested, some sort of fight-or-flight reaction in his eyes as they shifted around the room, taking in all of my scarves.

It was time to get everything out in the open. I'm not blameless; I've wronged him too. Time to say all the things we ought to have said before Mather was even born.

"That woman, Karen, from your school."

And then we heard the baby. Crick had succeeded in waking him up. I tilted my head; could he have *meant* to do that? Was his drawer banging intentional? Or could Mather feel the people who put him together starting to tear apart?

"*MAMA! MAMA!*"

Crick's face was still blank. He didn't acknowledge the screaming, just watched me.

Maybe it was the coward's way out, maybe I should have stayed in that room and shouted, let the baby cry himself back to sleep. But I went to the nursery. I cradled Mather in my arms and slid down onto the floor, leaning against the wall, his night-light showering us with pricks of color as I nursed him. His needs so simple. There's no grief my milk can't soothe: doctor's shots, lost toys, bumps on the head. I'm absolutely important to him. He swung one of his pajama-ed feet up, his toes stepping on my lips. I kissed them and wondered where these feet would lead my boy. Far and wide. And as upset as I was, I knew I wanted him to be like Crick. I wanted him strong and fearless and a little bit cruel, I wanted him to be nothing like weak and skinless me.

I wanted Mather to be the one who slams drawers instead of the one who cowers in silence.

I remember the night I told Crick I was having a baby. I took my cell phone and sat in my small San Jose yard, watching fireflies. Crick picked up right away; I could hear music, laughter, ice chiming in his glass. "I'm pregnant," I said. I heard him moving away to somewhere still and quiet. "We'll figure this out," he whispered. Then, "Are you sure?" I said nothing, my eyes tightly shut, waiting, hoping. "I can help you," he said. "I mean, if you don't want to keep it, I'll pay." *I'll pay.* As if money had anything to do with it. As if Mather's life was written with chalk, as if he could've been wiped clean, no trace left behind. We'd been together only a few months by then but I'd already seen Crick jerk and shudder in his dreams; I knew he knew that everything has repercussions, every single moment of your life clings to you, creates you, whether you're aware of it or not. Mistakes and accidents fill you up; they're like fingerprints pressing gently on your brain, and someday they'll start to squeeze.

That night, I didn't do anything but breathe into the phone and wait until Crick whispered, "OK, fine, we can do this."

When Little Man falls asleep, his lips pushed out, lashes fluttering, he's a prince, a gift. The perfect weight in my arms. All day he's voracious, wanting food, wanting the fragile glasses high on the shelf or the steak knives in the drawer, screaming, *Mo! Mo!* But here, he has everything he needs; he rests, whole and happy.

No matter what happens with Crick, I need to make sure I can always make my way back to Mather.

I put the sleeping baby into the crib and returned to the master bedroom.

I went to our bed, letting my eyes adjust to the dark. The body will adjust to anything, I tell myself, but that's not true. A frog fights like hell if his pot of cool water heats up, no matter what the murderous myth says.

Crick didn't speak. I could just make him out in darkness. He'd either fallen asleep or was pretending. I stood over him, still feeling our fight, the sad psychic residue lingering on me. Like a hangover. An ache.

For a moment I wished I'd listened to Robert Riding and filled this room with necessities, passports, cash, bags packed. I could've gotten the baby, caught a taxi to the airport, been on my way to San Jose before morning.

But there's nothing in California for me anymore.

So I stood there, useless, unable to run. The only thing I could do was slink into the dark bathroom, feel around the drawer under the sink for Crick's toiletry bag, tugging the zippers, until I got to the center, the tiniest pocket of all, the rip of Velcro tearing open in the stillness.

The photo was gone.

March 17

HOME

It rained today. We read. Mather understood this was the best I could do and sat still, looking from the illustrations to my face and back again.

The Pied Piper.

Little happy kiddos get walled up in a mountain and never see their parents again. One hundred and thirty children gone. I read, still hoping the ending would change, the people of Hamelin would pay the piper what they owed him, and their babies would be spared.

But it's always the same. Gone. Mather giggles when I go quiet at the end.

As soon as Crick came home from work tonight, I asked, "Where's the picture?"

He took off his jacket, concentrating on folding it neatly, resting it over the back of a chair. But he was ready. "I destroyed it."

I inhaled. Relieved he'd admitted the truth, that there was a photo, and yet part of me wanted to think I'd imagined it. "Why? What does it mean?"

He loosened his tie. "It means nothing. It was from a long time ago and I don't want to talk about it."

Mather yelled in agreement. I handed the baby a carrot and he put it in his ear. "Are you still in touch with her?"

"Mar, leave it alone."

"I looked in every single garbage can and didn't find any ripped pieces—"

"It's over and the photo is gone." He took his house keys out of his pants pocket and threw them in the key bowl so hard I thought the crystal would shatter.

I tried not to cry. "I held this photo in my own hands. I need to know why you kept it and what she means to you—"

He turned on me, eyes so incredulous and angry I knew he'd say something I'd never forget.

"I didn't know a fucking thing about you when I put a ring on your finger, did I? Did I question you? Did I ask you about the men you'd been with? I believed every single word out of your mouth."

This was it. The moment he trumped any and every argument. He was right. He never doubted me. Never asked for a paternity test or how I'd managed to get pregnant on the pill.

He watched me. There was so much he could have said and chose not to. "I don't pry into your past, Margaret. I don't pry into your life before we met, so don't do it to me."

And that was it, there was nothing more to say. I nodded my head and ever since I've made myself comfortable in this limbo of not knowing. Sleepless in this bed I made.

May 13, 2011

7:49 P.M.

I close the journal, run a hand over the smooth cover.

I know what's coming next.

My party.

They arrived late. Already I knew Crick was a man who did not like to be late; no military men or women do. I have been to Army functions where everyone sits in their cars in the street watching their wristwatches, and when the official start time comes, they turn off their engines at once, all get out and head to the front door. I also knew Margaret would be dragging her feet; she had resisted until I finally swore this would be a "casual" get-together, cocktails and appetizers.

I was delighted that nearly everyone I invited came. Margaret and Crick had worked their newcomer magic, offering something fresh to those of us who had picked over everyone else in the embassy community. People wanted to hear their stories. The Brickshaws had lived in America recently enough that they could tell us things we couldn't learn from Al Jazeera English. It wasn't all selfish; we also wanted to share hard-won gems like which Amman hair salon could properly highlight Western fair hair without frying the scalp a radioactive pink, or where they could find a real New York strip rather than the fibrous beef too readily available from Pakistan, or how to read the euphemisms (*grape beverages, draft selections, bubbly, mixed spirits*) to figure out which restaurants served alcohol.

We depend on this give-and-take when living abroad. You can't exile yourself from your homeland and not always feel that tidal pull of return. Those minor details, the commercial jingles and pop songs, the chain restaurants and decade-defining shades of our blue jeans, are details you don't even think about until you are face-to-face with a society that has very little to do with your own. Suddenly those one-hit wonders become a secret language, the very vestiges of American culture.

Those who have lived abroad know exactly what I mean. Our status as Americans creates an instantaneous, rarefied friendship. You are in a fast-food restaurant where they have odd things on the menu, *makluba, zaatar, soojouk,* and you are scrambling for something you recognize, pizza, or even pita, and then you hear that perfect *Hello* or *How you doing?* You gravitate toward that table of strangers, desperate, dear God, speak to me, fellow outsiders in inappropriately revealing clothing, speak to me American sweet nothings of sports and reality TV. It's the same everywhere. You reach for the known in an unknown place. You become friends with someone you wouldn't be able to stand if you actually had options. Our history of Super Bowl commercials and expectation of flushable toilet paper seal us together.

Crick entered first. I felt the pleasant sting of his stubble when he touched his cheekbone to mine. Then he kissed the other cheek, Jordanian style, which usually annoys me, but I found it charming coming from Crick, especially when I noticed he did not kiss anyone else in the room. He did crush Dan's hand. Dan tried not to wince, and, in response, he immediately led Crick to the bar, where I knew they would be engaged in a modern joust. They pretend to be adult by drinking single-malt scotch, but it's no different from college-boy days of shooting down tequila, all a race to pit manhoods against each other and see who can best keep their slurring in check. Then Margaret entered the room, carrying her massive bag as well as her massive baby. She dropped the bag on the floor in my hallway, reached inside, drew out a bottle of white wine, and gave it to me. She was wearing a black spaghetti-strapped dress with a hem that hit above her knee, and her hair was twisted up from her long neck. She was also wearing those dangling feather earrings (her mother's, I know now). Even with a peacock-patterned shawl draped around her upper arms, it was too little clothing to wear out and about in Jordan, and it was still quite cold in March. The other wives were more conservatively dressed, with loose pants and buttoned blouses, cardigan sweaters, scarves billowed up over bosoms.

"Thank you," I said, taking the bottle. She looked pale, her eyes red-rimmed and skittish. "Margaret, are you feeling OK?"

She balanced Mather on her hip. "*Mens sana in corpore sano.*"

I stepped back, baffled. She burst into her jarring laugh.

"Oh, I'm sorry, that's something my mom and I used to say to each other after a doctor's appointment. That's Latin for '*a healthy mind in a healthy body.*' It was funny because, well, I guess it wasn't actually funny at all, since my mother was incapable of either."

I set my smile. I wasn't going to let her vocabulary or deliberate weirdness ruin my evening. She did that when she was nervous, used words no one else had ever heard of. I'd been alerted to the possibility Margaret might not play well with others. Just a few days earlier I'd seen Deborah, the embassy employee who lives on the second floor in her building, try to help Margaret get her stroller out the apartment's front door. Margaret completely ignored her, almost pushing her out of the way with her hip. When I asked Margaret about it, she said she'd seen this woman kick a "clowder" near the building's Dumpster. I had to ask her what *clowder* meant (it's a group of cats, so why the hell couldn't she just say *group of cats?*). But that's Margaret. "If you're not kind to animals, well, you're just not kind," she'd said in her stubborn way. "I have no desire to become friends with a cat kicker." I had promptly removed Deborah from tonight's invite list.

This was Dan's and my first get-together in the two years we'd been here in Jordan, and, well, I would have kicked a *clowder* myself in order to make everything go smoothly. Throwing a party for Margaret wasn't a required task; my sponsor certainly didn't throw one for me. And, to be frank, I don't know the other spouses as well as I should. I've always felt like the women started treating me a little coolly after Becca Eisenberg left. Goodness knows what she told them. But surely it's my lack of children, which gives me less in common with everyone else. Without children, I have no reason to picnic in the embassy park or attend the American Community School events, the musicals and fund-raisers that everyone else is always rambling on and on about, coercing coworkers to buy raffle tickets. And I am too old for the younger set of single State Department folk, in their skinny jeans and heels, who go off to the *shisha* rooftop cafés. So this party felt like a way for me to prove myself, to show them I too am worthy of knowing. *Look, the newcomers are my friends, Margaret and Crick are mine, and yet I will share them with the rest of you.*

I told Margaret I was going to put her wine in the fridge, promised I'd be right back, then ferried a few more coats into the guest bedroom.

I could hear Crick's voice. He was always a note louder than everyone else. I wondered if he suffered from hearing loss, like so many soldiers who had shot off one too many rounds. He immediately started talking about the most recent protests with a staff sergeant from his office. Yesterday, five hundred people had set up camp in the capital. And today there'd been a clash between government supporters and two thousand protesters in Gamal Abdel Nasser Circle, and hundreds were wounded depending on what news source you listen to. The state-run papers say people are upset about the high price of grain, rice, and oil, but from what Americans on the ground have seen, they are really protesting to curb the power of the monarchy.

I'd been worried all day that we embassy folk would be on lockdown but other than a tepid text to stay away from large gatherings, no alarm bells had gone off.

When I got back, I caught sight of Margaret speaking with Joannie Lipson, who was squeezing Mather's lumpy toes in one hand while bouncing her own three-year-old daughter, Ella, on her hip. It appeared she was mingling just fine. As I walked around filling glasses, I tried to listen to their conversation.

"You must join our playgroup," Joannie was saying. "It's for embassy moms and children under four. We meet at the embassy park every Thursday, ten a.m., and do circle time and games."

Margaret nodded slowly. "Well, you know, Mather might actually be contagious? Ever since we got here he's had fluorescent poop. No fever, no vomiting—well, maybe a little vomiting but that's self-induced. Does Ella make herself throw up?"

Joannie immediately dropped Mather's foot.

Then she was on to Marc Smitz, who suggested Margaret join the coed embassy soccer team. "Oh, gosh, my husband is the athlete. My mother had an autoimmune disease? Lupus? It killed her last year. Actually, you're lucky if it's even diagnosed. And don't tell my husband but sixty percent of female offspring end up with the disease too. So sports have always been out of the question for me!"

I was relieved when I saw her speaking with Lorna Briggs. Lorna, the wife of Colonel Briggs, Dan and Crick's boss, is very proper, very capable. I find her a bit distant, but she is a reservoir of information, and I assumed she was giving Margaret a little introduction to a military spouse's role at the embassy. When I walked by, it seemed as if Margaret and Lorna were discussing breast-feeding, which must have been some bizarre ice-breaking technique on Margaret's behalf and not something I could ever imagine Lorna bringing up. When I passed again, I heard Margaret say, ". . . Take cows for example. I didn't think about it 'til I was nursing, but, I mean, *I'm* a milk-producing mammal. Cows are nursing mothers just like me. Humans are the only species that drink the milk of another animal. We take the calves away when they are only a day old. Can you imagine someone ripping your baby from you like that?"

"Margaret! I could really use your help!" I almost shouted, taking her by the elbow and dragging her into the kitchen. "You do know Lorna is married to Crick's boss, right?"

"I know!" She shook her head hopelessly. "I get so nervous I don't even know what comes out of my mouth." She grabbed my hand and held it to her chest. "My heart is about to explode. There are too many people, and I can see on their faces I'm not saying any of the things they want to hear. I'm sorry, Cass, I don't want to ruin your party."

"Don't be ridiculous," I said. I could actually feel her heart. It was the strangest thing; it made me think of a small piece of trapped material, the edge of a dress or a jacket, caught in a car door, flapping as the car careened down a highway. "Take a deep breath, you are doing fine. No one is judging you. They are people who want to meet you. Maybe you should stick to asking them questions about themselves until you feel more comfortable?" She nodded and let go of me. I put a beer bottle in her hand. "Can you give this to my husband?"

"OK, I can do that. I like Danny." I winced at her persistent use of *Danny*. No one had called him that since elementary school, but I tried to smile encouragingly at her. She nodded bravely, as if the handful of office workers in my living room had suddenly transformed into cannibals who only ate skinny people. I went to the doorway and watched, curious. I didn't think she would sidle up to Dan, *my* Dan, give him the beer, and then coyly point at the mother-of-pearl musket he had brought back from Afghanistan.

"Oh, Danny, there must be a story behind this," she purred, suddenly cool as a cucumber. "It's terrific."

Dan left Crick holding the bottle of single-malt and followed Margaret to his mounted gun. I sipped my wine and watched as he pulled it down from the wall and let her slide her fingertips along its length.

The baby reached out and Margaret laughed softly. I saw Crick lift his head and watch her, as if he recognized the tenor of that certain strain of happiness, some rare birdcall. Dan started to put the gun away but Margaret hooked her fingertips into the crook of his elbow to stop him. I straightened, my eyes watching her hand on my husband's bare skin, and for a moment I wondered if this sort of thing would have bothered me if we were in America, or if I was so much more aware of the delineated space between the sexes here in Jordan. But Crick was also keeping his eyes trained on them.

Dan continued telling his story; I knew it well, the small, dirty *souk* hastily set up outside of Bagram Airfield, how he had to drink vast quantities of weak tea with different carpet sellers until he spotted this gun, which they claimed was over a hundred years old and yet had also shot dead three Russian soldiers in the 1980s.

Mather grappled for the trigger and Dan lifted the gun so the baby could splay his sticky fingers on the pearl triangles set into the wood. Margaret kept her hand resting on Dan. *Mine*, that touch seemed to say. As if she didn't have enough already, I thought then. As if she didn't have everything.

Out of the corner of my eye, I saw Crick leave the room.

We moved to the backyard after everyone had a drink or two. The sun was setting nicely, the white Christmas lights I had strung up over the fence giving everything an ethereal feel. Dan began to grill the prized protein of the evening: pork. I had raided the embassy shopette as soon as a new shipment arrived, securing a cart full of frozen chops, sausage, brats, and cutlets. I hadn't been much of a pork lover in the States, but there's something about living in the Middle East that makes me crave all that is *haram*, or forbidden by Islamic law. Ah, the embassy minimart, it is exempt from customs' inspections and taxes and therefore acts as an oasis of all that is naughty: pork, yes, but also booze and tampons.

Margaret hovered over the flowerbed my lazy gardener had yet to plant, pointing rocks out to the baby. I found myself filling plates and glasses instead of going to her. You know how it is when you are hosting; you are always busier than you think you will be. And yes, fine, I couldn't shake the image of her pointer finger resting on the sensitive skin of my husband's inner elbow. I preferred her when she was in a state of cardiac distress.

She came over and asked me if she could nurse Mather in my bedroom.

I nodded. I had been careful to arrange our room just in case someone needed to use it for some sort of unpleasant childcare—diaper changing and the like. I'd found our wedding photo and propped it up on Dan's bedside table for all to see. Such a beautiful, crisp autumn day on the Charles River. How young we look. How sharp he is in his Army dress blues. How naked our smiles are. We don't smile like that anymore. We hide our teeth primly, no longer hungry for what the other has to offer. Our smiles are the mere ruse of musculature rather than any indication of joy. I hoped Margaret would ruminate on this picture and leave Dan alone for the rest of the evening.

Crick was standing next to Dan at the grill. They both seemed unsteady from however much scotch it took to prove they were equals, and now they were talking intently, not the stuff of parties, no, I knew that sideways glance of my husband hiding something. I brought over two icy Hefeweizens and tried to eavesdrop but my husband was no fool.

"Cassie!" he said loudly, elbowing Crick to shut up. No fool, but utterly lacking subtlety.

"—leaving soon," Crick continued, ignoring Dan's cue. "But I'd rather handle our own goat rodeo than one created by an international shit show." He grinned and reached for one of the bottles I held. "You're a sight for sore eyes. How'd you know I was empty?"

"I can read your mind," I said lightly, cocking my head at my husband. *Leaving soon?* "Which international 'shit show,' gentlemen? There are so many."

Dan's eyes widened in alarm but Crick kept talking. "Libya. Uncle Sam has decided we don't like creating failed states by ourselves, and wants Europe and the Middle East in on the action." He took a long swallow. I watched the motion of his Adam's apple, up and down, as oversized and yet oddly sexy as the rest of him. "But that's what makes the job exciting, right?"

Dan quickly plopped a charred pork chop on Crick's plate. "There's Margaret," he said, pointing with the tongs. I glanced at him, he who was suddenly so aware of our guests, before looking over my shoulder.

Margaret stood in the frame of the sliding glass door watching all of us, lit from behind. She was alone; her species-appropriate milk must have knocked her baby out immediately. I wondered where she had stuck him.

Crick sat down heavily at the plastic table nearest the grill and began to saw into his pork. Dan put a platter of meat out on the little buffet table I had set up next to the outdoor bar and people began to help themselves, settling into the few tables we'd borrowed for tonight. Crick continued to speak to Dan as my husband put more burgers on the grill, his voice loud enough to carry over the din of guests and the music I had playing in the background. He was telling a story about Morocco, something about asking for directions to his hotel. I glanced at Dan, raising my eyebrows, wondering if he too noticed that Crick's volume was off. I wanted to share something with him, one of those mundane moments, that comfort of togetherness that makes up for the sizzle long ago lost. We used to send so many wordless messages to each other at parties like these, always knowing what the other would find amusing or tedious. It was half the fun of hosting—the rolled eyes, the half smiles, the recounting of our guests' foibles when we were cleaning up late into the night. This was one of the perks you were left with, part of the bargain you make at the altar: I am purchasing a future made up of a median of good and bad, I am trading the unpredictable excitement of the single life for the pleasant mediocrity of marriage. But Dan avoided my eyes, watching Margaret as she came slowly toward us holding a plate of strawberries.

"Oh my God, are these local?" she asked over her husband's voice. Only a Californian would say something like that. "I think they're the best I ever tasted." Her mouth full, staring at Dan as if he was the one who had bargained with the street seller for the stained Styrofoam containers of bruised fruit.

Dan swallowed, watching Margaret's pleasured mouth too closely.

"So this shady little fucker approaches me . . ." Crick continued over his wife, not acknowledging her interruption. He sawed away with his knife as he spoke. Glasses on the table rattled.

"Let me get you a drink, Margaret," I murmured. She followed me a few feet away to the bar. "Did Crick happen to mention anything to you about Libya?"

Her eyes widened. She put her strawberries down next to a stack of used plastic cups. "Libya? What's going on?"

I shushed her; some of the guys from Dan's office were standing around the grill laughing at Crick's story.

Margaret immediately reached for the bottle of rum, poured a healthy portion into a plastic cup without bothering to add any ice, then topped it off with the remains of someone's discarded Diet Coke.

"You don't think they might be going?" she asked, her voice lower but fast and frightened. She shivered in the dark.

"Oh, I don't know, you'll have to ask Crick," I said.

I could hear him droning on, ". . . back at the hotel. Five dollars instead of the agreed-upon two!" The chill of darkness was settling on us. The temperature must have dropped twenty degrees from that afternoon as the desert recalled its world the way it did every evening. Margaret's arms were unattractively goose-fleshed in the twilight. I considered offering her a sweater but thought I would wait just a bit longer, wanting to hear Crick's conclusion.

"I'm livid," he said. "'*Two dollars!*' I told him. He threw the money on the ground, demanded five." Crick's voice shifted into a high-pitched and vaguely Mexican accent: "'*Such a very good tour, sir!*' Right, like I wanted to waste an hour seeing every brass lantern workshop in the friggin city."

Margaret swallowed her entire drink. She wiped her mouth off with her knuckles, smearing her glossy lipstick onto her chin. I didn't tell her.

"In the end I had no choice but to just walk off," Crick said.

"You could have given him the money," Margaret said.

We were right in front of him but he glanced at her as if he'd forgotten she was even at the party. "What?"

"Five dollars."

Conversation stalled; guests turned to watch. I immediately stepped away from Margaret and began to clear plates of watermelon rinds and uneaten, ketchup-bloodied hot dog rolls.

"We agreed on two," Crick said slowly, as if Margaret had just proven herself mentally deficient. "I wanted directions, not a guide. It was the *principle* of the thing, Mar."

"Five bucks." Margaret wasn't letting up. "It would have proven you were a good person. Is that so *unprincipled?*"

Crick's eyebrows lifted and his voice dropped, intimate somehow, as if he thought he could pitch his voice in such a way it could be heard by his wife alone. "What're you trying to prove here?"

"You're the one who told the story about being an asshole." She glanced at the dozen or so people standing around, holding their breath and empty glasses, then she pressed her free hand to her forehead. "Excuse me." She ran into the kitchen, leaving Crick in front of all those averted eyes.

Dan closed the lid on the grill with a bang. "Who needs another beer?" he asked.

Crick stared off into the direction Margaret had gone, then tipped his bottle back and poured the remainder down his throat.

Maybe a half hour later, on her way out the door with a crying Ella, Joannie Lipson told me we were almost out of toilet paper in the guest bathroom. I wandered around picking up trash, the party winding down. Most of the guests with children had left; just a handful of the heavier drinkers joked loudly from the back patio. I carried two nearly empty bottles of beer in one hand, the last bit of my red wine in the other. The light in the hallway wasn't working, of course. It had gone out that day, and since every light in my apartment required a different sort of odd lightbulb and the ceiling was just high enough to require an actual ladder, and the embassy forbade anyone not officially vetted by the embassy to do any sort of interior work on our apartment, I had to wait until the following week to set up an appointment with the embassy maintenance crew. So much work involved just to change a lightbulb. It sounded like a bad joke.

The bathroom door suddenly opened, light catching me in the dark hallway like a camera flash.

"Just the woman I was hoping to see," Crick said, slumping against the door frame. "One of those for me?" He nodded at the beer bottles I held.

"No, these are empty, but I can get you another if you'd like." Though it was clear it was the last thing he needed.

"I could definitely use another." He smiled. *Rakishly* was the word that came to mind. "How about another . . . *wife*? You happen to have one of those too?"

I stood absolutely still. Was I supposed to laugh?

Crick didn't need any encouragement to continue. "I don't see you abusing *your* husband in front of everyone. I see you smiling and handing out alcohol. And pork. Margaret's a goddamn vegetarian, you know that? If she makes me eat another fucking eggplant I'll lose my mind. And she can't drink for shit." He glanced at the ground, shaking his head; I couldn't tell if he was disgusted with the thought of eggplant or if he realized he had gone too far and was regretting his tirade.

"We all have our flaws," I said softly. "I'm sure Dan could rattle off a long list of things he doesn't like about me."

Crick blinked. I was struck by how sad he seemed. Without the distraction of his usually arched eyebrows, his brown eyes seemed younger, defenseless.

I don't know how we got to what happened next. Honestly, no matter how many times I think about it.

I watched Crick begin to straighten. He was pushing himself up from the wall when he must have accidently brushed against the light switch with his shoulder.

Everything went dark.

I quickly stepped into the bathroom to put the light back on. He must have reached to do the same, and our bodies slammed together. There was a confused fumble as I tried not to spill my wine, the two beer bottles clattering to the ground. Crick had both of his arms around my back and he held me tightly, protectively, as if keeping me from falling. I could smell the lager and filthy ash that splashed on my shoes and thought, *I need to clean that up right now.* I steadied myself and laughed uncomfortably in the dark room, waiting for Crick to realize I was firmly on my feet. But the embrace went on. Then one of his hands slowly untucked the material of my blouse from my jeans, slipped underneath, and slid up the bare skin. I gasped, his palm hot as it moved up my naked spine, resting over the clasp of my bra. Such heat in his hand. He leaned me against the tiled bathroom wall, his face close to mine.

"Sometimes you end up with the wrong woman," he said into my ear. I held my breath. What did I want to happen next? Did I want to cross that line, did I want to snap my marriage in half? I had a split second to make a decision that could change everything.

I stood there, letting him decide for me. After a moment, three heartbeats, maybe four, his palm moved down to the small of my back, hesitated there long enough that I waited for it to slip under the waistline of my jeans, beneath the silk of my panties, and bring me up hard against him. Instead his hand was suddenly gone, and cool air flooded under my loosened blouse.

He released me. Pushed himself up off the wall. I put my arm out, holding the edge of the sink to steady myself, immediately missing his weight pressed against me.

"Whoa, they're not joking when they say drinking at a high altitude can fuck you up, right?" he said, looking out the bathroom door and down the hallway, straightening his shirt.

Without another glance in my direction, he walked away.

I could feel my blood pulsing erratically through every artery in my body. I told myself it was an act of drunkenness, pure silliness. Good thing I didn't act, good thing I didn't reach for him and have him reject me. Anyone could have seen us; after all the drinking everyone was doing certainly many bladders, right this moment, were full to bursting. I told myself it was only a flirtation. Crick was so drunk he didn't realize he was taking it too far.

But it was undeniably exhilarating to know that, even if it was only for a moment, Crick had wanted me.

To wonder if there might be a moment in the future when he would want me again.

After making sure he was no longer in the hallway, I flipped the bathroom light back on, blinded for a moment, and avoided looking at myself in the mirror above the sink. I put a fresh toilet paper roll next to the toilet. Then I got down on my knees to work out the beer and ash from the tiles, unable to wipe the smile from my face.

Now, after reading Margaret's journal, *Sometimes you end up with the wrong woman* takes on a whole new meaning. He might have meant the right woman for him was this Karen.

He might not have meant me at all.

That night, after tidying up the bathroom, I returned to the kitchen with those bottles full of cigarette butts. I found Margaret and Dan standing at the sink, Margaret up to her elbows in soap suds, Dan next to her with a towel. I hesitated, wondering if Dan would sense I had been handled by another man.

Then I saw Margaret's wet arm lift and hand Dan a serving platter, their fingers touching at the rim. He took it from her and carefully dried it.

He never, ever dried dishes for me.

I stood there and watched an alternate universe unfold. I saw Dan with a woman whose ovaries worked, a woman simpering, needy, sweet to the point of stupidity. A woman who could offer him ordinary simplicity, hot meals and warm slippers and Cheerios crushed underfoot.

"Where's Crick?" I asked, my voice clanging in the quiet kitchen. Both turned quickly.

"There you are!" Margaret said so forcefully I took a step back, afraid. Had she been in that dark hallway watching, listening? But she turned a radiant face toward me. "He went outside to hail a taxi."

Dan put the platter carefully on the countertop.

I went close to Margaret, invited by her smile. "And Mather?"

"Hopefully still asleep in your bed. I'll get him when the cab pulls up." She glanced at Dan. "I've been trying to get it out of Danny, but he won't tell me," she stage-whispered.

"Tell you what?" he and I asked at the same time.

"What's happening in Libya. What it means for our husbands."

I was alert to that *our*. She and I on one side, the men on the other. I could see Dan was too.

"What did Cassie tell you?" Dan asked, but it was too late. I was standing closer to her now. I was the recipient of her shimmering gaze.

"You're leaving us, aren't you?" I asked him. I thought I was bluffing but once the words left my mouth I realized I had actually deciphered the evening, all those male heads leaning into one another, making sure none of the women were in earshot. The men drinking too much, the way they did when they knew alcohol might soon be scarce. I had seen this behavior in the past. All those deployments, all those training exercises, all those absences that started exactly the same, with vague uncertainty coalescing into Dan's leaving me again.

"Damn it, Cassie," he whispered, moving from foot to foot.

I turned to Margaret. "Whatever happens, it's you and me." Perhaps I was trying to annoy Dan, trump whatever flirtatious moves he was putting on her, show him I too could seduce, I too could offer something desirable. But Margaret's tremulous eyes, the mixture of fear and trust, the full wattage of every blond and breathy ounce of her, were trained on me. Needing *me*. It was as if she had suddenly shifted fully and clearly into my sights.

"You and I," she whispered. As if she feared nothing. Such a smile. Such emanating warmth, the air crackling just below consciousness.

Dan was outside of the circle, excluded. "When we know exactly what's going on, we can share it with the spouses. Until then, please don't say anything."

Neither of us paid any attention to him. Margaret raised a sopping arm, water sloshing over the side of the sink and dripping down onto her fine dress, none of it of any consequence. She reached for my hand and squeezed. I could smell her, lemon soap and strawberries, but under that sweetness, I could smell Crick, his smoke in my hair.

"To us," she said.

Both of them touching me within moments of each other, it was too much. I felt light-headed, sure Dan could see an outline of desire glowing from my skin.

"I'm going to wait with Crick," he said, and walked out of the kitchen. I heard the front door slam shut behind him.

I squeezed Margaret's hand.

March 20

HOME

Last night was agonizing. Cassie couldn't understand why I didn't want to go to her party, she didn't believe me when I told her I get so nervous talking to more than one stranger at a time. She thought I was being modest but I just knew it was going to be awful. Bad enough with my usual low-grade panic attacks, but with everything happening with Crick, it's no wonder I called him an ASSHOLE in of everyone he knows from the Unites States embassy. And their spouses. Oh my God. Every single word out of my mouth screamed crazy. I keep cringing every time I remember something. I let ugliness get inside. Do other people feel that? Every argument, every time I've wronged someone or cut someone off, yelled at a poor telemarketer for only doing her tedious job that alas woke Mom when she finally fell asleep after being awake three nights in a row, the residue of it stays. In the back of my mind, a soreness; it makes me look over my shoulder, like trying to remember something important

I need to do immediately. But then I remember: I was a jerk. I hurt someone. I'm not nearly as nice as I think I am.

We'd like to think guilt is some old-fashioned by-product of the Catholic Church, but it's as real and palpable as hunger or thirst.

Crick sat up front with the taxi driver on the ride home from Cassie's, slinging local Jordanian dialect, while I held a sleeping Mather in the back and looked out the window. I was wondering if I had to apologize to him. I mean, he really is an asshole, right? I had only stated the obvious, though my method of announcing it to his coworkers and boss was totally nuts.

The whole ride, he never looked back at us once, never indicated to the driver I was his wife or Mather his son, didn't say one word to us, nothing.

But when we pulled up at our apartment, he made sure I saw that he gave our driver a generous tip.

March 25

HOME

❧

Cass is right. They're leaving us. Not for Libya, but for Italy's NATO headquarters. Yesterday Crick came home from work and said, *Oh, don't worry, we won't leave for at least a couple of weeks.* But already it's, *Any day now.*

Leaving me.

Everything I tried to make is toppling down.

This is a war, Margaret, of course I have to work late.

Last night, he was home at nine, tonight after ten.

I was in bed.

"Sorry to wake you." Sounding pretty unapologetic.

I wasn't sleeping. Waiting in the dark, as always. "It's OK. Did you see the dinner I left out?"

"Yeah. Thanks. But I ate at the embassy."

"Oh. Maybe you can tell me that in the future? So I don't make a special meal for you?"

"Right. I'm sure you cooked just for me. How the hell do you even find *tofu* in Jordan, for Christ's sake?"

"It's a tofu *burger*. You love burgers. Did you taste it? It tastes just like beef."

"You're telling me curds of soy milk taste like beef? We need to end this conversation right now before I have an aneurysm. Go back to sleep."

I went to sleep. Or pretended to. Really I waited to see if I had the guts to have a real conversation. I'm no better at it than he is.

He got into bed. It's impossible for me to even imagine how he can fight with me, turn off the light, and be unconscious in the time it takes me to roll over, sit up, turn on the bedside lamp, and turn toward him, finally ready to talk.

What would I have said to him? That it really was super difficult to find tofu? Cass had to bring me to three different supermarkets, and she did, such a good sport, sitting in the backseat with Mather while I ran into each, desperate, as if the right tofu might be the cure for my marriage. Thinking that if Crick took a bite, he'd be wowed, he'd be won.

When we were leaving California, he said he'd start eating healthy, he'd at least *try* the recipes I make. Like smoking. He was supposed to quit. I know he doesn't smoke around me and the baby. He says smoking is a nervous habit, not an addiction, and use of his BlackBerry will overrule the need to keep his hands busy with a cigarette. But that BlackBerry is never out of reach and I still smell smoke on him every night, smoke and the inability to keep a promise. I want to believe he's trying; isn't that what this is all about, what *everything* is all about, marriage, parenting, life? Just *trying* to do the best you can as often as you can?

He isn't living up to his end of the bargain. *Bargain: an agreement between two or more people or groups as to what each will do for the other,* or *a thing bought or offered for sale much more cheaply than is usual or expected.*

A transaction. I banked on his marrying me and he did. I expected him to be a better person than he was, and he expected the same of me. Both of us swindlers.

So much meanness flooding through me. I can't shut it off.

I gave Mather his name to remind myself, every single time I say it, *Mather,* that I need to be a better person. From our trip to Camp Mather. We are all capable of such cruelties. I was twelve. Mom woke up wheezing so badly in our cabin on the third morning we had to go home four days early. Dad had promised to teach me how to skip rocks and I'd spent the previous day collecting the smoothest, flattest, prettiest. I still have that jar, somewhere in a box in a storage unit in San Jose with all the things I couldn't bring to Jordan, all those unskipped stones. That's the first day I noticed how thin her hair had gotten, as I sat in the backseat glaring at the back of her drooping head. The air was thick in her throat, and every twenty minutes or so, she'd whisper, *I'm so sorry to ruin the trip.* Dad and I didn't say a word. No *It's OK,* not once. I wanted her to suffer, I wanted her to know how hard things were for me, with a mom who never came to school plays or brought my class cupcakes, an invisible mother trapped in a dark house, a mom who made me live this somnambulant half-life. Until that day, Dad had been so patient, the one to cook, the one to clean, but during that ride he must have been thinking, *How much more can I take?* I bet he'd told himself a thousand times he couldn't possibly leave a sick wife, leave a kid to sort out pill bottles, doctors' appointments, homeopathic cures. But he did. You can only do the right thing until you can't.

And now Crick is leaving us. After all the things I've done to keep him.

Stop it. Stop it stop it stop it.

I got out of bed to turn off my head. Went to the window, looked down on the street. I like the silence of night, though when you listen for a while you realize there is no silence, just unnoticed noises. Air-conditioning. Water gurgling in pipes above and below. Elevator moving up and down on its trapped track. Cars on the faraway streets outside. Thrum and beat of the music playing from the work site. Cats fighting or mating, desire and hatred sounding the same.

Then I saw a kitten, tiny, orange, tail puffed, standing smack-dab in the center of the road.

What could I do? I wrapped Crick's cold dinner in a paper towel, grabbed a fleece jacket to put on over my sweats, pocketed my keys, and was out the door, in the elevator, and down to the street before I could think anything else.

The kitten was gone. I made that *pss pss pss* noise humans think attracts cats but probably just lets them know a human invader is near. I unwrapped the burger and put it on the sidewalk near the Dumpster, got down on my hands and knees to peek under parked cars. I looked around from that angle— cat's-eye view. Mather's baby's-eye view. I heard the clicking hum of electricity you only hear at night when everyone is sleeping, the buzzy whine of streetlights and power surges. Looking up from the street, the air so cold, I couldn't help but roll over on my back and put my palm under my head. My breath streamed out of me. The moon is bigger here. Only half-full, but its light was so bright my free arm was casting shadows.

Something moved and I turned to see Saleh at the side of the building, looking scared that I'd been hit by a car or a seizure and wondering what in the world to do with this dead, foreign lunatic. I hopped up, pulling a twig from my hair. I was being stupid. If Crick almost had an aneurysm over a tofu burger, imagine his reaction if he looked out the window and saw me stretched in the street. *Mar, goddamn, are you out of your gourd?* But Saleh only smiled, and it drew a smile out of me too.

"Did you see a kitten? Orange and white? Real tiny?" I asked.

He nodded slowly, like he didn't understand a word out of my mouth. I noticed the embroidered script over the heart of his jacket said *Mike*. I didn't know if it was a bad *Nike* knockoff or if it had belonged to an American tenant who handed it down to Saleh. Both scenarios made my skin go warm.

"Meow! Meow!" I said, my hands cupped together to show something small.

He smiled like maybe he got it and motioned for me to follow.

We walked around the block, circling the construction site. Quieter than during the day, but people were still moving around. A couple lights glowed in the darkness; I could hear a generator, muted hammering and digging. We passed men lifting concrete blocks near a metal drum filled with fire. Whenever we walked by any workers, they'd stop and stare at me. Saleh would speak a burst of Arabic, then he'd look at me and I'd meow on cue and make the cupping motion with my hands. The men would usually shake their heads, amused, or say something unintelligible to Saleh in reply.

We finally made it back to the front of the building; we'd heard some noise in the bushes but not one cat had emerged. Saleh was telling me a story; his cousin had married a girl, a foreigner? His cousin, also from Egypt, met a girl when he was a waiter on a Nile cruise? He was trying so hard to communicate. He struggled with every single word, shivering as he spoke, but he wasn't giving up, he wanted me to understand. Makes me think I'm better off with people who don't speak English as a first language. Maybe if you only understand half of what a person says, you can more readily read the sincerity of their gestures. Maybe language is much less important than I think it is, and therefore much less frightening.

He stopped speaking and I realized he was waiting for a reply. I'd lost the thread and wasn't even sure what sort of facial expression to make. Happy, worried, surprised? I smiled and nodded but didn't fool him; he started to repeat what I thought was *eyelash, EYELASH!* over and over again until he was almost shouting and I was poking myself in the eye to no avail, when suddenly I realized he was trying to say that the girl, his cousin's new wife, was *Irish*. They now owned a snack shop in Dublin. That his lucky cousin gets to eat chips all day. They're rich!

I burst out laughing like a hyena and Saleh seemed very pleased with himself. "Wow, Saleh, that's really great."

He watched me with those lovely non-Irish eyes of his like he wanted to say more. Like he could talk to me all night long.

I hesitated. It was late, too late in this space between morning and night for me to notice the eyes of a man who is not my husband. "Good night," I said. "Thank you for the walk."

He made no motion to follow me inside, just stood under the streetlight, watching me as the door closed between us. I took the elevator up. I made a hot cup of chamomile tea and sipped it slowly, heating up my hands so I could write these words. Now it's time to crawl into a chilly bed with Crick and stop thinking about Saleh's eyes.

May 13, 2011

8:08 P.M.

✧

I close her journal, pressing the pointed corner of the cover into my forehead. Oh, Margaret. There she goes. Wandering around a construction site. In the middle of the night. With Saleh.

I reach for my phone. She's been gone four hours now.

It suddenly vibrates in my hand, a message.

But it's from Dan.

Just ran into Crick, what's up? You still at her apartment?

I hesitate before replying.

Yes. No word from Margaret.

I want to call him, but surely he has heard about everything that's been going on here, and surely Dan, being Dan, will immediately realize my role in it all. What if this really is the last straw, what if Dan has decided he'd rather be in a different time zone than with me forever?

I get up. I carry the journal into the kitchen.

I need to think about Margaret. What could she possibly be doing right now? She can't be at the station unless they threw her in a prison cell. Considering how she was behaving at the scene of our accident today, that might not be so far-fetched after all.

I go to the window. It feels terrible, claustrophobic, the apartment closed up like this. I consider cracking the shutters to look down in the street again but I don't want to see Saleh slinking around.

What did Crick tell Dan? And why hasn't Crick called back? I think of the last time I saw him, a few days after the party. I was at the embassy, picking up mail. I had called Margaret that morning to see if she wanted to come with me, but she had just put the baby down for a nap. I was heading toward the parking lot carrying a box in my arms, probably an order from Amazon, probably more Campbell's cream of chicken soup—certainly something I will never make for the Brickshaws again—when I saw Crick sitting under the little "smoking section" gazebo. I almost dropped the box. Instead I made a quick left, hoping he hadn't seen me, even though I had been thinking of him that morning when I got dressed, thinking maybe, just maybe, I might run into him, so why not wear the blue shirt that best highlighted my cleavage? Why not leave the cardigan in the car?

"Cassie?"

I had no choice but to stop. "Hello there."

"Let me get that."

He took the box from me. His eyes snagged on my breasts before he quickly looked away.

"I've been meaning to thank you for having us over the other night."

I could smell smoke on him. I've always hated cigarettes but right then I had a disturbing image of myself sucking on this man's nicotine-stained fingertips.

"It was entertaining," I managed to reply.

He glanced my way, very deliberately looking at my face and only my face. "I had a hangover all week. Your husband's gener- ous with his scotch."

"Mmm. I drank a little too much myself." I tried to smile. There was silence between us until we reached my car and I opened the trunk.

He put the box inside, closed the trunk, adjusted the embassy badge around his neck. "So, Cassie, can I ask a favor?"

"Anything," I said, holding my keys tightly.

"Will you keep an eye on Margaret for me?"

I exhaled. I walked to the driver's side. "Crick, you don't even need to ask me something like that. Of course I will. Thank you for your help."

"Can I call you?"

I froze, turned to face him. He lifted an eyebrow, back to his good old snide self.

"When I'm in Italy. You know, to see how you geographical bachelorettes are handling yourselves in big, bad Amman."

I shrugged, unsure; was he asking me to be his spy or was he flirting? I got behind the wheel, made a point of gently posi- tioning the seatbelt strap exactly in between my breasts. If

Crick was glancing away uncomfortably, then he only wanted me to tattle on his wife. I looked up to assess his reaction. His eyes were unabashedly staring at the straining buttons of my blouse. "You can do whatever you want," I said, and then I drove away.

April 1

HOME

❦

A pril's Fool.

Crick's gone.

It happened so fast. Last night he came home and said, "Well, we just handed the whole clusterfuck to NATO today. I head to Italy in the morning." Big grin. "Now it's time to bring the Jordanians into the fight. Prove this isn't just another example of Western aggression. This is one we're going to win, Mar, you'll see. We've got Benghazi sewn up."

He went into our bedroom and started putting all his camouflage uniforms out on the bed, spreading them out gently with his palm as if they could feel his touch, as if he's missed them, as if he was glad to be putting them on again. He'd be at NATO headquarters, Naples, safe, accompanying Jordanian Air Force officers, to make sure they felt involved, felt like allies. Make sure the world could see this mission, at least, had some honest-to-goodness Muslim Arabs onboard. He talked as he packed, excited to be leaving us. I folded his underwear and socks and wondered about all the things Crick's been longing to do but couldn't because I've been in his way.

Then this morning.

His alarm went off at five.

I thought I'd be frightened, and maybe I am, all the uncertainty ahead, but I feel something different from fear. That slow ratcheting ride up a roller coaster. The distance below is dizzying, you know something's about to happen, you should be scared, the wind's in your hair, you're looking up, not down, and holding on for dear life the whole time. *Please, God, let it be OK*, you say, and then you plummet, screaming and smiling at the same time.

Crick was getting ready to leave and part of me was glad.

I made him cocoa while he was in the shower. That's one of the things I love about him: he doesn't drink coffee, he thinks it is socially acceptable to walk his six-foot-three-inch self into Starbucks or Peet's and ask for a hot chocolate with whipped cream because that's exactly what he wants. It makes him seem harmless, like he has an undiscovered source of sweetness deep down. Like when he's surprised, really and truly surprised by a breaking glass or a deer running out in front of the car, it triggers an insolvable case of the hiccups. I love the sound, the breathy gasp of each one, the bounce of his chest, the way he has to surrender, helplessly letting them seize and release him over and over again.

I put together a ham, egg, and cheese sandwich. Pretty obvious who won the vegetarian debate in this household. I also made one for his Jordanian driver, minus the ham.

I folded tinfoil around each one and drew a smiling pig face on Crick's.

"Hey there, buttercup," he said softly. I jumped. He was leaning against the kitchen door frame as if he'd been there awhile. No side smile, no arching eyebrows. "You gonna miss me?"

Easy to say *yes*, he wanted me to say *yes*, but shyness crept up my throat. It's been a week of late nights and early mornings, so many evasions. I had just one question, and forced it out before I could stop myself. "Actually, please, we need to talk? About Karen? Crick, she's on my mind now, I can't stop thinking—"

His gentleness slid away; he stood up straight and tall and made every millimeter hard. "You're going to bring this up now? When I'm about to walk out the door?"

I pulled my shoulders back the way my dad used to tell me to when I was a kid. Then I patted his sandwich; it was warm and round and soft, like a little tinfoil-wrapped baby. *Breathe, breathe,* I thought. "I need to know. You might be gone for weeks and weeks."

He took a step toward me, wearing his blue polo shirt, khaki pants, a hint of that rosemary lotion on his smooth cheeks. I could see his bags all piled up at the door.

"C'mere." He took me in his arms. "I know something better we can do now that we won't be able to do for weeks and weeks."

I stiffened.

I suddenly wanted him gone, out of the kitchen, the apartment, my life. *This is anger*, I thought to myself, and it made me feel strong. I could feel his body against mine, one long, taut muscle. He ducked his head, half shyly, as if he didn't like my resistance but was pretending he didn't notice. He angled his chin, pressed his mouth against mine. My lips were a line, not returning his kiss. I drew back farther, craned my neck to look at him.

He cupped my cheek in his hand. I usually rub my face into his palm like a neglected cat but this time I turned my face away.

"Look, we'll spend a whole weekend in bed when I get back," he whispered. "Mather playing in the blankets with his blocks and board books, a big bowl of popcorn between us."

Popcorn. His little joke. The only thing he can "cook" besides bacon and grilled cheese sandwiches.

When I didn't respond, his words picked up speed. "Or we'll go on a trip. I know you've been wanting to see Petra." His voice, rough, thick, sexy. "We'll make a week of it, camp at Wadi Rum, then go south to Aqaba. Anything. Anything you want. I'll be gone a month, maybe six weeks, two months tops. I'll make this up to you, I promise."

My eyes were half open. I could see him through my blond lashes, indistinct, as if he was a long way off, as if he'd become too small to see in the distance. He was saying everything I'd always wanted to hear but now those words couldn't reach me. Would I be able to feel his touch if I surrendered? He knew my body, how to make my back arch, how to make me forget everything. I understood it would hurt him to leave me unsexed in a foreign country, strange men watching my every move.

But I didn't trust him. I wasn't entirely sure if I was still his. If he was still, or had ever been, mine.

I didn't trust anything.

In California, it was his grueling language school. Here in Jordan, it was his new job, then the uprisings in the region, now this NATO deployment. Excuse after excuse as to why he couldn't spend time with me. With Mather. And all along I believed him! Just merrily went along with whatever he told me, because Crick would never lie, Crick prided himself on absolute truth. Now I know how wrong I was. He may have done the right thing in marrying me, but that doesn't mean he ever loved me or ever will. And I realize that if I stay with Crick, this will always be my life, a husband at the edges, Mather and I alone.

Then Crick's phone dinged.

I asked him if it was his driver, Shadi, waiting. His concentration lost, he loosened his grip a bit. I could see his inner fight, to BlackBerry or not to BlackBerry . . .

I pushed away from his chest.

He said, "Shadi can wait, come back here—"

But I twisted my hips free.

His hands dropped to his sides. He stood there for a moment, shocked, almost out of breath.

"Do you want to say good-bye to the baby?" I asked.

"I don't want to wake him." His voice cracked. For a moment I considered going to him, begging him to put his arms around me again.

Instead I led the way to the nursery, to Mather, so he could see what he'd chosen. He hesitated, the way he always hesitates when it comes to his son. Again I wondered if I'm in the way. If I was gone, he'd have no choice but to take his son in his arms and hold on tight, to be the dad he ought to be. I watched as Crick went inside the dim room, how his hands gripped the wood of the crib and he stared at Mather's sleeping face. The baby, on his back, breathing deeply, almost snoring. Crick smiled. I stepped out, giving him a moment. I know this is a very different situation than his last deployments, but we don't know how long he'll be gone. How much does a baby change in a month or two? Already he's throwing balls, climbing sofas, trying to use a spoon. What if Libya drags on the way Iraq and Afghanistan have, what if Crick's gone six, eight, twelve months, what sort of child will he return to?

After a few minutes, he walked out of the baby's room.

I put the sandwiches in a plastic bag with napkins, poured the cocoa in Styrofoam cups, followed Crick as he swung on his backpack. He looked lost, like he was thinking he might actually miss us a little bit. He looked the way I feel all the time.

I handed him the cups stacked on top of each other and looped the sandwich bag over his wrist. I opened the locks on the front door. He stepped out into the hallway. I couldn't say the word *good-bye*. As he moved toward the elevator, I quickly shut the door, not loudly, but a solid, final sound. I imagined his spinning at the click of wood and metal, the confusion on his face.

I held my breath, listened to the elevator door close, to the sound of my husband leaving. I don't know what is happening, what will happen, but I do know I want Crick to be afraid of what I might do here in Jordan without him.

May 13, 2011

8:14 P.M.

✼

I remember when Dan left too.

The night before, he'd come home around seven thirty p.m.

I walked out into the kitchen wearing the lacy cotton night-gown I save for ovulation. Dan was standing at the open fridge and his look in my direction made it clear he felt extracting his semen via my vagina was about as pleasurable as removing his toenails with pliers.

"It's been a long day," he said, turning back to the fridge. I watched him as he reviewed the beer selection. He chose a bottle and popped the cap, the snap of it like a slap.

"Dan," I began, and I saw his back go rigid, as if he was afraid I was going to beg him for sex. "There's lasagna."

He glanced at me, nodded ever so slightly, crinkling the edge of his eyes in that way he has of almost smiling. He turned back to the illuminated shelves, noticed the plate I had wrapped in Saran wrap. It wasn't one of Tharushi's dishes; I had cooked this myself. Dan's favorite.

"Looks great, Cassie, thanks."

I went into the bedroom to change, listening to him micro-wave his dinner and then turn on the TV in the living room. Maybe we fared better when he was deployed a year, home a year, deployed again. All this "dwell" time was debilitating; too much *familiarity breeds contempt* without the dependable rejuvena-tion of *absence makes the heart grow fonder.*

"I'll be back before you know it," he said as we got into bed.

"We'll see." I didn't want to agree or contradict, hoping to fall asleep before one of us cracked this blurry truce. After I shut off the lamp I felt him move toward me. He leaned up on an elbow and placed a kiss on my forehead, then, as if he was afraid of my reaction, he quickly rolled back to his side of the bed. I reached for his hand in the dark, wanting to let him know that I under-stood the importance of that kiss. Here he was, actually trying.

"Come home to me, Dan," I whispered. He pressed my fingers in his.

"I'm glad you'll be here," he whispered. And then, "Take care of Margaret, OK?" I blinked in the dark. *Margaret?* I immedi-ately let go of him.

When I woke he was gone.

May 13, 2011

8:20 P.M.

❦

Is this an April Fool's joke?" I said when Margaret asked me to show her how to drive around Amman. I knew she hated driving. She'd told me that she'd only ever driven when she was taking her mother to last-minute doctor's appointments and they didn't have time for the bus. She had called, cheery and bright, the morning the men left. Why wasn't she a sobbing disaster?

"C'mon, Cass, what else do you have going on?"

I bristled at the implication that I had nothing better to do than be of service to Margaret Brickshaw. Weren't we spouses allowed to wallow, today of all days, croissants at hand?

"No one knows their way around as well as you do," she continued. I wondered if she had picked up Dan's method of persuading me through over-the-top compliments or if this came naturally. "What if the baby gets sick in the night? I have to be able to drive."

"You and Crick should have thought of that before he left," I said. There was a long silence and I regretted my words. "Fine. I'll do it."

So I went to her apartment. It was a Friday morning and therefore the best time to learn. The Muslim holy day. Shops are closed. Those who observe are in their mosques. The streets on a Friday are historically uncluttered, quiet, clear. This is when the expats go shopping without the crowds, sightseeing without the lines.

When it's safe.

Or *safer*.

Because Fridays have also become the day of protest. Hundreds of men filled with fervor, leaving the mosques at the same time after afternoon prayers. When better to unite and march? The Arab Spring started on a Friday.

We Americans are supposed to be especially vigilant and check the embassy texts and messages on Fridays, to know which parts of the city to avoid.

However this day was warm. Finally spring had come. Temperature in the mid-seventies, the world dappled in green. I arrived at Margaret's and saw her at the entrance to her apartment building, holding Mather loosely at her hip, speaking with Saleh. He certainly had no regard for prayer. He was standing too close, holding a small bag out to her, and Margaret hesitated; good girl. But then, as I parked, I saw her reach two fingers inside and pop something dark and grubby into her mouth. *Great, I'll be the one to take her to the hospital to treat her hepatitis*, I thought. When she bent over to retrieve something Mather threw on the ground, I saw Saleh's eyes slide over to where her T-shirt lifted and revealed the coral knobs of her spine. I honked my horn loudly and they all looked up.

We got into Crick's "new" car after she strapped the baby in his car seat in the back. It's a prehistoric Land Rover, which Margaret told me he'd bought cheap from a German heading somewhere else fast. Fortunately it wasn't a stick shift.

She watched Saleh sweep the sidewalk for a moment before putting the key in the ignition. "He's sort of sexy, isn't he?"

"Right, in a child molester kind of way. Turn the car on, Margaret."

"I'm a terrible driver, you know," she warned, and I nodded, trying to exude patience. "Crick said he'd have to be unconscious drunk to let me drive him anywhere in Monterey."

"Crick's an ass. But that's not a good enough reason to flirt with your *boab*. Now, let's start by looping around the block a few times." I was fully aware of the hypocrisy of my chiding her for finding her cleaning man attractive when I couldn't stop thinking about her husband, who was indeed an ass, an arrogant, condescending, unfaithful jerk, which did not stop me from being both thrilled and sickened every time I said his name aloud.

She pressed her thin lips together knowingly in her mirror. "Look at you blushing, Cass! You think Saleh is more attractive than you're letting on." Then her face went serious. "You know, I did ask Crick to teach me to drive but he said I needed to *grow a pair* first." She hesitated. "You know what that means, right?"

"Margaret, of course I do, I'm not an imbecile. Let's try pulling out—"

She slammed on the gas without looking, almost hitting a man on a bicycle. I reached up and grabbed the hand strap over my door.

"Remember the lamb balls at the grocery store? That's what I keep thinking of. Crick can't say, *Honey, you need to stand up for yourself.* Or *Sweetheart, you'd benefit from learning the art of defensive driving.* No, he sticks unpleasant images in my head. Me with a set of testicles."

She kept driving, barely pausing at the stop sign at the end of her block. "Margaret!" I shouted, and then, "Right! No, I said RIGHT! RIGHT!" Meanwhile Mather shrieked with delight from the backseat. Margaret kept the car lurching on, stomping from pedal to pedal as if they were keys on a piano. Thank goodness Jordanians drive on the same side of the road as Americans.

When she finally managed a smoother rhythm, I warned her that cars pass on the left or the right any chance they get here. Even if there is a red light twenty feet ahead, the passing car will pretty much run every other car off the road just to gain those few extra feet. Just like in the lines the grocery store.

"What lines?" she asked.

"Exactly! People don't wait in line here. If you leave a space between you and the person in front of you someone will wedge himself into it. Lines represent a democracy, everyone waiting for their turn, for things to proceed fairly and with order. That's our Western way of thinking. But Jordan isn't a democracy. There is no promise of *everyone getting a turn* here. People exert pressure for every single thing they want, and that's the only way they know."

I warned her about people parking cars wherever they liked. Especially during prayers, the main roads along mosques would have cars parked three deep, even if there was an empty parking lot within sight.

"It's nice to see that though, isn't it? How eager everyone is to pray? To connect with something bigger?" she said. "I saw a bus pull over the other day and all these laborers got out. I thought they were going to pee on the side of the road but you know what? They all had prayer rugs under their arms and they got down on their knees facing Mecca! It was incredible."

"Yes, Margaret, please pay attention. You just missed our turn."

She was especially hesitant at traffic circles, unclear about who had the right of way, no matter how often I told her it was whoever entered the circle first.

Lucky for her, Crick's old Land Rover was big. Bigger than most. There is power derived from being behind the wheel of the largest automobile on the road. I told her the muscle of her car gave her the upper hand. "Rules of the Jordanian road, Margaret. Might is right." As a woman, you are expected not to speak to strange men or show the nape of your neck or, God forbid, your sexy little ears, yet if you suddenly find yourself bearing down on a tiny Datsun full of bearded men in long *dishdashas*, you can cut them off, just like that.

"The embassy is straight ahead, right?" she asked. "And Cozmo grocery to the left? And you, your villa, three rights from this intersection?"

"Yes, you're getting it."

By the end she seemed to be enjoying herself.

The speed bumps, the unmarked construction that shut down lanes or entire roads, the taxis weaving with white doilies on their headrests, the jaywalkers suddenly stepping out in front of you, and the cars, dear God, the cars driving as if there were blind men behind the wheels. You couldn't help but be flooded with adrenaline.

"Keep your eyes on the road, Margaret," I cautioned. "And

while you're at it, grow a pair!" We both burst out laughing, more than the comment deserved. Maybe to release our fear at being left alone in this country without any balls at all to protect us. Just me and Margaret, who was about to turn the wrong direction down a one-way street. I gestured for her to pull over.

"Look! I drive like a local!" she said as she abruptly turned without using her blinker, then double-parked next to another car in a no-parking zone.

We laughed harder when someone beeped from behind. Staring at each other, we refused to look at the disgruntled driver.

"That's enough for today," I said. We swapped seats. I sent a throwaway wave of apology at the cars behind us and I drove us to a hole-in-the-wall coffee shop I thought Margaret would appreciate. I knew this place had great Turkish coffee, though of course you do not say that here, just like you do not say *the Persian Gulf*, and you never, ever, say *Israel*. It's *Arabic-style coffee*, *the Arabian Gulf*, and *Palestine*. Even our English translations are marked by war and occupation. I think Margaret was content with her small plate of sweets and sludgy coffee. She even glanced wistfully at the rainbow-hued glass *shisha* pipes sitting on the windowsill. I think she might have tried one for the pure novelty if Mather wasn't with us. We sat back on the rough woolen Bedouin cushions and she gave Mather a date-filled cookie and, inexplicably, a nail file from her purse, which he immediately started vandalizing the table with. Then she exhaled as if she had been holding her breath for a long, long time.

There are so many sides of a person, jagged edges like puzzle pieces; you never know when you'll snap together with someone else. But Margaret and I, we fit.

"You're so good to me, Cass," she said, grinning.

And now I am here, in her apartment, alone, no clue where Margaret is, suddenly feeling like she is an utter stranger. How have we gone from that day to this one?

Cass, was it you?

PART
TWO

May 13, 2011

8:28 P.M.

✤

My cell phone erupts. I've been waiting for it to ring for so long that my whole body jerks with anticipation. As I grab, it flies from my hand and goes skittering across the floor.

"Hello!?" I shout into the mouthpiece when I get it to my cheek. "Hello?"

"Is this Mrs. Hugo?" Not Crick. Not Margaret. A woman's voice.

I take a deep breath and reach out to touch the wall. "Yes?"

"I'm calling from the United States embassy of Amman to follow up on your earlier phone call. You requested embassy guards this afternoon?" The voice hesitates, letting me remember, letting me glance at the clock and calculate how much time has passed. Almost four and a half hours since Margaret left. An hour and a half since I spoke with Crick.

"It wasn't me," I said, adjusting my phone. I am sweating and it is slippery against my ear. I tell myself to remain calm. "I mean, I'm the one who made the call, but I called for Margaret. Margaret Brickshaw. She went to the police station around four o'clock."

There's a pause. "The embassy guards waited at the local police station but Mrs. Brickshaw never showed up. May I speak with her, please?"

"Wait—what? I don't understand. She hasn't come back. But are you sure she never went to the station?"

There's a concerned sigh and a rustle of papers. "The guards went to the al-Mahajireen Police Station near the Greater Amman Municipality buildings. Perhaps she went to a different station? Please have her call me if she needs any future help resolving this issue."

I mumble the woman's phone number as I write it down, then hang up. I go to the window, pull up the shades. Damn it, I can't take the shutters anymore.

I stare down at the construction site. Blue tarps are tacked up unevenly next to lopsided water jugs looking positively fetid, scrawny men milling about eating things wrapped in yesterday's newspaper.

All of my excuses for her are gone. Too much time has passed. Something has happened. She would not leave Mather for this long. Because for all of Margaret's flaws she is a good mother. I wonder if I have ever told her that. This is something she would like to hear, something she needs to hear. Why haven't I ever told her?

And what else has she not told me?

Still nothing from Crick. I pick up her journal and turn again to the final pages. It has to be here, the answer, the truth behind these last strange weeks.

I MUST FIND HIM.
I MUST MAKE IT RIGHT.

I push the journal away, let it slide onto the floor with a thud that tugs my stomach.

I realize suddenly she never intended to go to the police station. The police station was never even a thought in her head.

Oh, Margaret, where are you?

April 7

HOME

*F*ault *n. 1) a defect or mistake 2) responsibility for an accident or unfortunate event 3) a break in the layers of rock of the earth's crust*

It's been one week since Crick left. And I realize all the time I've spent, all the time I've wasted, thinking about the ways to make him happy. Trying my clothes on again and again before he came back from the embassy, would he like this green blouse, would he notice lit candles in the bedroom, would he appreciate my asking about the Muslim Brotherhood? Or would he put on the same expression of slightly skeptical glee he wears when I say *Mather said* minaret! *Mather drew a perfect circle!* All the things I've done to make him love me, *love me love me love me,* always trying, simpering. Since the day I met him he's filled me up. I thought he was *vital: full of life, absolutely necessary, essential for life.* I'd wake and his name would be in my head. Go to sleep with his name echoing. He was my call to prayer. But then I found the photo.

Karen. Writing her name, seeing it on the page, real and damaging, makes my head hurt. The root is *katharos*, Greek for *pure, unsullied.* Maybe he had this relationship with her before I was a part of his life, but he won't tell me. He held on to that photo the way someone holds on to a moment in his past when he looked his best or liked himself the most.

I know, because that's the way I hold on to the moment I met Crick.

Mom and I in our off-kilter, aquarium world. *Let's pretend it's New Year's Eve!* she'd say, but by the time we got back from the grocery store she'd be defeated by the sun, or fluorescent lighting or cleaning supplies, who knew? No one, certainly not the doctors. First a rash, then she'd be on the couch. *Pop the cork, Margaret! Now!* She'd tell me about Times Square, make me promise I'd see that ball drop someday. Then ask me to help her back to bed. That was my life. Short peaks of joy followed by an inevitable crash.

By the time I was fifteen, Dad had a new wife, new house. *Your father doesn't understand commitment, he doesn't understand vows, but you show him you and I still do. Margaret, don't let him leave you, too.*

He'd drive up from San Diego. We'd spend the day at a mall, art gallery, bookstore, but I never left Mom to stay with him. I never left Mom. No senior year of high school class trip to Spain. No slumber parties. Then I chose community college, followed by local temp jobs. That was my rule. For ten years just Mom and me.

Then there was Crick.

Crick at my favorite spot, the Rosicrucian Egyptian Museum, a few blocks from my house. I was jotting down lines from the cat exhibit to have something interesting to bring home to Mom.

The Egyptians didn't name their house cats out of respect, instead calling them Ta-Miew, or the Meower. They adorned them with jewelry, sometimes earrings.

Families would go into mourning at the loss of these pets, shaving off their eyebrows, turning the little corpses into mummies. They found a mass tomb with eighty thousand cat mummies inside.

The penalty for killing a cat in ancient Egypt was death. In 60 BC a Roman soldier accidentally ran over a cat with his chariot. A mob gathered and ripped him limb from limb—

A man's voice: "That's actually pretty standard practice for how a mob deals with an invader."

I spun around. There was this man, scars on his knuckles, smelling of cigarettes and Bengay, clearly peering at my notes over my shoulder.

He grinned.

"Excuse me?" I pulled my notebook to my chest. Had he gotten me mixed up with someone else?

"I just don't think an anecdote about a mob killing one Roman guard is proof that Egypt had a death penalty for *cat killing*. It makes an odd footnote but there must be more to it. There's always more to it."

I looked at him for a moment in confusion, then turned away.

"Are you going?" he asked.

I glanced back. "Where?"

"To Egypt? Planning a trip?"

"That's none of your business." I couldn't believe I was being so rude.

He smiled like he liked it.

"I'm a spy," he said. "I can't help it."

I walked out of the room, half mortified, half exhilarated.

He followed. "Maybe you like cats?"

"Allergic." I knew he was hitting on me and it didn't make sense. I just wanted to get away from him. He wasn't my type. I certainly couldn't be his. I came here to be invisible, to be alone.

He continued. "My name's Crick. Rhymes with *brick*. That's what happens when you play hockey in high school and get hit in the head too often."

I stopped, spoke without thinking. "Did someone once make the mistake of telling you you're charming?"

This made him laugh, a charming laugh.

"I can tell you're having a bad day," he said. "They teach you to detect that sort of thing in spy school. I'm actually on a mission to make you smile."

I didn't. I couldn't understand my reaction to him; where had my shy and nervous self gone? Who was this person who wanted to be seen, to engage? I could feel the lightning of adrenaline surging through my limbs, quick-firing my brain in ways it had never fired before.

He pestered. "I think the best cure for you would be a San Jose Earthquakes soccer game."

"I hate soccer."

He took a step closer and tripped over a wrinkle in the carpet, not seeing the electric cord under the rug. My defensiveness seeped out. It took one stumble, and I thought maybe he was awkward like me.

He righted himself, glanced down at the floor. He didn't get so close this time. "Well, how about I just follow you around and continue to trip over things?"

I could tell he was losing steam, that he was about to give up.

"If you do that, I'll scream," I whispered. It was my last-ditch effort but I could feel the moment had passed me by; I was suddenly too aware of myself, my words, my faded Old Navy jeans. I felt like a popped balloon without my indignation to keep me afloat, like the only sound I could make would be a high-pitched yelp of inhaled helium. "I'll yell for help."

"I dare you," he said, instantly brightening, charm reclaimed.

I hesitated and could see my wavering disappointed him. He wanted me to resist, to banter, to shock. But the few boys I'd dated had been self-conscious and worn glasses; I could have swiped their lenses and they'd have blinked up at me like moles. We'd go to the beach, wear hats and sunblock, wade up to our ankles in the surf. Already I knew this man had perfect vision. Already I knew he'd dive right in, that any beach he visited would have a dangerous undertow.

"Guard!" I shouted. "Fire!" I'd never shouted in a museum before. I'd probably never *shouted* before, anywhere. Crick's eyes widened. And you know what? No guards came running; no one even checked on me. But I'd impressed him. And then, without even calling my mom to explain where I was or why, I went to my first soccer game, drank three lukewarm beers, cheered for a team without knowing any rules of the game. It was delicious, all of it. *This is what the rest of the world is doing*, I thought. Afterward, Crick brought me home, walked me to the front stoop. I was wondering if I'd see him again when he grabbed my elbow, pulled me in, and crushed my mouth with a kiss.

I felt the burn of his stubble on my lips for days.

How could I resist? Why would I? My mother and her sickness. Our dark and muted house. How could I not latch on to

Crick? I wanted to be whatever he thought he was seeing in me. I wanted him to look at me with surprise, as if I was someone who could enchant him. Someone who could keep him.

He followed me that day at the museum and it made me long for him to follow me forever. But I've been the one following him ever since.

Until now.

April 10

HOME

I went to the embassy today to check out language lessons.

At the front gate, the guard who always has candy ready for Mather, Hassan, said, "Good afternoon, Miss Margaret." Not even glancing at my badge.

"*Marhaba!*" I shouted.

"Please." He waved to the guards behind him. "Please, this spring day, you must join us for chai."

I hesitated only a moment; there was no Cassie, no Crick, no Robert Riding, no car honking behind me, no one to stop me at all. I said *yes yes yes!* I'm so tired of *no*.

I parked on the side of the road, got Mather out of his seat. Hassan led us to a small white guard shack, its door held open by a rock. There was one stool and the young man sitting on it jumped up, wiping its chipped paint with the heel of his hand, motioning for me to sit. Hassan handed me a Styrofoam cup with a fresh tea bag inside, then poured hot water from an electric kettle attached to a very long extension cord that snaked off into the embassy grounds. The tea had barely steeped before he spooned in two heaping mounds of sugar. Another guard slipped Mather something that he ferreted into his mouth before I could get a look at it. Fortunately Little Man didn't choke.

Then a guard picked Mather up and started throwing him in the air. The baby shouted in pleasure or terror, I wasn't entirely sure, and I burned my tongue on the sweet tea, sipping and watching and not sure if I should ask the nice man to please stop. More guards swarmed, lifting thick eyebrows and mustaches. Their English was iffy, lots of "big boy" and "welcome, welcome." All of them were fascinated with Mather, squeezing his dimpled elbow or knee, finding endless candy in their pockets.

By the time I got to the classroom for Conversational Arabic, I was late. I hesitated at the door. The room was set up with all the chairs in a big circle while the teacher, in a flowered *hijab*, stood in front of a large chalkboard up front. She was going around the circle dialoging in Arabic with each student. Every one of them was wearing a suit; they must all work here at the embassy. I felt my heart speed up, accelerating to clang against my rib cage.

"Can I help you?" the teacher asked. She walked over to Mather, touched his foot, and whispered, "Beautiful. *Ilhamdilallah*."

"Thanks." This had to be lunch hour, all these people with full-time embassy jobs spending their break here, cramming more into an already full workday, and they managed to be on time. Here I am, nothing to do all day, bedraggled, with my baby, and LATE. All eyes were staring at me. I wondered if they could hear my heart, see how my dilated veins were pumping splotchy red into my face. "Um, I wanted to find out about class." I tried to smile. "Is there babysitting?"

"No, so sorry, there is no childcare. But this a good idea. Perhaps next session, I will ask. Yes?" She had a gentle face, no makeup, lines around her eyes and mouth as if she often smiled.

"Yeah, thank you, I'm so sorry, I meant to come early to talk to you before class, but, well, I should go—" And I ran out of there before she could say anything else.

I took Mather to the park and tried some of my breathing exercises. I'm so used to bringing Mather with me, it hadn't occurred to me this wasn't going to be full of mothers with their own small kiddos running around underfoot. I'm an idiot. Who would I leave Mather with? Cassie? But could I really sit in that class and go around in that big, exposed circle and speak?

"Ms. Margaret?"

I turned around and saw Hassan at the gate to the park. His smile faltered when he saw my face and he walked toward me. "Are you not feeling fine?" he asked.

"I was going to take Arabic at the embassy, but, well, I don't think the class is for me."

"Arabic is not so difficult as English."

"Maybe you should teach me." I was joking. It was one of those mortifying things I manage to say and wish I could shove back into my mouth as soon as the words are released.

He shrugged good-naturedly, glanced at his watch. "Perhaps. You have a paper? When I will see you, I will write words. Even if you learn only one every time, that will be one new word. Five words, that is a sentence. Good idea?"

I wanted to cry. "Yes! Would you really do that?" I pulled a grunting Mather from the swing, dropped him on the grass with his bouncy ball, then dug through my big old purse and took out this journal. Hassan sat down at one of the benches in the shade and began to write:

na'am	yes!!!
la	no
ahlan wa sahlan	welcome
Allah ysalmik	God protect you

We stayed like that while Mather tried to rip up the sod near the base of the slide. Hassan told me he had one child, also a son, who lived in New Jersey now. "He too was a fat, fat baby. Always a piece of candy in his fist, like this one," he said, opening up Mather's sweaty palm to reveal a melted Mento covered in grass that the baby either forgot about or was saving for later. Mather immediately shoved it in his mouth, grass and all. We laughed as I pulled strands of green from the sides of Mather's lips, then Hassan stood, stretching his knees, telling me he had to finish his round of embassy checks.

Can you imagine if we can manage to do this three, four times a week? And I study during nap time? It makes me feel like so much is possible.

Then, on the drive home, I saw the nice produce man who sells fruit near our apartment. I usually walk over to him with Mather in the stroller, but somehow he spotted me behind the wheel. I could see that he'd added a row of white tubs jammed with flowers to his wares. I wonder if selling flowers is higher on the street vendor hierarchy? They're transitory, a luxury. If he doesn't sell them, he can't feed his family carnations. I hope it's a sign he's doing well. He reached into a bucket of bouquets, water flecking his clothes as he ran into traffic.

I rolled down my window.

"*Saba al-khair!* Good morning," I said.

"Hello, baby, baby!" he said emphatically, peering through the window at Mather. He always looks at Mather rather than me but today he seemed even more uncertain, as if he was new to the dodging-traffic game. So many cars around us. I don't know street etiquette; surely it's fine for this bearded man outside his mosque to talk to an uncovered Western woman in her big car as long as a sale takes place? He held tulips out to me. I've never liked tulips, they wilt quickly, tragically, stalks going limp, petals opening and falling like withered tongues; is there anyone who can look at a tulip and not think of the morbid Sylvia Plath we all read in high school? But they were the only thing he'd brought out to me so I scrambled to get my wallet from the passenger seat. He ripped a head off one and held it out, motioning for me to give it to Mather.

I knew Mather would eat it and babies ought not to eat tulips, but I also didn't want to hurt this man's feelings. So I handed the decapitation to my child.

The man glanced at the red light, pressed the bouquets to his chest, and held up seven fingers. As a well-trained disciple of Cassie, I offered five. He glanced again at the light and nodded his head yes, put the damp bundle on my lap so I couldn't change my mind.

I flipped through my bills and saw I only had a ten-dinar note; what is that, fifteen American dollars? I gave it to him and as he started to riffle in his pocket for change I shook my head no. He seemed confused. It's terrible, what I was doing, paying him to like me.

Light turned green, street buskers quickly hopped up on the median and out of the way of moving vehicles. The man shoved my dinars into his pocket as if embarrassed, then waved again at Mather, who was gumming petals and stamen. I was afraid my attempt at generosity was insulting, and the car behind me honked. But the man turned toward me and smiled. I wanted to grab his hand and kiss it with gratitude but of course I didn't. Instead I clutched the tulips in their smeared newspaper. "Ma-salama, good-bye!"

Out of sight, I twisted around and slapped the tulip out of Mather's mouth. He howled, mouth furred with yellow and black like he'd swallowed a hive of bumblebees.

Is it possible I'm finding my way, comfortable here, of all places, in Jordan?

May 13, 2011

✴

Aha. So this was the beginning. This was when she started to lie to me. I had no idea.

All along I thought I was the one giving her what she needed.

But I advocated caution. She didn't want caution.

She wanted men. Tea and tulips, Hassan and Saleh, even this unnamed flower man on the corner. I remember the first time she mentioned him to me, months ago. She said she'd been pushing Mather's stroller when a total stranger flagged her down, came running over, split a fig with his two thumbs, and then fed her half. And she ate it. "Margaret! Please tell me you didn't let him feed the baby, too!" I asked. But of course she had. I was thinking of unwashed thumbs and the fecal matter used in fertilizer. I was thinking that Margaret allowed a complete stranger to put something in the mouth of a child who hadn't gotten all of his shots. Yet the only thing Margaret found remarkable was the man's generosity.

I wonder if Crick sensed it first.

It was late, past midnight, and I'd been sleeping. But an Army spouse knows to never ignore a ringing phone when her husband is deployed.

"Cassandra," a man's voice said, dragging out the S's.

"Who is this?"

"C'mon, don't pretend you haven't missed me."

"Crick? What's the matter? Is it Dan?" I lurched up, swung my feet off the side of the bed, ready for anything.

Crick snorted; was that a hint of derision in his voice? "Dan's passed out in his room. You wouldn't believe how much this Jordanian colonel we're babysitting can drink. Thank God he's a Muslim. If he was a debauched Christian like the rest of us we'd kill ourselves trying to keep up. NATO headquarters sure knows how to throw a war."

"Oh." I blinked in the dark room. "So why are you calling?"

"Just checking on my ladies," he said. "Everything going well over there?"

"Yes, fine."

"Margaret seems happy to you?"

I felt a wave of annoyance. "Happy enough. Why don't you wake her up in the middle of the night and find out?"

His voice went low. "I figured you might give me a more honest answer. She's been a little . . . *emotional* lately, have you noticed?"

"No. Crick, do you know what time it is?" But I pulled my legs back under the blankets and got comfortable. Dan's calls had been brief, sporadic, during daytime coffee breaks.

Crick asked, "Do you want me to hang up and let you go back to sleep?"

I didn't want to answer that. "We've been keeping busy," I

said quickly. "Margaret's been on a quest for adventure. *Show me something real*, she keeps saying. Did she ever tell you about the time we nearly got killed by a gang of ruffians near the citadel? They threw rocks but we ran away. It was quite a daring escape."

"Seriously?" I heard the gasp of a lighter and then Crick inhaling deeply from a cigarette.

"We ended up at the animal section of the *souk*. Margaret cried when she saw the pastel-dyed chicks."

He chuckled softly. "Jesus, Cassie, of course she'd cry at the animal *souk*, you're a freaking sadist to even bring her there. All those miserable creatures crowded together in tiny cages." He exhaled and I closed my eyes, imagining the smoke sifting out from his full lips. "She tell you she says a prayer every time she goes by a butcher shop? Something about hoping the animals inside had peaceful deaths. I swear she does it just to make me feel bad for craving meat."

"Well, you're lucky she's allergic or you'd have ten feral cats in your apartment by now. She keeps a Ziploc bag of cat food in her diaper bag right next to Mather's snacks. She'll pour it right out on the sidewalk whenever she sees a stray." Unlike my own husband, Crick seemed to be enjoying the sound of my voice. Crick wasn't upset that I was maybe exaggerating the tiniest bit. "I also took her to an olive wood carving factory run by the American Christian group who only hires hearing-impaired employees. Margaret bought one of everything, wooden spoons, salad bowls, soap dishes, a Christmas nativity set. Mather had the Virgin Mary down his throat before Margaret even got a chance to pay for it."

He laughed loudly; my phone shook with it. "Cassie, stop the charity tour, already. Can't you find something *normal* to do in Amman? Take Margaret to buy high heels? Get your nails done?"

I scrambled to put another vivid image in his head. "Next, I was thinking we'll go to . . . the Turkish bath."

"A *hammam*? You're getting naked together?"

I smiled, pleased. "It is a bath."

He groaned in my ear and my entire body rang with the carnal sound. "Cassie, you're killing me."

I waited, listening to him breathing. "Then maybe it's time to hang up. Good night, Crick. Sweet dreams."

After that, I kept my cell phone under my pillow when I went to bed, and I replayed that groan over and over again.

And I took Margaret to the baths: the Pasha baths on Rainbow Street, in downtown Amman. The *hammam* was the perfect compromise. She could participate in a rite that had infiltrated the Middle East during the Ottoman occupation, and I could get a massage.

I had gone once before and knew the routine, nodding to the covered woman at the front desk and heading to the locker rooms so we could change into our bathing suits. I assessed Margaret's body in the fluorescent lighting while she changed. She wasn't flawless; there was a crooked C-section scar that sloped from the left to the right under the soft curve of her belly, a tight, purplish line that snagged through the top of her fair pubic hair. But she was less shy about her nudity than I expected, not nearly as hunched over and embarrassed as I was. She seemed fine with her imperfections and it made me think Crick must love watching her strip her clothes off, slipping one slender leg, with those unpolished toes pointing down, into her blue bikini bottoms, wiggling them up her boyish hips.

But he'd called me in the middle of the night.

The interior was steamy and dark despite the effort of the few ornate, flickering brass lanterns and the colored glass spheres that were cut into the ceiling to filter in sunlight. And there was an almost overpowering smell—burned cedar mixed with soap, sweat, olive oil, and, ever so slightly, urine.

We underwent a delicate torture: showering in cold water, dipping into the bubbling hot tub, scalding in the pitch-black steam room (which left me blind, breathless, and claustrophobic to the degree that I tried to leave but instead slipped and landed savagely on my tailbone; Margaret cackled while helping me to my feet, that nimble little bitch). We were laid out next to each other on slabs of marble, stripped from the waist up, and exfoliated, the women working on us with what felt like a Brillo pad sewn into an oven mitt. There was something medical, almost gynecological, about the way they handled, inspected and cleaned us, lifted our legs and arms, scrubbed at our breasts, and how no one seemed the least bit alarmed when bits of my old skin piled up around on the marble slab and were then rinsed away. Then we were violently massaged, my masseuse splashing every part of me with water and olive oil, and she finished by walking along my spine. By the end Margaret and I were exhausted and beaten, and sent to the hot tub to soak ourselves back together again. I sat carefully on the edge with my legs in the water. Margaret was mostly submerged, water splashing along her ears, her face so close to my thigh I could feel her hot, damp breath, as intimate as women can get and still remain heterosexual. She did not look pretty now, no, she was redfaced and blotchy, her thin hair matted against her scalp, her eyes bloodshot. But somehow the very ugliness gave her a beauty she didn't have otherwise. Something tougher, stronger, not so easily broken.

In the intimacy of that bath, it seemed only natural that we'd strip away even more.

She told me she'd only slept with one other man before Crick, but this young man had ejaculated so quickly she wasn't certain they'd actually had intercourse. I laughed and she looked stricken, then burst out laughing too.

She scooted closer and said she had a theory that Crick's arrogance sprang from an insecure place, from his having been short throughout puberty, his growth spurt coming late. I held my breath. I wanted her to keep talking. "Before he was *Crick the Brick* in college, he was *Crick the Midget* in high school," she whispered. "He claims when he was seventeen, he could hear his knees cracking in the night, that he was growing so fast, he could feel the muscles tear."

She looked up at me. "Do you think he would have been different if he hadn't grown so tall? Do you think he could have been, I dunno, *nice?*"

I was dizzy from the heat, the sweat, her proximity. Thinking about Crick sent a shiver across my skin. I glanced around for the woman who was handing out cold glasses of sweet hibiscus tea. "Are you saying this because you see Dan, and he's short, and you think he's nice?" Her eyes widened and she bit her lip, as if I'd made her aware of her thoughts before she'd even been able to think them. "Well, you're wrong," I continued. "My husband is not nice, and even six inches shorter, your husband wouldn't be either. We married career soldiers, Margaret. Men who chose jobs that might put them in a situation in which they will kill another human being. So maybe there are times they can be kind, and fair, and good, but they will never be 'nice.'"

I thought she'd be scandalized but she drew closer. I was hoping she'd keep whispering secrets about Crick but instead she started talking about her mother, the medicines and side effects and failed therapies. I realized for the first time how her mother's illness had circumscribed Margaret's life, especially after her father left. Her father supported them financially but that meant Margaret never needed to think about a career; her only job was to care for her ever sickening mother, and when she managed to work she only took on short office temp schedules that allowed her to be at her mom's beck and call. No wonder she didn't know how to behave in public, no wonder Jordan seemed so delightful. She had nothing but a dank little bungalow on a side street in San Jose, full of prescriptions and books, to compare it to.

Maybe because she was practically sitting on my womb, I found myself telling her about my trials in infertility. How the very act that should have been bringing Dan and me closer together was now pulling us apart.

"Sex has been completely ruined," I whispered. And then, without thinking, "Sometimes I'm afraid he's begun to hate me even more than he ever loved me."

I looked at her. I half hoped Margaret, with her dictionaries, her bottomless optimism, would have an answer for me. Her eyes seemed to swell with tears. "At least you know he loved you once," she replied. Then she took a deep breath and disappeared under the hot water. It seemed like ages before she rose up, streaming water off the planes of her greenish-gold hair and the strut of her clavicles, the line of her arms held straight at her sides. I had a dim memory of a long-ago Christmas, my Scottish grandmother telling me to beware of ashrays, translucent water creatures often mistaken for sea ghosts. When captured and exposed to sunlight they melt. Only a puddle of water remains.

That's when an attendant came over, clapping loudly as if afraid Margaret was going to drown herself, and abruptly told us to leave. Women's hours were over. Men were waiting at the door.

April 12
HOME

H assan is my window.

It's only been a few days, but I've seen him every time I've gone to the embassy. If he isn't at the front gate, I send him a text, play in the park with Mather until Hassan does his checks and has a few minutes to talk. He writes out vocabulary, we practice simple dialogues. I never feel embarrassed or shy no matter how much I screw up. Mather attacks Hassan's knees and then reaches high, wanting Hassan to lift him.

Yesterday he told me he's a widower, that his wife died two years ago of cancer, and as he spoke he moved his hands across his body, his fists opening and closing over and over again as if to show how the cancer had radiated from every part of her. I told him about Mom, the doctors, the slipping away. He understood. Then we talked about his son. He hasn't seen him in years; he has never even met his two small granddaughters.

ummi   my mother
ibni   my son

eayilati   my family

habibi   my beloved (either friend or spouse)

Crick Skypes maybe twice a week to tell me NATO anecdotes ("All I do is make sure the mess hall pork is properly labeled so the Jordanians don't eat it"). He's relaxed in a world of men in a way he never is with me. When he switches to family mode, it comes out stiff: "Margaret, be careful/pay attention/stay tuned to what's happening, OK?" It makes me defensive, makes me want to do something he doesn't think I'm capable of doing, makes me sign off sooner than I should, so both of us hang up feeling unsatisfied. Then I spend the rest of the night imagining him at dodgy nightclubs, a woman, dark like Karen, shimmying next to him on the dance floor, saying she wants to practice *this thing called pillow talk*. Wait, no, he's no dancer, he'd be at the bar, or back door, leaning into the alley beyond, smoking his face off now that he can. A woman comes over; takes the cigarette from his fingertips; puts it in her mouth, red ember crackling; then blows smoke into his lips. Crick knocks the cigarette from her hand, presses against her, *Isn't this what you really want?* See, I'm driving myself insane with these visions in my head all night long.

But that's better than going over the last moments of Mom's life, the way I have, and do, and will forever, because when I think dark thoughts about Crick they get knotted up with all the things I did and shouldn't have.

What if I had never told her about Jordan? What if I had never married Crick?

We visited her every other weekend. Mather and I on the bus, giving Crick time to study. Or time to see Karen. Then that final visit. Mather was six months old and crawling, grabbing, pulling everything down. After Mather went to sleep I made batches of soup, ginger and carrot for the anti-inflammatory properties and vitamin D, sweet potato and cumin for vitamins A and C. I should've been in her room talking, listening. I should've been dabbing apple cider vinegar into the angry red of her skin, rubbing coconut oil into the wolf-bite rash, all those quiet, soothing things I did before Crick came along.

Lupus, the Wolf, the body attacking itself.

That last Sunday, I packed up the portable crib and toys and small suitcase. I sat down on her bed. Her bloodshot eyes were bright in the dark room. She sat propped on pillows, her breathing difficult, pneumonia again, full of corticosteroids. The nurse would come to check on her in two days.

I told her Crick got his official orders for Jordan. I let it sink in: *Jordan*.

"But I'm not going, Mom," I said. "Mather and I are going to move home, take care of you."

I thought my plan would fill her with relief.

"You didn't marry him to stay with me," she whispered.

"Crick'll come back for Christmas. Mather and I will visit him. It'll work out, don't worry."

She pointed to the bookshelf.

"*The Pied Piper*. Take it with you."

I went to the shelf, pulled it down. The book was in my mother's room instead of mine because I hated it. I hated the jester on the cover, a 1960-ish trippy illustration with tremendous black eyes facing the reader. I hated his leering, smiling mouth, the flute in his hands, and most of all the long line of faceless, smudged children following behind him. Had Mom forgotten the nights I woke up screaming? Yelling for Dad to *get it out, get it out, he can see me!* No matter how hidden on the shelf it was I felt his black eyes watching.

"Thanks," I said, unsure.

"Your body might be a time bomb too."

I felt everything stop, my heart, my breath, my hands holding the book in midair. A prophecy. Not that I hadn't thought of it before, certain that every headache and menstrual cramp, every cold or random nosebleed, was the onset.

Your body might be a time bomb too.

"I know," I said quietly. I turned to Mather, who had crawled into the room and was trying to pull the *The Pied Piper* from me. "Say good-bye to your grandma!"

She didn't get up, didn't hoist herself into the walker and stand in the kitchen as we left.

She must've said *I love you,* and other prosaic words I'd cut off the fingers of my left hand to remember. But I was shoving *The Pied Piper* into my bag, checking bus schedules, the clock relentlessly *tick tick tick*–ing. Selfish. I didn't realize the ticking I heard was coming from Mom, not me. We caught our bus with loads of time to spare; Mather sat on my lap. I'd opened the window, the wind cool in my hair; I could smell the loamy farmland of Gilroy and Salinas give way to the salt of Monterey.

Two days later, Dad called. Overdose. The nurse found her but it was already too late. Crick sat with Mather, watching college football, feeding the baby an entire bag of Doritos. As soon as I hung up, weeping, Crick held me and said, "Mar, Mar, shhh, she's out of pain now."

Tears down my face, sobbing so hard I couldn't breathe. I felt the strength of him, the rightness of his arms around me, how he propped me up. He was strong enough. In that moment, I had no regrets. Instead, I realized I'd be able to go to Jordan. Mather and Crick and me, we'd all be together. Finally, monstrous child that I am, I knew I was free.

April 17

HOME

A nother family Skype. Me, a screen-thin Skype image, trying too hard to be interesting while Mather flails about,
putting the computer's camera in his mouth and, though he's
been chanting it manically all day, refusing to say *dada*.

Crick glances at his watch again, our fifteen minutes up.

"Are we all right, Mar?" he asks, the closest he can come to
talking about us. Mar, Mar, Mar. Such an apt nickname. Just
like calling Mather *the Destroyer*. No need of Freud to see what he
thinks of us, of the impact we've had on his life. *Mar: to inflict
damage, especially disfiguring damage; to impair the soundness, perfection, or integrity of.* That's what I do. *Mar*, from the Middle English *marren*, from the Old English *mierran*, "to impede. To spoil."

I give him the answer he wants. "We're good."

"Well, got to go!" he says. "Work to do. Despots to kill. Pro-
democracy activists to save from certain genocide. Don't forget
to check the embassy texts before you go out."

I wanted *I miss you. I love you.*

I felt empty when Crick hung up. Even Mather couldn't shake me out of my funk, pressing his sticky fists against my cheeks, neighing into my face, *Remember how this made you laugh once, Mommy?* He pushed his fingers into my mouth trying to shape my lips into a smile and then released a pure and devilishly loud "DADADADADADADA," as if to say, *See, I am keeping this bit of magic just for you.*

So I started going through my cabinets, my fridge, the pantry. Pulling out random selections, a few pitas, Jordanian black olives, tomatoes, cheese, my goodness, maybe the very same cheese I bought during that early trip to Cozmo. Then I took the stairs down, afraid that if I waited for the elevator I'd lose my nerve, holding Mather in my arms, grocery bag dangling from my left elbow.

"Saleh?" I called outside of the room in the parking garage that really ought to be a storage closet, next to a wall of circuit breakers and the furnace. The door was held ajar by a small crate of car cleaning supplies. I wondered for weeks when we first got here why there were sandals outside a weird little closet until one day, bang, lightbulb going off over my head! I realized that's where Saleh lives. "Excuse, me, Saleh, are you here?" I tapped on the pressed-wood door.

Then he was standing in front of me, his hair tousled wildly, as if I'd woken him. I lifted the shopping bag.

"*Tafadhali,*" I said. "*Please take!*" He opened the door wider, sweeping his hand across the air to welcome us in. His smile was enormous. I glanced around, hesitated, took a small step so I stood in the doorway but not actually inside his room. It smelled like sleep, the way sheets get when they need a washing, plus curry, kerosene, a dash of his sweet scent. There was a small TV showing people setting up camp in Tahrir Square, a frayed prayer rug folded on a plastic crate, a portable gas-burning stove precariously close to a futon mattress, and grease smudges on the unpainted cement walls.

"I wanted to bring you something." I faltered. "I mean, there's only me and the baby now, and too much food in the fridge." Pita and old cheese? What had I been thinking? That I didn't want to be alone. I wanted someone to look glad to see me. I hated myself, so needy, so desperate, trotting out leftovers in order to force this poor man to act grateful at my putrid largesse. He took the bag, nodded as if he'd been expecting it. Then he placed it on the floor next to his tiny fridge, blinking his long lashes at me.

"I shouldn't have bothered you—"

"Please." He walked quickly over to the opposite wall, and as if conjuring up a genie, he lifted a cardboard shoe box from behind the television set. Hidden like a treasure, as if that box was the only thing worth stealing in the whole place. He carried it to me and I leaned over to see what was inside. Photos of his family? Jewels? A membership card to the Egyptian Muslim Brotherhood? Nope. Candy. Wrapped in gold foil. I glanced up; I couldn't take one! But I couldn't refuse. I moved Mather away so he wouldn't grab all of them and I chose the smallest. I peeled it slowly, trying to show how much I appreciated it. Inside, the chocolate was striated with white the way old chocolate gets. I put it in my mouth fast, before Saleh could notice.

"Yummy, thank you!" I said, mouth full. Mather screamed and hit me in the chin, *Where is my chocolate! Where, where, where! DADADADADA!* I saw Saleh's eyes widen; he was thinking, *Oh no, do I have to offer more?* So quickly I chomped mine in half, reached into my cheek to fetch a piece, and shoved it, dripping with saliva, into Mather's furious maw.

"Good night," I said, wiping my wet mouth on the back of my wrist, then running out before Mather realized the chocolate was not, indeed, yummy. I could hear Cassie's voice in my head, laughing at me for expecting anything other than some third-world *assumption* of chocolate. It tasted like brown crayon, talcum powder, crunchy with too much sugar.

We raced up the steps again instead of waiting for the elevator. I bounced Mather and chanted the ABCs. Somewhere between the first and third floor, Mather either spat out the chocolate or swallowed it. I was skeptical he'd swallowed it. A toy dinosaur or fistfuls of Mentos still in plastic wrappers, sure, but candy I actually *wanted* him to swallow? No way. I put him in the bath, got him ready for bed, did the things a good mom should. When Mather was finally sleeping, I crept out of the apartment, tiptoed down the stairwell until I found the fingernail-sized pellet of melted brown, picked it up with a tissue, and thrust it in my pocket quick. At least tonight, while I toss and turn over mistakes I've made, I don't have an image of Saleh finding the spat-out gift and having to get down on hands and knees to clean up his own kindness.

May 13, 2011

9:13 P.M.

I wonder if I ought to take a trip down to Saleh's basement lair right now. Is that where Margaret has been, on that filthy futon, breathing in the fumes of his kerosene heater perched dangerously close? Turning to Saleh for solace? But that can't be right, I've seen him angrily storming around. No, it must be someone else.

I scroll through my phone until I find Crick's number. I have never called him in Italy, not once. He was the one who would call me, six times total. Then he got angry and stopped.

I stare at the clock on my cell phone and do the math. More than five hours have passed since Margaret left me. I spoke to Crick two hours ago but he hasn't called back as promised; someone else taking me for granted as a babysitter who has all the time in the world.

I press his number, put the smooth phone to my ear.

I hear that long exchange of clicks for an international call, but there is no answer after twelve rings.

I assumed Crick was spending the last couple of hours frantically tracking down his wife when he may really have been typing memos, attending meetings, or maybe sipping coffee, watching predator drone footage of Libya.

I could call Dan. Dan will have plenty of advice for me, and plenty of criticism too. Dan will tell me the obvious, that I should have gone with Margaret. Dan will likely take it even farther and tell me that this, like so much else, is my fault.

No. I'll call him when everything is done, when I have been proven blameless. Already, reading her journal, I know much more than I ever did. I will be a better friend to her in the future.

I have to tread lightly this time, I know.

Better to just keep reading, to just keep waiting.

I flip through pages of Arabic in Margaret's little book. Here she is learning the Arabic alphabet and writing the letters over and over and over again. I skim ahead, impatient; it should be coming up, right about now.

You see, Margaret and I didn't have a fight. You wouldn't call it that.

But we did have a falling-out.

I'd started to notice she was beginning to spin beyond my reach. She was good-natured, always glad to see me, seemed to appreciate our time together, but she didn't *need* me anymore. I had been necessary in her life, and then I was not.

There was the day we went to the Dead Sea. I let her pick the beach—big mistake—and of course she chose the *authentic* experience, rather than my suggestion of paying an entry fee to use the Marriott facilities. We could have gained access to the infinity pools and lockers and showers and fluffy beach towels, as well as the pretty sliver of salted sand at the Dead Sea's edge.

Instead Margaret made us go to the one with a young boy ran-domly riding a camel through the gravel parking lot, where the public restroom was flooded and all the lockers full, where it seemed as if half the women were covered in slick Batman-like burkini suits, covering them from crown to ankle, and men en-tered the water fully dressed.

Margaret didn't care. We'd both worn modest one-pieces and still could feel eyes on us, men taking photos of our cleavage and rear ends, or maybe just Margaret's blond hair. But there were a few Europeans or maybe Russians who helped take the attention off us, sunburned women with breasts stuffed into too-small bi-kini tops, pulling at skimpy bottoms wedged into the cracks of their cellulite-dimpled asses.

Margaret spotted a man with what looked like pots of black tar at his feet—it was a mud that smelled of petroleum and dead fish. Supposedly it would draw "the poison" out of you, and before I could back away Margaret had handed him some money and slopped the disgusting stuff along my right arm. I screamed, and she nearly choked to death laughing at my alarm, and then both of us threw the sludge at each other until we were black and terrifying to poor Mather. We trudged up to the weak showers at the top of the beach and rinsed what we could off of us. Then I took a picture of Margaret floating in the densely salty water, feet and hands up in the air, Mather astride her belly. Yes, it was that day, because then we went back to Margaret's house. I re-member because I can clearly see Margaret undoing her blond hair from her ponytail at the kitchen table, shaking her hair loose, and it was still damp. I could smell the briny scent of sea from where I sat across from her.

She had a bulging notebook she'd filled with cutout recipes spread out on the table. "Aren't you just famished?" she asked.

I was. I assumed Margaret would pull out cheese, the only appetizing thing in her haphazardly vegetarian fridge. Big square chunks of feta with mint. Rubbery slabs of halloumi cheese she'd fry until it was golden and crispy and we'd eat hot enough to singe our fingers. *Shanklish* that she bought in thyme-covered balls, then chopped and mixed with red onions and tomatoes. I usually thought it best not to remind her cheese was made from the milk of cows and sheep and goats, from all those farmyard mammary glands of a maternal workforce she identified so strongly with.

Instead she unfolded a piece of paper, clearly pulled from a magazine, and slid it over to me. *Recipe for Reproduction!*

"I'm going to make you a fertility smoothie. Not that you should be trying to procreate with Dan gone, but it can't hurt to start the regimen now. Don't get freaked out if it's green."

"A *fertility* smoothie?" I said, at a loss for words.

"I couldn't find maca so I'll just add a little more bee pollen and Yemeni honey to cover up the chalkiness of the whey powder."

Where in the world did she find something like whey powder? And why is it always *Yemeni* honey? That's what the little honey kiosks in the malls always advertised: *Honey from Yemen!* Huge glass bowls of the precious, viscous stuff lined up on shelves, always manned by an angry-looking man in a white *dishdasha* and long black beard fingering prayer beads.

She plugged in her blender, threw in ingredients, fitted on the lid, and pressed the button. We both watched the blender twist and churn out something greenish gray and hideous.

"Hmmm." She took off the lid, smelled it, glanced at me with apology, poured it into a glass. "What is it that Queen Victoria said?" she asked. *"Just lie back and think of England?* Well, just toss this back and think of children."

I sipped. The honey was not helping. But I drank the entire thing.

She nodded, delighted.

Then she peered at my mouth very closely. "Pesky spinach. Smile."

I pulled my lips away from my teeth, curious, my mouth open for her as if I was a baby. And Margaret stuck her pinky inside. A quick, unthinking motion. I felt the salty tip of her finger, the shard of nail scratch at the center of my front teeth.

It was just a split second but it felt tremendous even then, her hand in my mouth, that intimacy between us. Mather was at our feet; why need anyone else in the world, ever, when we could be so free and open? No embarrassment, no awkwardness, just talking and telling and listening. No men to ruin it all and make us feel inferior, weak, silly, demanding, not attractive enough, not thin enough, just not *enough*. Why did we think we needed more than this, all the mess that men make and break? Her touch said: We do not need them. We are complete in ourselves.

"Got it," she said. She wiped her hands on her jeans.

I ran my tongue quickly over my teeth. They were as smooth as could be.

And then someone rang her buzzer.

Margaret pulled away, turned her back to me, quickly went to the intercom by the front door.

"Hello?" There was no answer. She glanced at me and shrugged. "Who's there?" She started to walk back to the table when it rang again. She returned to the intercom. I followed. "Hello," she said. "Hello?" She looked at me. "Someone must have forgotten their keys."

"Don't you dare buzz them up," I replied. "That's what your *boab* is for."

We went back to the table.

A few minutes later, there was a knock at her door. We froze. Margaret and I got up slowly, went and peered out the peephole. No one was there. Mather started shouting from the kitchen stool he was trying to climb.

"It must be Saleh." Margaret seemed unconcerned.

I grabbed her arm as she reached to open the door.

"Don't!" This was no game. "Who is it?" I shouted, and heard loud Arabic in return. I could understand the word *look* but not much else. *You look, we look, they look?* Still, we couldn't see anyone in the peephole but we could hear someone on the other side of the door, moving from foot to foot. Maybe examining the lock with a crowbar.

"I'm calling the United States embassy!" I cried. I found my cell phone. "Let's go into the panic room. It's in your master bedroom, right?"

Margaret smiled. She got the baby, put a pacifier in his mouth, and tried to pass him to me. "Don't you think you're overreacting a bit? I'll just step outside and see—"

"We need help," I began, trying to refuse Mather. I thought of all the men in the construction site below. Who knew their political affiliations, where had they come from, Lebanon, Iraq, Afghanistan, Pakistan? Had they seen Crick in a US Army uniform at some point? Had they noticed he'd been gone for weeks? There had been anti-American protests in Zarqa just a few days ago. *Down with Israel, down with the USA!* the Salafists had chanted.

"I'm going to see what they want," she said. Calmly. "You can wait in the panic room with Mather if you'd like."

"I'm not leaving you."

She shrugged and threw open the door. Two men stood outside, paint-dappled strangers. They glanced at each other and said something to Margaret and she nodded. One of the men beckoned for her to follow him.

"Oh my God, don't even think about it, Margaret!"

"It's all right, I recognize them. Give me ten minutes before you call the Marines," she said.

"Margaret, it only takes seconds to slit a throat!" I called after her. I stood at the top of the stairwell as they walked down, listening to them trying to communicate. Was Margaret meowing? As soon as I heard the clang of the heavy front door, I called the embassy.

Margaret returned seventeen minutes later, smiling her smug, still-attached little head off.

"We found the kittens!" she said. "Those workers from the site, they've seen me looking for them for weeks. They found where the mama cat hides. Good thing you called those embassy guards, they were able to translate."

Was she being sarcastic? If this was a new side of her I didn't like it. "And, Cass, you know Hassan? He explained the men step back from the door after they knock; it's a sign of respect here."

"Hassan?" I shook my head; none of this made sense. "Slow down! What kittens?"

"The ones I've been tearing the whole neighborhood apart

searching for!" She leaned her head as if shocked at my igno-rance. "Oh, Cass, it was just *hilarious*! Hassan went to the shop on the corner and got them some milk."

I stared at her. I hated the word *hilarious* with a passion. I de-spise people who use the word *hilarious*. It's a word designed to make the listener feel excluded. Always with that emphasized pause between syllables, always that implied *You who missed out and couldn't possibly understand*. I handed her the baby and walked back toward the kitchen. I stood at the table, waiting for her to step close to me again, to enter the warm hazy world where only the three of us mattered.

"Yikes, I almost forgot, Crick's supposed to Skype tonight!" She used her free hand to touch her messy hair. "Don't tell me it's already eight o'clock?"

I waited a beat. I didn't know Crick Skyped with her; she hadn't mentioned it before. I wondered how often they spoke. And I wondered when he would next call me. "I guess I'll see myself out," I said stiffly.

Margaret ran over, gave me a quick hug. It seemed cheap, her shallow show of affection after the intense day we'd had. I col-lected my car keys, my purse, and walked out of her apartment alone.

April 21

HOME

This morning, as I was shoving the stroller into the hallway with one hand and swinging a heavy bag of trash in the other, I walked straight into Saleh.

"Oh, hey, I was hoping to see you!" I put my palm on his shoulder, thought, *Yikes, NO TOUCHING!* Then sort of giggled at Cassie's shouting voice in my head. "Guess what? Last night we found the kittens!"

His eyebrows lifted. He didn't back away; we were so close I couldn't move the stroller.

Then he noticed the garbage bag. Disappointment shadowed his eyes. He stepped aside to give me room to pass. Put his hand out for the trash. I stood there; I couldn't give him the bag now, it felt too belittling. "I'll bring this down to the Dumpster myself."

"No, madam, my job."

Oh, so terrible, the shift from friends to employer and servant.

"Don't call me that." I moved the trash out of his reach, overcompensating with a smile so big it hurt my forehead. "I told you, please call me Margaret."

He centered his attention on my eyes. Maybe I should have looked away like Cassie says, but it felt very important to acknowledge he was a person at that moment, a human being.

"Nice name, Mar-Gar-Rat."

I thanked him. My name never sounded so hideous.

He took a step closer and reached for the bag again.

"Oh, right." I lifted it as he moved toward me. His hand slid over my knuckles, and, as he tried to get a better grip, his hand squeezed mine as it tightened around the bag's neck.

I froze. His hands were so soft. Skin on skin. I stared at his fingers, thought of what they'd feel like running over my shoulder, my thigh, my stomach. Something in his dark-rimmed eyes told me he was thinking the same thing. I flushed from ribs to hairline. This liability of mine, always looking guiltier than I am. Or maybe I'm guiltier than other people?

I let go of the bag.

"Help more?" he asked. "More? I take?"

I had more trash in the apartment, loads, a full Diaper Genie in the nursery, overflowing bins in each bathroom I'd been too lazy to dump. Ask him inside? Would that lead to my fingertips tracing the embroidery of another man's name, the mysterious *Mike*, over Saleh's heart, feeling the beat of his blood beneath? I'd have control, power, in a way I never did with Crick.

But I stepped away.

Then Mather, silently observing while nibbling cereal, banged the tray of his stroller with both fists and the little O's burst out all over the smooth hallway floor.

"Gosh, I'm sorry!" I felt cool air on my face as I bent to stop Mather's fists.

Saleh carefully placed the garbage bag off to the side, picked up his broom, began to sweep up our mess.

"Bye, Saleh, thanks!" I said, nearly running to the elevator before I could say or do something I shouldn't.

When the doors shut behind us I pressed my hands to my face, tried to catch my breath, to still the heat radiating off me. I always muck up ordinary social interactions. I misread facial cues, laugh too long, miscommunicate and mislead; somehow I always get it wrong.

I looked out from between my fingers, imagined myself in an *abaya* with a *niqab* over my nose, my cheekbones, my mouth. In America clothing is all about revealing the best parts of our bodies, but here it is all about obscuring those very same curves. Would it be nice to be anonymous, unknown, completely veiled? Even if someone was watching, he'd see nothing but a swath of black cloth. All of you private, no emotion, no features, no size. If no one is watching, can you finally be absolutely yourself? If no one is assessing you, are you able to clearly assess yourself, be confident in your small, dark space? Or maybe you become a nonentity, invisible without your individual details setting you apart. I stood behind a woman on an escalator at the mall the other day; she was covered in black, head to toe, the tiniest opening for her unmade-up eyes. But the way she'd tied her veil in the back, it looked like braids. Small, intricate knots; there was something pretty about them, something that must have been intentional, something about that woman that made her decide she'd allow that bit of string to say, *Look, this is me.*

I think of my mom, how she wore sickness like a shroud, our home her shell, keeping her far from judging eyes. It was her choice to live like that, to re-create herself as a shadow, a ghost. Afraid of everything. Easier to never leave, never risk, never be.

I have to make sure I don't ever let that happen to me.

May 13, 2011

9:24 P.M.

❧

I skim ahead in the journal, skipping a list of home remedies for insomnia in Margaret's loopy script. Then I see a long entry about Jerash. Jerash over and over again. It makes me furious just thinking about that day.

"I have a favor to ask, my dearest Cass," she said over the phone. *My dearest Cass*; those words buzzed sweetly through my caffeinated blood. "Can you watch Mather for me tomorrow?"

"What are you doing?"

"Arabic class," she replied, coy girl. "We have a field trip!"

"I certainly never had a field trip," I said. "But fine, I'd love to watch Mather."

When I got there the next morning she was filling a string of baby bottles. She was humming as she poured out bags of her milk and screwed the plastic nipples on. I helped myself to her French press of local-style coffee. She was actually making me like the taste of cardamom.

I assumed her class would go to a Jordanian café so they could practice ordering food. "Margaret, you won't be gone that long," I said, looking at all the milk lined up.

"Oh, right. So I'm actually going to Jerash? Hassan's showing me the Roman ruins."

Hassan? I tilted my head. "What are you talking about?"

She looked a little sheepish. "He's my Arabic instructor! Today's his day off so he offered to walk me around his hometown. Mather will nap for you. I'll be back by dinner."

"Wait. You said you were taking classes. That the teacher let you bring Mather."

"It was kind of a class. Listen, I have to run, you know how to warm up the milk, right?"

"But you don't know this guy, Margaret. He's a guard."

"Hassan's giving me a tour. That's it." She leaned over to pick up the baby, then turned to me, challenge in her blue eyes. "If you won't watch Mather, that's fine, I'll take him."

"It's miles of sand and stone, you can't take a baby to the Roman ruins." I scrambled in my confusion, reaching for my coffee mug to keep my hands busy, finishing it off so I didn't have to look at her. "Margaret, you shouldn't be so trusting."

"Well, I can't say no now. I'm meeting him at his house."

I stared at the bottom of my cup, pretended there was a final sip of the imaginary, bitter liquid. What happened to *Don't you want to come with me and Hassan?* What happened to *My dearest Cass?* Just *Will you watch the baby?* It was one thing to babysit so she could take an Arabic class I had no desire to repeat, quite another when she began making elaborate social plans without me.

I said, "He is not your friend." I was sure Hassan was a perfectly nice man. I always enjoyed chatting with him at the embassy gate. But he had never invited me to Jerash. I tried to think of something to stop her from going. "You're not supposed to be alone with a man who's not your husband or a member of your immediate family."

She burst out laughing. Then hesitated, waiting for my punch line.

"I'm serious, Margaret. Arab men do not take an interest in Western women unless they want to test our supposed loose morals."

"Cass, racism doesn't suit you," she said, the mirth draining away.

My eyes stung. She wasn't going to listen to me. She had probably never listened to a thing I said. "You'd better at least change into a long-sleeved shirt and long pants if you are going outside the city limits."

She glanced at her freckled arms. She was wearing her daily uniform of short-sleeved fitted T-shirt and khaki capris with hiking sandals. Her hair hung in a loose braid. I could see her bra strap slipping down her shoulder.

"These legs aren't worth looking at." She craned her neck to see her bared calves.

"Margaret, this is a bad idea."

She stamped her foot, a short and angry thud on the tile. It made me go rigid, the violence, the frustration in that kick. "I've been here over three months. Three months! And haven't been anywhere but grocery stores. I want to see Jordan!"

I could feel every vertebra in my neck. I thought of all the things we had done together, those glorious days. How could she sum up our marvelous adventures, our trips to the Dead Sea and the citadel, as *grocery stores*?

I recovered enough to say, "Wait for Crick. If you'd like, Dan and I could watch Mather for a whole weekend so you guys can tour Jerash by yourselves—"

"Who knows when that'll be? I can't sit in my little Western apartment anymore, eating Western food at the embassy cafeteria, buying tablecloths at tourist shops aimed at Westerners! This is my chance to experience the *real* Jordan. Cassie, you and I aren't even scratching the surface."

I told myself Margaret hadn't had time to long for home and therefore couldn't appreciate all things American the way I did. Sure, maybe I had kept her from "real" life—water-borne, food-borne, mosquito-borne diseases, hepatitis, typhoid, measles, brucellosis, sandfly fever, rabies, and schistosomiasis. So many options thanks to the overcrowded refugee camps. Just a touch of food poisoning and Margaret would no longer hunger for small roadside restaurants with their bowls of unrefrigerated meat and unwashed parsley and mud-splattered tomatoes.

How can I forget the day Dan and I ordered *shawarma* from a little corner stand on our way out of Aqaba last year? How we raved about its being the best we'd eaten in all of Jordan, by God, in the entire Middle East! So tender, so fresh, we would write a review for Lonely Planet, for Zagat! We would tell everyone to eat there! We didn't even make it the three hours home before Dan shit himself and had to change into the sweat-stiff clothes he'd worn to the beach the day before. I did not leave our bathroom for two days, curled around the toilet in a miasma of vomit and bile. One bout of such explosive diarrhea and Margaret, too, would be afraid of the ice in her soda, would wonder where her *tabbouleh* had been, would check the state of the bathrooms before even considering ordering lunch. One good sunburn, no matter how religiously she applied that SPF 30, with the skin peeling off her perky little nose, hot blisters rising up on her wrists and chest and forehead, and she would tire of these local desert sites. Or this desperately sought Jerash. Let her walk around in those capris and snug baby tees, let her get damning looks from the conservatives who live out in the sticks, who have not been raised in cosmopolitan Amman. Here residents distinguish between the corporeal rules of tourists vs. the spiritual covering of their own people. Not so outside of the city limits. Maybe then she will understand. Maybe then she will be satisfied to sit at the embassy pool in a bathing suit, shaded by an umbrella, with Sri Lankan pool boys in their white polo shirts bringing her a piña colada and a real hot dog.

I tried not to be stung by her words. I tried to tell myself Margaret hadn't meant to insult my entire life.

"I'll keep Mather. Jerash is no place for a baby." I meant it as a reprimand, a reminder of her duty as a mother, but Margaret only hugged her child and then handed him to me.

"Thanks a ton, Cass. I'll make it up to you!"

But she didn't. She didn't even try. She smeared sunblock into her face, leaving long streaks of white along the sides of her neck that I didn't tell her to rub in.

She packed up that big purse of hers, dumping out Mather's diapers and toys, replacing them with her guidebook, her journal, her dictionary, one large Ziploc bag of trail mix, a water bottle.

I watched her. I did not offer to help and I did not offer any more advice.

According to her dictionary, *jealousy* is derived from the Greek word *zelos*, the same as *zeal* or *zealous*, as in *"emulation"* or *"ardor,"* with a root connoting *"to boil, ferment."* So many chaotic emotions involved in a word we use too easily, not realizing the complexity, the love. Maybe everyone ought to carry a dictionary, look up each word we utter so blithely, finally understand the layered richness of everything we take for granted.

I'd spent so long feeling neglected, unseen, and then Margaret came along and centered her attention on me whenever I spoke, nodding with enthusiasm as if she agreed with me wholeheartedly. Even that horse laugh of hers, it felt like a triumph to be able to get her to make such a noise. It made me feel as if whatever I said was exactly what she needed to hear.

How could it not have hurt to have her focus taken away? To witness it turned on someone else?

Margaret was leaving me behind.

April 24

JERASH

How are small terrorist cats?" Hassan asked yesterday. I nearly spit water all over him I laughed so hard. Oh, Cassie! Calling embassy security when the men just came to show me the kitten hideout! Hassan hitched his uniform pants, sat on the bench next to me, and began to write the Arabic names of animals in my journal. *Cat. Dog. Cow. Goat. Lamb. Chicken.*

When he got up to complete his walk around the embassy, he handed Mather a chocolate bar and said to me, "You must come to my home tomorrow."

I jumped. Yes yes yes!

He leaned over the picnic table and drew a map under his latest vocabulary.

Today I convinced Cass to watch the baby.

Today I went to Jerash. All by myself. Such freedom. It felt like the first time ever, in my whole life, I didn't have to worry about someone else.

Drove north, up, up, up to where everything is green and

growing, an hour on the highway. Then first right off a traffic circle, right at the cell phone shop, left at the house with the barbed-wire fence, right at the apartment building with three goats in the yard, and two blocks down I found his home. Cement blocks, a grapevine growing on the front porch.

Hassan was waiting; he looked different in regular clothes. He was wearing dress pants with sharply ironed pleats and a light blue button-up shirt with the collar opened. Leather loafers with small tassels, and I thought to myself, *Mather would love to try and swallow one of those.* Hassan stood under the vine, arms up in air to flag me down.

"It is a joy you have come."

I got out of the car and closed the door softly, suddenly feeling shy without my baby, without his uniform. "This is a really nice neighborhood."

"These are my family, all." He pointed down the entire block.

I looked at the houses neighboring his, all simple, one floor, many with unfinished roofs similar to Hassan's own, rebar sticking out like lightning rods. "Are you adding another floor?"

"All of our hope. May someday our children they return to us, to live, *inshallah.*"

I joined him on the porch, noticed that his small trellised vine grew from four coffee cans evenly spaced out in the shape of a rectangle. Vines had been looped lovingly through a combination of twine and wire hangers.

He motioned for me to sit on one of the white plastic chairs under the fragile canopy. "My family very much anticipating you."

"Family?"

"Yes. My brother's family visiting from Ma'an, you will have meal with us. All of us will be eating at my sister-in-law home, very near, and you are of course invited."

"Oh, no. I mean, that's super. But can we stop somewhere so I can pick up cookies or fruit, I don't know, something to bring? I can't show up empty-handed."

He smiled. "This is Jordanian invitation: you are expected to bring nothing but eat everything!"

He went inside to get tea, and I leaned back in the chair. I closed my eyes; it felt indulgent, sitting in the sun quietly like that, not having to make sure Mather wasn't breaking anything. Hassan returned with two narrow-waisted glasses full of black tea. It seemed like a perfect moment, hot glass in my palm, warm sun on my face, a whole day ahead with no diapers to change or naps to schedule. That's when a woman stopped at the gate below. She looked at me, a withered face peeking out from a gray *hijab*, black *abaya* covering the rest of her, small eyes staring at my bare arms. I should have listened to Cassie and put on a sweatshirt. Hassan spoke Arabic, tried to hand her his glass of tea, but she shook her head, eyes not leaving me.

He introduced us. Karida, his wife's sister. She was hosting the dinner this evening. She nodded to acknowledge his words but said nothing in reply, just stood sentinel while we emptied glasses and I stood nervously. I waved good-bye but she didn't wave back, just crossed the street and stood on the porch of the house directly across from Hassan's.

Hassan got into my passenger seat. While I belted up and put on sunglasses, Hassan watched her watch us.

"Ah," he said, speaking without moving his lips as if fearful she might read them. "She has the sour face. She is married only one year when husband leaves her, long time ago; there are no children. Please, drive straight now, and then left."

"Are you sure about dinner?"

"Yes, yes, it is absolutely. Karida good woman. She watches all nephews and nieces. Children do not misbehave because, what is the phrase, she scare the living bowels out of them?"

"That's one way to say it," I said, giggling, and he laughed too, wiping at his right eye as he directed me out and onward, through a clogged roundabout, the road gutted with construction, cement trucks and drills and lots of orange flags flickering in the wind. All the cars drove single-file, past more shops and restaurants, until we were in the city of Jerash.

He pointed upward, to the hill on my left. Suddenly ancient ruins stood pristine in the distance, as if cast off by spoiled gods. I'm not very good at taking photos but I wanted to take a picture of every single thing.

"My wife second cousin make bad suggestion and tell me I should marry Karida. You see, *ilhamdulillah*, Karida take good care of my wife when she was ill, and I am very grateful. But her sour face is no company, it is better I am alone. I think this cousin also tell Karida so maybe she waits for me to marry her. It is unknown."

I nodded, thinking to myself, *Oh, joy, Karida thinks I am competing for Hassan's affection? This is going to be awkward.*

Before I could get too freaked out thinking about the ways I could make her like me, we pulled into a small gravel parking lot next to the ruins.

It's impossible to sum it all up.

There was Hadrian's Arch. With Hassan pointing out recent

reconstruction, I could see the new smooth lines above the two-thousand-year-old base. "Like a woman who should not get the plastic surgery," he whispered. "You always see the make-believe against the beauty of the real."

There were the stark pillars of the temple of Zeus. The curved rock of the amphitheater. The hippodrome's track glinting with actors reenacting chariot races. Flowers dotted the rocky slope, petals floppy like the purplish ears of Doberman puppies. Hassan said, "These are the very famous black irises of Jordan. You are very lucky to see them." I wished I had Crick's huge camera but I made do with my phone. In the stadium, bagpipers in red *kaffiyehs* and tan *dishdashas* surreally played "Amazing Grace." Finally. This is what I dreamed when I dreamed of Jordan.

I looked at the "modern" city of Jerash that ringed the ruins. Neighborhoods built on top of one another, on top of time, all made from the same sandstone as the earth below. It seemed like only fragile satellite dishes and telephone wires connected the buildings to the modern world. I could feel the past whispering, *This is what you need to see. This is Jordan, right now, in this moment, breathing, alive.*

It started to drizzle and we ran to a small umbrella-covered stand for shelter. Three teenagers stood over a table of jewelry and one of them gave me a necklace of reddish-black beads.

"Jerash stones," he said, pressing his hand to his heart, waving away my money.

"I can't take them—" I started to say.

"It is a welcome gift. To reject will insult him," Hassan said, nodding at the young man.

"*Shukran.* Thank you." I put my palm over my heart in return; I'd seen Hassan do this loads of times and I loved the sincerity inherent to the gesture, no language needed to understand, *You touch my heart.* The beads were heavy in an earthy kind of way, not light like a man-made thing but something created deep in the ground. I put them on, right then. I remembered the trail mix in my purse; I'd eaten all the cashews on the ride up but I shared the rest, and we stood around the table, reaching into that bag, watching the rain. I didn't once say something alarming. The whole world shone, the grass a mighty green, wild cats mewing from bushes. If I'd had Mather, I would have wanted to stay forever. But then Hassan's cell phone began to ring.

"*Yalla, yalla!*" Hassan said, hanging up, then speed-walking his way back through the ruins as I tried to keep up. "The nieces are waiting! It is time of dinner."

When we were getting out of my car in front of his small house, Hassan looked at my bared arms. "Come, I have warm clothing."

I followed him, his home simple, walls a light green, linoleum flooring peeling but pristine. I waited in his kitchen, looking at a picture of his wife, round and happy, with her arm around the waist of a teenager who grinned with Hassan's squinty smile.

Hassan entered, handing me a turquoise cardigan. I loved it immediately; it felt soft and warm, like a splash of joy, such a rich, underwater color.

"Please, let us go to sister-in-law home now. English maybe not so good so maybe they will be shy."

"Don't worry, I understand shy," I said, donning the sweater. We crossed the narrow street and entered another house without knocking, and as the door opened I saw Karida standing at the picture window, holding the curtain as if wanting us to see that clearly she'd been standing there, watching, ever since we pulled up. She motioned to me, hit her chest with her palm, and I touched the shell buttons of the sweater—oh God, it was her dead sister's and she wanted it, of course! I made a move to take it off but Hassan put his hand out, almost touching my elbow. "Please, it is yours now. As I said, you cannot reject a gift."

Karida clicked her tongue, loud, like a metallic snap. I felt it go round the room, eyes glancing around corners. I heard Hassan say something and I was surrounded by women smiling, welcoming, taking my hands and tugging. So many of them, it's a wonder they all fit inside. They pulled me down to sit on pillows arranged on the floor. It seemed as if they'd been waiting for us to eat and as soon as I was sitting two men carried huge, steaming platters into the room and put them down gently in the center of the circles we had made—one circle of women, one of men.

"*Sahtayn!*" Hassan called to me from across the room. "May you eat with two appetites!"

The women all wore *hijabs*, flipping the ends of the scarves over their shoulders as if they were long hair. One niece, Shahad, smiled on my left and kept passing me a small cup of cinnamon tea. I never knew for certain if this was my tea glass or if I was sharing with the whole circle of women; the glass came smudged and half full, and as soon as I finished, it disappeared down the line and then returned the same way, partly refilled, steaming, sweet, wonderful. They called me *Um-Mather* instead of Margaret, "*Mother of Mather.*" If I thought about this too much maybe I wouldn't like it but tonight it felt right, made me feel part of the group to have a Jordanian name, and it's Mather I have to thank for giving me this life, giving me the husband and everything that followed, so it all made sense.

At first I tried to eat only rice from the *mensaf* platter, but women next to me kept picking out the best bits of yogurt-covered meat, pinching thin pitalike bread closed around rice and lamb, no utensils, just fingers, then placing it on my tongue. I'll have to tell Crick how delicious it was. I promise I'll be vegetarian again tomorrow. I glimpsed men in the other circle rolling rice into a ball and tossing it into their mouths but I didn't dare imitate. Only Karida, across the circle, staring, wouldn't smile at me.

Tea, tea, and more tea. Then dessert, *kanafeh*, cheese pastry soaked in syrup with pistachios crushed on top. I thought I'd burst, and I put my hand on my heart the way I'd seen Hassan do, and said *ilhamdulillah*. Before anyone could put more food on my plate I took out my purse and showed photos of Mather. None of the photos made their way back to me and I was charmed that anybody would keep a picture of my baby.

"The women very sad you are leaving already," Hassan said when he walked me to my car. Two women waved from the window above us.

"I'm sad too. But I'll come back, and I'll bring Mather to meet them!"

"You are like daughter to me. Anytime you are welcome. You will understand how to find your way?" He had drawn me another map, names in both English and Arabic, in case I needed to pull over and ask for help.

"I'll be fine." I was brimming with joy. "I'll see you soon?" I got behind the wheel.

"*Inshallah*," he replied.

As I drove home, I thought of my mom, how she would have loved hearing about this day, the food, the tea, the hands pressed warmly against mine, and Crick, won't even Crick be impressed when I tell him? That I managed to get an invitation to such a feast, to sit at a circle with real live locals? Or will he be angry it was dark and I drove back to Amman alone? Maybe it's better to not even mention it so he can't tell me to never go to Jerash again.

May 13, 2011

9:51 P.M.

I look at the time, filled with an unshakeable sense of déjà vu.
I waited furiously that day too.

She didn't come home from Jerash until almost ten o'clock. I was sitting in her living room with all the lights out, on the velvet love seat that faces the front door, my phone in my lap. Margaret came in quietly, perhaps assuming I'd fallen asleep on her couch. I watched her carefully close the door behind her. I noticed that necklace of glossy beads right away—it looked so cool and expensive against her tanned collarbones—and the turquoise sweater made her blue eyes glow. She hadn't been wearing either when she left. And they certainly didn't look like souvenirs from a hike through Roman ruins. They looked like indulgent gifts from a lover. I'd tried to imagine Hassan giving them to her but couldn't. Was Hassan a lie? I wondered. Like her supposed embassy Arabic lessons? Was there someone else entirely?

"Finally."

"Oh my God!" She jumped, put her fingertips to her throat. "Cass, gosh, what are you doing there in the dark?"

I stood up, crossing my arms over my chest. "I was about to call the Marines at Post One. I thought I was going to see you getting your head lopped off in an al-Qaeda recruitment video."

She switched on the overhead light. We both blinked. I waited for her to apologize for being so late. I could see she had new freckles on her nose, darker than the rest; they were starting to merge together, a map of her time here. They might be adorable now but in a few years they would be ordinary age spots, lost amid all the sun spots of all the other places she would go without me.

She walked up close. "Silly, Cass!" she said, teasing. Gloating. "Here I am. Alive!" She did jazz hands.

I stiffened. So the ingénue act was wearing thin and the real Margaret was peeking out.

And maybe I *had* hoped something would happen. Not something terrible, but something annoying, small, to prove I was right. A detour thanks to protests. The Desert Highway closed. A flat tire. But she stood in front of me resplendent and self-satisfied. It wasn't fair. I was the one who listened. I was the one who followed rules. I was the one stuck here all day watching her child.

She glanced around at the immaculate room, not a toy out of place. Much cleaner than it had been when I got there.

"No, really, I'm sorry it's so late," she said, slightly chastened. "It was terrific of you to watch Mather. I did try to call on the way home but my phone must have died during dinner. When I get it charged, I'll show you the photos. Oh, and I had *mensaf*—"

"You let your phone die?" I tried to keep my voice calm.

"I was with a security guard. I couldn't have been any safer!"

It was useless to argue. I yawned behind my hand. It was harder than I thought it would be, those hours on the floor with Thomas the Tank Engine, trying to amuse a fourteen-month-old baby. There are only so many times a grown-up can read *Elmo's ABC Book* with a high-pitched, headache-inducing voice. I wanted her to ask me about my day, I wanted to share those inane details I often overheard mothers sighing over. I wanted to complain with authority, feel infused with that warmth I'd felt when I found his lost pacifier hidden under the couch cushions, and Mather, in the middle of a tantrum, sat up and clapped with delight. I had earned that much of her attention, hadn't I? But Margaret was already fiddling at the series of plugs dangling from her kitchen wall, hooking up her cell phone, looking at it intently and not at all at me. No *Oh, Cass, you are so good to me* tonight. I noisily gathered up my things. Really? I had changed two, yes, two diapers full of human feces today, and this was all she had for me?

She absently tugged at her messy braid, her hair falling loosely around her shoulders, around her new treasures.

"Where did you get the sweater and necklace?" I asked.

She glanced up from her phone, touching one of the cardigan's buttons in a way that seemed nervous. "Oh. Hassan gave it to me. And a boy gave me the beads."

I went to her, reached around the back of her neck, lifted the tag from under her hair, peered at it. "A security guard gave you a cashmere and silk sweater?"

"Cashmere?" She stepped away as if she didn't want to know how much the gift was worth, turned her big guilty eyes on me.

"I shouldn't have accepted it. I didn't know how to say no . . . Cass, would you mind terribly if I show you the pictures another time? I'm suddenly exhausted."

I walked out her door without another word.

Downstairs, I saw Saleh pacing up and down the walk. He stopped when I stepped outside, his eyes wide, but when he saw me he turned quickly away, acted as if the curb needed all of his concentration. Clearly I was not the woman he sought. I wondered if he too was on the outs now that Margaret had found this new mysterious pal.

As I opened my car door, I heard a noise behind me, a low whine, and I lifted my head. I thought it'd be Margaret running toward me, apologizing for being so distant and strange.

But no, she wasn't there. I slipped my fingers into my key chain, putting a key between each knuckle, and spotted something moving by the Dumpster.

I took a step closer. Four minuscule cats were mewing in a disturbingly human way, pushing one another aside to get at three bowls full of cat food. Ah, the sought-after kittens. They looked like hungry rats. She must have fed them before she even came up to me and her son.

Crick called me that night.

He didn't wake me. I was lying there, staring up at the ceiling, still fuming.

"So what sort of mischief has the missus been up to?" he purred in my ear. He rarely said her name. The pronoun *she* was impersonal enough to keep her presence, and therefore any twinges of remorse, away from our innuendo-heavy conversations.

I bit my lip. "Well, actually, she *has* been up to something."

He whistled low, his voice still light. "Please don't tell me she adopted a friggin cat."

"I wish." I waited a moment. "Did she tell you she was taking an Arabic class?"

"Yeah. In the last couple of weeks she's picked up more than she did the past year trying to study my workbooks. Jordanian dialect too."

"Well, let's just say she's not taking lessons at the embassy. And Arabic might not be all she's pursuing."

The sexiness went out of his voice. "What're you getting at, Cassie?"

I hesitated, unsure of how far I should go. But Margaret had been disloyal to me, hadn't she? Wasn't it my duty to tell Crick? If there was a wedge driven between them, it certainly wouldn't be my fault. "She has a lot of days unaccounted for, and she hasn't been telling me the truth. That's all I know."

"You're fucking with me, right? Is this like when you told me a taxi driver offered you five camels for her?"

"No. I think Margaret's been lying to us all."

There was a long pause. Then his voice loud and clear, sober as a judge. "You're talking about my wife. My goddamn wife. You call her a liar again and I will personally rip the tongue out of your head."

I stared at the disconnected phone in my hand, my eyes so wide with horror my lids ached. I slid it away from me to the farthest corner of the bed and knew Crick would not be calling me again.

May 13, 2011

10:09 P.M.

I remember feeling sick for three days, upset stomach, headache, persistent sadness, knowing I had destroyed whatever tenuous connection there was between Crick and me. I was convinced Margaret would come; she would make me soup, take my temperature, bring me to the embassy clinic. But I refused to call Margaret. She would notice my silence, I told myself. Any moment now, she'd realize she needed me. She'd miss me.

She didn't even call.

By the morning of day four, I got out of bed when Tharushi came to clean the house. I couldn't take the walls of my villa anymore. The loneliness of Dan's absence, combined with Crick's silence and Margaret's indifference, was too much.

When the men first deploy, it's wonderful. No rules, no timetables, eat when you like, watch what you like, spread out and sleep in that sweet hump in the center of the king-sized bed. So much freedom.

Then it starts to sour. Too many days of being able to do

whatever you want makes you realize you behave that way because nobody cares. As in nobody actually gives a damn about you. Then it becomes paralyzing. You could die, and who would find you? A *boab*, three weeks later, when he comes looking for what you owe him for washing your car? You stop shampooing your hair and shaving your legs; you start to drink too much. This is when it would help to have a job. This is when it would help to have a child.

But this time, I had thought I'd have Margaret to keep the desolation away. It was a small thing, wasn't it, her coming home late from Jerash compared to the emptiness of the looming days? Did one rude gesture on her part warrant my being all by myself for the unknown remainder of Dan's deployment?

And just like that, showered and wearing clean clothes again for the first time since I left her apartment, I decided to see Margaret. I was so relieved by my capitulation that I drove straight over without even calling.

I pressed the button of her intercom.

"Hello?"

"Margaret, it's me, Cassie."

"Cass? Hi there. What's up?"

I stood for a moment. Why wasn't she immediately buzzing me up? *What's up?* The implication being that I needed a reason to be at her door? I had never needed a reason before. Had Crick told her about our calls?

"I was in the neighborhood," I said. "I haven't seen you in days and days. Buzz me up!"

"Yeah, of course."

I found her standing in her doorway. *See, there she is smiling, everything is fine,* I thought. She looked especially pretty, her hair smooth and loose, lip gloss on her mouth, wearing a linen tunic and dark leggings I hadn't seen before.

And then I realized there was a man standing in her living room.

"Hassan's never had Mexican food, can you believe that?" she gushed, taking me in her arms and pressing a kiss on each cheek. Just the way she always did, as if there was nothing different about today, nothing at all, with this interloper watching, looking so very at home in her apartment. "Seven years in the Bronx and he never tasted a taco! It's criminal. Join us, Cass. I got Taco Bell kits at the embassy shopette yesterday. Cass?"

I looked at him, standing underneath Crick's framed photographs. He didn't look like a security guard today. He wore a light green dress shirt and dark gray slacks, and even with his mustache and sideburns shot through with silver, he was much more handsome than he ever looked in his badly fitted, industrial-grade guard uniform.

Hassan seemed to notice how uncomfortable I was and his smile wavered. Mather, who was sitting at his feet, tugged at his pant legs.

"Cass, don't you know Hassan?"

Hassan nodded. "*Salaam alaikum.*"

Margaret quickly filled up the silence. "I invited Hassan here to help him with the online tourist visa paperwork for the US. He was going to go to one of those cybercafés where you're charged by the minute but this is so much cozier. Have you ever looked at the visa paperwork, Cass? It's a nightmare!"

I nodded soundlessly. I wanted Mather to toddle over to me but he was too intent on dropping grapes into the cuffed hem of Hassan's slacks and then fishing them out again.

Hassan touched his mustache nervously. "I think I interrupt. Perhaps we will attempt visa another day? Maybe today is no good."

"Today is very good." Margaret put her hands on her hips and watched me.

"Can I get some water?" I asked.

Margaret glanced at Hassan. He bent down and began playing with the baby so he didn't have to look at us.

When we were in the kitchen I turned toward her. "Margaret, what are you doing?"

"I told you. Making make-believe Mexican food. Trying to help a guy visit granddaughters he's never seen in Jersey." She went to her cupboard, took down a glass. "What are *you* doing?"

"You shouldn't have a man alone in your apartment."

She turned on the water filter over the sink, filled two glasses, and slid one over to me. "You sound like Crick. Hassan's old enough to be my father."

I pushed the glass away without taking a sip. "In America, he'd be old enough to be your father. Here this is grossly improper."

"So you don't want a taco?"

"Margaret, listen to me, your neighbors are surely watching and thinking the worst. They all know your husband is away. You don't understand."

She took a calm swallow from her glass. "If you're not hungry, then I guess you should go on home."

"*Go home?* You are kicking me out, just like that, for that stranger?"

She stared at me as if she couldn't believe the words coming out of my mouth. "Oh, I'm sorry, am I supposed to clear my day so we can sit around, drink coffee, and I can listen to you bitch about how Danny doesn't understand you anymore?"

"Don't you dare. You don't know anything about my marriage."

"I know your idea of a relationship is stifling!" She reached for my water, dumped it in the sink, slammed the glass on the countertop. "No wonder you're having marital problems!" She put her palm to her cheek, suddenly shocked at herself. "I shouldn't have said that. Cass—"

Too late. "At least my husband trusts me," I hissed.

Her hand dropped to the countertop, her nail-bitten fingers spread across the granite for traction. "What are you talking about?"

"Crick. He calls me. Did you know that? In the middle of the night. He claims he's checking up on you. *What has she done, Cassie?* he asks. Or: *What sort of mess has Mar gotten herself into now?*"

She stared. I could see her eyes fill with tears, her blue irises distorted and glittering.

"Please go, Cass," she whispered. "Please, please leave."

"Fine."

I walked out of the kitchen, glared at Hassan, who was now sitting on the living room couch, leaning protectively over Mather. The baby shot his arms in the air as I walked by, holding a block in each hand and grunting at me to join the fun. Hassan very deliberately did not look up as I left.

I took the elevator down and walked quickly out the door of her building, tripping over Saleh and his broom in my hurry.

"What the fuck are you doing here?" I said, banging my elbow on the stone wall.

Saleh glanced at me, a half smile around his lips at my stumble.

"You thought you were special, didn't you?" I asked, pulling myself up to my full height. I was almost as tall as he was. "You're not. Margaret's cooking lunch for someone right now. A man who actually understands English."

"Madam?" He stopped sweeping. He leaned on the broom handle in an attempt to seem casual but his face was very alert.

"How many other men does Margaret have in her home?" I asked again, slower. "Men? *Shababs?* Does she *feed* them all?" I pantomimed bringing a fork to my mouth.

Saleh looked up at the third-floor windows above, confused.

"Oh, forget it," I hissed, and went out to my parked car.

I drove home. I didn't understand what had happened. Just a week or two ago, hadn't she touched my arm and said, *You're an incredible friend?* We'd gone for falafel at the Mecca Mall; Mather had fallen asleep in the stroller, and she and I had sat in the food court, sipping tea and whispering, flanked by women in colorful headscarves.

"I don't even miss Crick now that he's gone," she whispered, as if it was a confession.

I'd lifted my paper cup in agreement. At the time, I thought Margaret was saying she didn't miss Crick because she had me. Of all the women Margaret could have chosen for her intense and pure strain of friendship, the women with children or toddlers, the women who believe in chakras or are vegetarians, Margaret had chosen *me*. But in fact, once again, someone had decided I was not good enough.

Now I return to her journal. *What else, Margaret*, I think, *what else did you keep from me?*

April 28

HOME

I tried to help Hassan today. Then Cassie showed up like a madwoman, raging and stomping, *At least my husband trusts me.* As soon as she was gone Hassan packed his old briefcase, his passport and birth certificate and all those documents he had so carefully laid out on my dining room table. I told him to stay but he said he'd come again, *inshallah.* I handed him the Taco Bell kit box. Then watched from my window as Saleh met Hassan below. Hassan's hands were full; I thought Saleh was going to offer to help him. Instead he seemed angry, Saleh holding his broom in a way that was anything but friendly. Hassan got his keys out, put the food in his car, turned to Saleh, his hands on his hips. They had some sort of exchange, Hassan pointing around the property, then at my apartment. Was he reprimanding Saleh for the night a few weeks ago, perhaps, when Saleh wasn't at his post and the construction men had been able to get inside? Saleh looked up as if he could feel my eyes watching them, and his face was red, humiliated. Hassan followed Saleh's gaze and saw me as well, waved quickly, got in his car, and drove away.

I wasted the rest of the day. Should call Cass but am upset with her for all her ridiculous suspicions, for ruining a day that could have been wonderful. So we stayed inside, Mather and I, watched TV, listened as Gaddhafi government forces threatened annihilation of whole towns in Libya. The news went somewhere else, and for a moment I thought it'd be good: *The people want to overthrow the regime.* But no, a program about self-immolation. It started in Tunisia; Mohammed Bouazizi set himself on fire and the whole Middle East changed. Now people are setting themselves on fire in Algeria, Egypt, Saudi Arabia, Mauritania, and Syria, but nothing is changing. *Immolate*: from the Latin *immolare*, "*to sprinkle with sacrificial meal; to sacrifice.*" First recorded use of *self-immolation* was in 1817, used as "*setting oneself on fire, especially as a form of protest.*" Now back to images of people in streets and squares, with signs and flags and rocks and Molotov cocktails, facing off against a wall of massive, armored black, with tear gas and water cannons and guns. So many attempts to change your life, every desperate action worth it in order to find the smallest bit of freedom, of meaning.

At least my husband trusts me.

Why is Crick calling Cassie? What are the two of them saying about me night after night? My husband and my friend. Conspiring. Crick calls Cassie to ask how I'm doing but he can't ask *me* how I'm doing? All his Skypes, so rushed and distracted. But he calls a woman he barely knows, a woman he makes fun of, and tells her he doesn't trust me.

I cuddle Mather on my lap, breathe in his newborn chick–fuzz hair. He gives me more comfort than I could ever give him. I think of Mom, how I could go to her no matter what time it was. Always happy to see me, lifting the blanket, scooting over in her bed. Moms don't always have money or time, but they can usually smile, right? A soundless *Everything is better now that you are here with me.* I need to remember this. No matter how much pain she was in, she'd make room. Her hand softly on my back, the reassurance that, through the dark night, she'd be there.

I want to stop thinking but my brain goes round and round and round. Crick. Cassie. Karen. Mom.

I put Mather to bed. Then I tossed and turned in my own bed for hours. I got up, found the book Cass gave me, *Women in Islam* by Dr. Muhammad Ali Alkhuli. She said she got it at a grocery store, that it was one of the few books there printed in English so it must be meant for the likes of us. I looked over the passages she highlighted:

THE WOMAN'S CLOTHES

The man is the man wherever he is, and his natural instincts and strong sexual motives cannot be changed through education or civilization. The human female body remains an irresistible stimulator for the human male. Therefore, the female must cover her body so as not to add fuel to the man's already blazing fire.

MAN WOMAN DIFFERENCE

In court testimony, two women's testimony equals one man's. Empirical data have supported the fact that women forget very much more than men, almost four times more.

But Cass missed the best part! This is what I have underlined:

*And among His signs is that He created for you mates from
among yourselves, that you may dwell in tranquillity with them,
and He has placed love and mercy between you.*

Tranquillity. Love and mercy. I wanted Crick and I to find that.
He said *I do.* He must have thought it was possible.

And now?

I look up *disappointment: sadness or displeasure caused by the
non-fulfillment of one's hopes or expectations.*

I wonder if you can maintain such low expectations that you
are never disappointed. And does that equal happiness, not
being disappointed? Being grateful for everything you have,
rather than desiring what you can't?

If only I'd been content with Mom. I had everything I needed.
I was safe. And loved. Why wasn't it enough?

It's never enough. Adam and Eve. So desperate to know
what only God knows. Reaching. The writers of Genesis had us
pegged more than two thousand years ago, realized exactly what
a human being boiled down to, Eve on her tippy-toes grabbing at
that apple, forcing the fruit on Adam. We're never happy with
what we have even if it's paradise; there's always something else.
MO, *Mommy,* MO! You can see the whole striving human race in
my fourteen-month-old baby.

That's the true original sin, that's the spark that separates us
from the beasts, not opposable thumbs or reason or language or
even the ability to walk upright. But desire. Insatiable in every
way. It makes us cross continents, build airplanes and subma-
rines and trains, topple rulers and dig for oil and fall in love even
when it's doomed. Always reaching, needing. More.

I'm so tired of reaching. I'm so tired of needing.

May 1

HOME

May 1.

    May Day. *Mayday*, from French *m'aider*, *"help me."*

My hands are still shaking.

Don't want to write this down.

How?

For the past two days, Saleh didn't bring out my trash.

Today, he said, "Mar-Gar-Rat. You bring strays to this place."

I jumped up from where I was crouched next to the cat bowls. I smiled because that's what I always did when I saw Saleh.

"Landlord not like you feeding."

Mather was sleeping in his stroller. "OK," I said softly, wanting Saleh to whisper.

"Tenants not happy. Cats must go." His voice too loud.

I felt a prickling of sweat under my armpits. His face looked wrong. I dusted my jeans off, pushed my hair behind my ears. Could it have been Cat Kicker on the second floor, had she ratted me out, gone straight to the landlord to complain? Had I gotten Saleh in trouble?

"But the construction workers, they feed the cats too," I said. "Saleh, is everything OK?"

I should have strolled away right then, given a stupid little wave and said I had to get the baby to bed. Saleh was staring at my mouth. It made me brush my fingertips against my lips, wondering if I had a Mather-sized handprint of applesauce there.

"Maybe food in garage," he said.

I shrugged. No way would Cat Kicker allow cats to eat inside the garage if she was pissed off about their eating near the Dumpster, but I followed Saleh because it didn't occur to me that I shouldn't.

He stopped outside his small room. "Here," he said, pointing at the flip-flops piled up outside his door.

I tried to laugh. Was he teasing me?

"Here," he repeated louder, not liking the laugh. "People think you here to feed cats."

His English was confusing me. What was I missing? Did he really want me to put cat bowls by his door and invite random strays to mill about his shoes?

"You like man?" His voice echoed in the quiet garage.

I glanced at Mather, relieved he was still sleeping. "What man?"

He smiled but it was loose on his face. "Man who comes to you."

"Hassan? My friend?"

"No friend." He stepped in front of me, standing between me and the baby. He put his hand on his chest. "I friend."

"Wow. OK, well I ought to get Mather upstairs—"

"I friend." He was too close and the wall was behind me. Saleh reached out and grabbed my wrist. I gasped, it was so unexpected. Before I could tug free, he pulled me into his chest and pressed my back against the wall.

I smelled sweat under the baby oil.

"Saleh?" I kept my voice light. This was a joke, this was impossible, what was happening?

"Always I see love in your eyes." His face close, his breath damp on my cheek.

For a split second, I wanted to sink into him. That was the easiest thing to do, with Mather asleep; what if I felt this man's body around me, what if I let him put his mouth to mine? Would that be so terrible? Would it balance the scales between Crick and me?

"Every day I want to receive your smile," he whispered.

I couldn't do it. I didn't *want* to do it. "I'm sorry." I tried to extricate myself. "Saleh, please, I'm married." I wedged my arms between us and I felt him tighten his grip. The sweet and dank smell of him was becoming too much.

He started to drag me toward the open door of his room. I knew I had to stay out of there. I had to do whatever it took to remain here, where anyone parking a car could see us.

"No," I said, my feet starting to slip as he pulled. I looked at the baby, Mather sleeping at an odd angle, his head completely sideways, his beautiful fat cheeks and perfect lips and chest rising slowly up and down. I didn't want him to wake and see his mom in the arms of another man. No matter what they say about a child's memory, I couldn't have him see me fighting. Failing.

I lifted my knee and pressed it between Saleh's legs. "I'll scream." I thought of how I had screamed at the museum with Crick and no one had come.

Saleh's face was so close. Watching, smiling as if certain I'd come to my senses, throw my arms around his neck. I pulled my knee fast into his groin.

He managed to jump away so the full impact grazed his inner thigh. He held me at arm's length, a hand tight on each shoulder. I took a deep, relieved breath, pushed my arms into the space between us.

His face was surprised, genuinely surprised that I didn't want him. He started to squeeze my shoulders. I thought he was going to apologize, say this was a misunderstanding, when instead he pulled me toward him, held me close to his chest, and then shoved me hard.

I felt my head crack against the cement wall.

Everything went white. Then gray. Then red. Every vein behind my eyelids etched in scalding color. I couldn't breathe.

I opened my eyes and his hands still held me pinned to the wall.

I quickly looked at the stroller. Mather was OK. Mather didn't see a thing.

Then Saleh let go. I fell down, forward, landing on all fours, gasping to retrieve the air that had been knocked out of me, my head pounding, the whole world in a crooked orbit. I stood very slowly, locking my eyes on Mather's angelic sleeping face, sliding my right palm along the wall for balance, telling myself to breathe. I took the five steps to the stroller, got behind it, put both hands firmly on the handlebar, not once looking at Saleh, the fire of my face, hair in my eyes, ringing in my ears, my heart not beating as much as tornado-ing through my chest.

I turned the stroller around, walked one foot in front of the other, keeping my knees straight so they wouldn't buckle, careful, careful, did not look back, praying a car would come into the garage, fill it with headlights, but it stayed dark and quiet. Just the roll of my wheels over the box of cat food I must have dropped. It crunched beneath my wheels; I didn't stop. *Let Saleh clean it up*, I remember thinking. I got into the elevator, went into my apartment before anyone could see me, hands shaking so much, trying to stay calm, calm, calm; as soon as the door closed I completely broke down. I couldn't stop the quaking or the crying; it seemed outside of me, a physical affliction I had no control over, as violent as vomiting. Only now—what, three hours later?—has the shaking stopped. Mather sweetly quiet and watchful. Now he is patiently emptying all his wood puzzles on the floor, watching me put his little world back together again and again and again.

May 13, 2011

10:20 P.M.

There are spots on these pages of Margaret's journal. Tears, maybe.

I close the book, get up from the bed, walk around the dim room. It's as if her distress has lifted up off the page and become my own. I am finding it hard to breathe.

It's inconceivable she carried this around and never uttered a word.

Why didn't she tell me? Because we'd had a silly fight? I would have had Saleh fired by the next call to prayer. Margaret, how did you keep this to yourself? You could have packed a bag and come to me, stayed in my guest bedroom, Mather in a Pack 'n Play nestled near the couch. How could I help you if you chose to hide so much?

And, though it is terrible to even think right now with Margaret out in the night doing God knows what, I've been waiting for something like this to happen.

I warned her. *You play with the bull, you get the horns.*

Which must be why she didn't tell me.

I press my fingernails into my scalp. I wanted to hurt her. I wanted her to need me again, and only me.

May 2

HOME

It must have happened differently. He couldn't have done what I remember.

All the times I came home from trips to the embassy, park, grocery store, and I'd see him sweeping, cleaning up the forgotten bits and pieces of everyone else's lives. I'd empty Chiclets into his hand, leftover pizza, maybe a warm sandwich I'd picked up for him at the *shawarma* stand down the road. Small gestures of thanks. Was I taking steps in the direction of seduction? Nighttime trips to feed the cats—did he think the cats were an excuse to see him? Thus, cat bowls outside his door? All of it so matted and melted together. My head throbs enough to know someone hurt me, someone slammed me into a cement wall. *Slammed.* Or not? Maybe I tried to get loose, hit my own head? It's all such a blurry convoluted mess of arms and knees. How did I manage to again draw a man into something he didn't intend?

May 13, 2011

10:26 P.M.

I reread Margaret's last entry. May 2. The day the US killed Osama bin Laden.

I remember that day. We all got the text from the embassy: **Exercise Extreme Caution. Remain Highly Vigilant.**

I put my TV on right away. People were celebrating in Washington, DC, college kids holding up posters of bin Laden with a target over his face. American flags over their shoulders. Shiny exuberant faces, fists raised. Then the screen switched to Pakistan. Youths holding up posters of President Obama with a target over his face. *War Criminal USA. Beloved Sheik bin Laden RIP.* Crowds burning American flags. Anger and chanting, fists raised.

I was frightened. I swallowed my pride and called Margaret but she didn't pick up. So I sent her a text: **Osama bin Laden dead. Stay close to home.**

She sent me a text a few hours later.

Yes.

I pondered over it for so long. Yes? Yes to what? She knew bin Laden was dead? She would stay home?

Dan called me that night. "Finally!" he said. "'Merica, fuck yeah."

"I miss you. I want you home. Now." I was shocked at my gush of words, and even more amazed to realize I meant them.

"Really?" he said loudly, laughed a little awkwardly, and for a second I dreaded what he might say next. "I miss you too, Cass," he whispered, maybe surprising both of us. "Libya's going well for a civil war, we should be back soon." We were quiet, and I imagined both of us just grinning dumbly into the phone. Then he said, "You holding up? Keeping busy with Margaret?" and I stopped smiling. I considered telling him everything then, spilling all of my suspicions into my clearheaded husband's ear. Margaret's so-called Arab classes, her trip to Jerash, the jewelry, all of it seemed to be adding up to . . . what? But Crick's threat was still reverberating. I didn't want Dan to say anything to him, have Crick think I was gossiping behind Margaret's, and his, back.

"Everything is fine," I said, willing it to be.

May 4

HOME

The call to prayer woke me, the world still dark, 4:15 in the morning.

Hassan told me once that the morning prayer is called *fajr*, which has the same root as *explosion, infajar*. It starts at the first breath of morning twilight and ends with the dawn exploding light across the sky. It was beautiful, the way he explained it, lifting his palm up to demonstrate a rising sun.

The call to prayer was so lovely when we first arrived, incredible that the entire world would open with it every couple of hours. That song, haunting, echoing, felt divine, even if in a different language, different faith. I feel the urge to make the sign of the cross in reply, *Amen*. This must be like church bells in the old days, I would think. An inescapable God reminding us: *Do not forget Me, I am here.*

But now the call sounds different, less gentle, more insistent. Now the prayer says: *You do not belong; you do not understand; you fool, you fool, you terrible fool.*

PART

THREE

✳

My phone rings and finally it's a number I recognize.

"Crick? What the hell, it's been hours and hours." I quickly walk out of the bedroom and into the living room, away from Mather's door. "Crick, hello?"

No answer.

"Crick, is that you?"

"Yes."

It doesn't sound like him. There is nothing in that *yes* that carries the confidence of the man I know.

I wait, almost holding my breath.

"It must be a mistake," the voice whispers.

"I don't know what you're talking about. Crick? Have you been drinking?"

There is a long silence, then he speaks slowly, a breath between each word: "Has . . . she . . . come . . . home?"

"Margaret? No. I still haven't heard from her. Did you track her down?"

Again a long pause. "They must have gotten it wrong." Then his voice pitches wildly. "You said she was going to a police station. What are you hiding?"

I swallow and try to stay calm. "Nothing. I'm confused. Crick, please, tell me what's happening?"

I count his exhales. He takes four deep breaths before continuing. "She was in an accident."

I lean against the couch. An accident?

He continues. "It was a clusterfuck." I try to be patient as his words lurch out. I push myself up and start to pace in time with his broken words. "Mistakes were made . . . unlicensed paramedics . . . ambulance didn't know the way . . . fuck." His voice dips unintelligibly, as if the images in his head are too much. ". . . found her embassy ID . . . took hours for someone to realize and . . . the embassy just called me."

I hear what sounds like a sob and I stop.

"It's bad, Cassie."

I feel dizzy and start to sink down; it seems like this is what I have been expecting all day, maybe this is what I've been expecting for weeks, or a lifetime. All the dread and anxiety and fear crescendo in my ears for a moment and it is almost a relief to find myself sitting on the floor, this man still breathing raggedly in my ear.

"Can I go to her?" I whisper.

He makes a terrible noise in reply. I wait for him to start shouting, to say I was supposed to take care of her but look, look how I failed her. He doesn't.

"Yes," he manages to say. "You need to bring . . . passports. Diplomatic. And regular. They're in . . . drawer, by bedside table. Do you know the Medical Center, near Fifth Circle?"

"I'll find it."

"I'm driving to Rome. I'll be on the first flight to Amman."

"OK."

His breath is uneven, the phone too close to his mouth. "I'll be there as soon as I can. I don't, I can't . . . Please go, go to her now."

I'm unable to reply. I just listen to him weep on the line until he hangs up.

I return to Margaret's room, pull open the top drawer of her bedside table, and there are her passports. Fresh and crisply navy blue, just her one stamp to Jordan inside, with so many pages she means to still fill. Then I collect her big purse from the floor, check to make sure there are a few diapers and wipes, baby books, a rattle that seems too big to stopper a windpipe. I riffle through her drawers for comfortable capris and the light gray sweatshirt I know she likes, find underwear and bra, socks. I go to the edge of her bed and stare at the journal; should I bring it? I hesitate for a moment. I don't want to touch it, afraid of what it might still reveal, but I put it in her bag, back where it belongs.

I go to the kitchen and stand in the middle of the room, making a mental list:

Bottles.

It's bad, Cassie.

Snacks.

She was in an accident.

Jar of baby food.

What are you hiding?

All of it confusing. I want to be able to think straight, think in an organized manner; this is what I am good at, right? Making plans, following the rules. But my brain is chaos. I have to sit down. How much did I drink? One glass of wine, or was it two? Surely I can I drive. But where is the hospital, exactly? What do I do without a car seat for Mather? Perhaps I should take a taxi so I can hold the baby on my lap. Margaret will also need a toothbrush, hairbrush. Her dictionaries. No matter how injured she is, she'll be so happy to see Mather. I have to go to her, I have to go now. All this time I wanted to be the only one here for her, and now I am.

It's bad, Cassie.

I find a taxi in less than five minutes; Mather sleeping in my arms has helped, I am sure. In the backseat I wrap him in a blanket and manage to get a seat belt around both of us. Absolutely not legal in America. Here, I'm not so sure what is legal or not; I have seen children sitting on the laps of fathers driving, talking on cell phones, and smoking cigarettes all at the same time.

She was in an accident.

I keep telling myself it's fine. We will get to the hospital, we will talk to a doctor, everything will be all right.

The driver ignores my awkward, *How are you tonight?* I want anything but Crick's voice tolling terribly in my head, I want a stranger's small talk, but the man speaks rapidly into his cell phone. Every time we go under a street lamp, the light seems to flash on Margaret's journal poking out of the bag at my feet. So I reach carefully with my right arm, free the journal, try to read by street lamp as we go.

May 6

HOME

So many days trapped in our apartment, so many days trapped inside my head. Couldn't make sense of anything.

Until I realized.

Saleh and I are the same.

Irish, he said during that walk we took in the middle of the night, circling the apartment building. I missed all the cues. His cousin's wife, the woman who got his cousin out of the Middle East. He wanted me to do the same. Certain I'd be the one. All of it must have seemed so cruel, an offer of another life, and then snatching it away.

How could I not understand from the beginning? Crick was my Irish. Those early days, what was it, two months, three? His waning interest. My texts going unanswered; longer gaps between dates. Then he took me out one night in Carmel; I thought it'd be romantic, I wore strappy shoes and pinned my hair up, but instead of a nice dinner alone we were meeting a group of other Army officers from his school who were also preparing to work overseas. Classmates. Everyone talking about *terrorism, insurgencies, recruitment techniques*. While I silently tipped back margaritas, I watched Crick chuckle at his cell phone, angling the screen away from me. I knew he was texting a woman. When he brought me back to his apartment I was drunk but not as drunk as I pretended, reaching for his belt buckle and tugging him toward the bed, wanting to erase whoever had been sending him quippy messages.

"Wait, wait a second, hold up." He laughed into my neck, my hands doing things my hands had never done before. "Hey, Mar, you're on something?" He'd never asked this, he'd always been incredibly exact, reaching for his wallet each and every time, finding the little silver square, putting it on, never letting me do it, oh no, careful, careful Crick. He must have had too many margaritas himself. "Whoa there, filly, seriously, Margaret, you're on the pill, right?"

It was a given, the way he said it; how could I say the truth, how could I say no? He looked at me with so much trust. I was desperate, *love me, not anyone else, please.*

"Of course," I said.

I need to get out. Right now. Get away from all of them, Cassie, Crick, Saleh. Pack a bag: diapers, clothes, pacifiers, water bottles, snacks, sunblock, hats, guidebooks. Go. Get out of this apartment and away.

May 7

OUR HOTEL

❧

I'm here.

Petra.

We arrived last night and found a hotel, the Petra Moon, right outside the entrance gates. So many people, I could feel the excitement in the front lobby, snippets of French, Chinese, Russian. A woman in an embroidered caftan served us small cups of cardamom coffee and sticky dates while we waited to check in. I looked up at all those huge framed photos of Petra hanging grandly on the wall, knowing all of us in line together had been dreaming about this trip.

Mather woke me this morning. *Where are my twinkling night-lights?* he seemed to yell, standing up, clutching the rail of his strange hotel crib. We got out of the room as the sun was rising. And not five minutes into the walk he was asleep again in his baby backpack. First we walked through the Siq, along a path through a single block of stone split by violent tectonic force. I was trailing a tour group of Italian women who were filming every step of the way. And it was beautiful enough to video, how the light trickled like paint, spilling pinks and oranges and yellows down the pale sandstone. Cobblestones underfoot, all echoes and shifting light, the subterranean silence only broken by random horses and carriages that crashed past to retrieve tourists at the front gate.

Then a fissure of light, the crevice opening, abruptly giving way to the Treasury, pillars and carved figures on horseback. It felt impossible to emerge from solid stone and see rock tamed into Platonic ideals of civilization.

There were dark-haired young men everywhere, something flashy and pirate-like about them with their eyeliner and earrings; they were on horseback, or leading donkeys, mules, and camels, beckoning to me while shouting, "Air-conditioned taxi." I waved them on, not looking at them, nervous and flushed; I have no desire whatsoever to be alone with a man. But then a child guide, Ali, came up and introduced me to his mule, Marilyn. The boy—he told me he was eleven—had a scar on his cheek I wanted to touch, to heal, and when he offered me a ride I didn't hesitate, climbed up on the beast's back with Mather on my back and let him lead me in.

Ali guided us toward the eight hundred rocky and uneven steps leading steeply up to the Monastery. I had to fight not to close my eyes. Hadn't realized how steep the cliff face would be to my right, how sheer and deadly, how being perched on a mule with a baby strapped behind me would be so harrowing. Marilyn kept slipping on the shale-like rock, her hooves too big for the minuscule steps shallowly cut into the stone. Ali tried to ballast her with all of his seventy pounds, pressing against her right shoulder to keep her from the edge, which only made me worry about Ali's toppling off instead. Mather was either petrified into silence or sleeping—he didn't make a sound the entire time.

If I fell off this cliff, would I have lived enough?

Mather has so much ahead of him. A whole big world to conquer. Yes, *Mather*, for Camp Mather, but also *Mather* for *conquering army*, because I want my boy to be stronger than me.

We got to the top. Saw what seemed to be all of Jordan. Stubborn cypress clinging to dry and rocky earth. And of course the Monastery; it looks like a palace built into the mountain, an uncompleted sandcastle made by giants.

Industrious Bedouins had set up a tent to sell cold canned drinks, hot tea, instant coffee. A few women stood nearby selling jewelry. One young girl with a Yankees baseball cap over her *hijab* sat next to a piece of plywood that was covered with rocks of all sizes, all striated with color, chipped from this place. I imagined how much time they all must spend getting their goods up here, so determined. So many people reaching for more.

Now, back at our hotel, I can hear Little Man snoring from his crib. Just the two of us. We're in a new place, alone, but it's not nearly as frightening or as lonely as I thought it would be. When I was in San Jose, I was afraid to drive to the Safeway for groceries, but today my baby and I scaled an ancient civilization, and tomorrow we will do it again.

Mather and me. Maybe this is the way it always should have been.

May 13, 2011

10:55 P.M.

※

Crick didn't give me any details so I go directly to the hospital emergency room. It's dingy but recognizable as a place of medicine: the walls are green and gray, the fluorescent lighting hums, the smell of bleach doesn't entirely mask the almost sickly-sweet musk of body functions gone awry. The waiting room is empty except for a man sitting stoically with his left hand wrapped in newspaper. I notice it is dripping a slow circle of blood onto the tiled floor. I give him a wide berth and approach the reception desk.

"I'm looking for Margaret Brickshaw," I say to a man at a computer. He glances at me briefly, continues typing. The head-scarved woman next to him ignores me completely, counting out cash.

"I'm from the American embassy," I say, louder, lifting Margaret's diplomatic passport to eye level. "I was told my friend Margaret Brickshaw was in a serious car accident and has been taken here. If neither of you can help me, let me speak with a supervisor."

The man slowly rolls his chair over, takes the passport, then just as slowly rolls back to the computer and types. He glances between the screen and the passport.

"There is not this name here."

I see a large book on the table next to him; it looks like a book where patients sign in. "What about that?"

He goes to the ledger, peruses one or two pages, shaking his head, slides the passport back over to me with a shrug.

My hands itch to grab the book. "Maybe you've misspelled her name. How many people came in today after being in a car accident?"

The man's mouth pulls into a humorless grin. "Jordan is very famous," he says. "We have more than one hundred forty-five automobile accident for each day. Almost every patient automobile accident."

The woman next to him puts her tray of money back into a drawer, wipes her fingertips on her pants, *tsk-ing* him under her breath. She comes toward me, looking up into my horrified face with empathy. "Someone good English coming."

"I don't need someone with good English! Just let me see Margaret Brickshaw!" My voice is borderline hysterical. But I want Margaret to hear me from whatever room they've stuck her in, I want her to know I'm out here, loyal and true. The empathy slides off the woman's tired face and she dips her head in the direction of a security guard at the end of the hall. The guard, reading a Koran, doesn't give a damn about my theatrical voice. But the woman's look is enough. I don't want to be put out, I want to make sure they let me see Margaret. So I cling to the baby and scurry toward the seats against the wall.

I scan through Margaret's bag and find an antibacterial wipe to clean off the chairs with before putting Mather down. Then I find a board book for the baby, who is sleepily sucking his pacifier and blinking at the bright lights, looking around at the other people in the waiting room. Certainly, if they already called the embassy, the embassy must have a representative here somewhere. What happens when you are in a serious car accident and sent to a local hospital? I know so many rules but I don't know this one. Mr. Robert Riding's brief has failed me.

Margaret. Her journal is in my lap with the baby books. I open it with my free hand. Petra. I hate the very sound of it. Why did she have to go to Petra? It was the worst decision Margaret could have made. For three days she didn't answer any of my calls or texts.

And I tried, I really tried, not to worry about her that first night.

I thought she had lost her phone, dropped it on one of her meandering walks. It would have been just like her to not bother to get a new one. But the next day, while she was in Petra riding a damned mule up a cliff, I was knocking on her apartment door, getting more and more worried.

Saleh let me into the building, rode the elevator with me. He stood at the end of the hallway watching as I stepped over the limp trash bags piled up at her door.

"What are you standing around for?" I asked him. He grinned as if he didn't know what I was saying, but there was a surliness about his eyes that told me he understood every word. "How about you clean up this trash? That is your job, isn't it?" I was seething. The self-satisfaction left his face. He walked past me, grabbed the smallest bag of garbage, made a big show of hefting it, and trudging down the stairs.

After I rapped loudly for a minute or two and there was no answer, I realized I should have tried to sweet-talk Saleh into letting me into her apartment. If he didn't have a spare set of keys himself, he may have known how to get one from the landlord.

I tried calling her again, then knocked harder in case she was napping or outright ignoring me. Finally I went downstairs to see if her parking spot was empty. That's when I saw Saleh's little basement room, the door ajar. I walked up to the door, wondering if I should go inside and search for a key to Margaret's door. But that was crazy, right? To break into his apartment in order to break into Margaret's apartment?

I went outside and paced in front of her building and saw those damn cats near the Dumpster. Clearly she hadn't fed them in a while; they were mewing in their migraine-inducing way, almost as if they were saying her name, *Merow-go-ret, Merow-go-ret.*

I need to do something right now, I told myself.

For all I knew, Margaret had been abducted in retaliation for bin Laden's death. The embassy had been on high alert since the attack. Paramilitary vehicles ringed the embassy compound; military dogs were jumping and barking and sniffing at every car that entered. Or maybe she was in her apartment, had slipped on her tiled floors and hit her head, was bleeding out in the kitchen while Mather whimpered weakly with dehydration from his crib. I remembered how, maybe two months after her arrival, she'd confessed she still hadn't figured out how to radio the Marines, and then she said she may have misplaced the key to the armored door of her panic room. When I gasped and said,

"Margaret! You need to find that key immediately!" she had let out her sea lion bark of a laugh and squealed, "Don't PANIC, Cassie, HA!"

There was every reason to think she was in trouble. There certainly was.

Though, yes, perhaps I was a little upset with her.

For the cell phone that rang unanswered. For not telling me where she was, where she had been. For the invitations she never bothered to extend to me. For the promise of friendship she revoked without any explanation. For choosing someone else.

I searched through my purse and squinted at my cell phone, scrolling through my contact list, wondering who I could call, who might know what to do.

Contact: Robert Riding, Regional Security Officer, United States embassy, Amman.

This was less than one week ago. I stood right in front of her building, looking up and down the street, half expecting her Land Rover to appear so I could say, "Oh, wait, there she is, false alarm!" But there was no sign of her ambling along in her merry Margaret daze.

It took me all of five minutes.

I told Robert Riding that Margaret had been missing for twenty-four hours. I waited and heard something like an exasperated sigh. My news did not elicit the response I had hoped for.

"I'm sure it's nothing you need to worry about, Mrs. Hugo," he said. Was that *boredom* in his voice? *Annoyance?* Here I was, being a dutiful embassy spouse. Was I not reporting suspicious behavior and activities just as I had been exhorted to do?

So I continued, telling him how Margaret and Hassan had

been spending an awful lot of time together, that I'd seen Hassan in her home. "Both of them were acting strange."

Again I waited. Clearly he was a busy man. He was letting me know I was being a pain in his ass. I heard his hesitation; I could imagine the shrug of his shoulders. This is where the police detective in an American movie would say that there was nothing he could do for at least seventy-two hours. But we were in the Middle East. He was the regional security officer. We both knew his job was to be paranoid for the rest of us.

"I appreciate you bringing this to my attention," he said finally. He waited, perhaps hoping I would say, *It's nothing, I'm sure this will turn out fine*. I did not.

He continued. "Please do not share these . . . *suspicions* with anyone else. I'll do everything I can to track her down."

"Thank you," I said.

I got into my car, turned the radio up loud. I felt a momentary elation; Margaret had not listened to me but she had to listen to Robert Riding. He would do something. He would sort this out. He would speak to Hassan.

That's when I felt the first stab of regret, a tingling dread.

I shouldn't have mentioned Hassan.

May 8

HOME

I'd just put Mather down to bed when I heard Skype gurgling from our computer screen, saw the little icon CRICK.

As soon as we'd walked in the door from Petra, I'd plugged in my dead cell phone. Immediately the display read *Crick. Crick. Crick.* And *Crick* again. Seven missed calls. Maybe he wanted to wish me a happy Mother's Day, I thought. Maybe he missed me so very much he couldn't help himself. Maybe this was the key, I had to be less available in order to be appreciated, had to disappear on him more often.

I answered. His face clicked into focus; he leaned in, said, "Christ. Margaret. You OK?"

I started telling him about Petra, how *petra* is Greek for *stone*. It's Jordan's most visited tourist site but there's no P sound in Arabic! The locals can't even pronounce it!

I didn't expect him to be pleased, exactly, but I thought he wouldn't be able to stop himself from feeling the tiniest bit impressed.

"What the fuck do you mean you went to Petra? I told you not to."

"Well, I 'grew a pair' and went. And here we are home, safe and sound."

"Jesus." He looked like he was unsure about how to arrange his features. "Who went with you?" The picture grew pixelated as it fought to maintain the connection.

"Mather, of course." I was still happy.

"Why didn't you tell anyone?" His image froze but his voice still came through.

"If I told Cassie, she'd just tell you, right? I wanted to do something on my own."

He snapped back into focus. "Margaret, the United States embassy has been searching for you. Rob Riding called me yesterday. He asked if I knew anything about you and a guard."

The floor seemed to shift under my feet. "A *guard?*"

"It's all over the embassy."

"Crick, what's 'all over the embassy'? You're not making any sense."

"No one has spoken to you in three days. You didn't pick up the landline or your goddamn cell phone for *three days?*"

"Well, I'll call Mr. Riding now—"

"It's too late. Everyone already thinks you're having an inappropriate relationship."

I started to laugh. "Inappropriate relationship?" Still I didn't understand. And then I did. Someone here in the building must have seen the scuffle with Saleh, thought it was consensual. And my mind filled with the image of Crick sitting on a bed with Karen, leaning against her, taking that photo, keeping it, refusing to tell me anything. I spoke without thinking, hissing rather than screaming, not wanting the baby to wake up. "Don't you dare expect me to be capable of what you are capable of."

My husband hunched his shoulders protectively, as if I had somehow reached through the computer, over continents, to cut him.

"So that's what this is about," he said softly. "Revenge?"

I shook my head. How could we continue to misunderstand each other day after day?

He suddenly seemed deflated. Ordinary.

I said, "I would never treat you the way you've treated me."

He kept his eyes on me, but it was in that strange way you look at someone while communicating through a tiny camera set into a computer; the person you are talking to seems to look through you, beyond you, at the past, the future, all sorts of places you will never see.

"What do you know about Karen?" he asked, still hunched.

I inhaled sharply, had to scramble to speak before he changed his mind and closed back into his hard-guy shell. "I just remember meeting her at your school. But that photo, that photo says so much."

He nodded, a slow, tired shake of his head. "I don't know why I kept it. We stopped sleeping together when you and I got married. So yes, I was cheating on you while we were dating. Or I was cheating on *her* with you, since she and I met first. But she wouldn't leave her husband. And you were sweet."

I felt all sorts of things seeping out of me then: hope, trust, any future happiness. I was *sweet?* That was the basis of my husband's affection? *She wouldn't leave her husband?* I'd never been the choice, I'd been the distraction. From the woman he was really pursuing, from the woman he really loved. *She and I met first.*

He must have noticed a shift in my face. "Mar, that was in the beginning. Did you hear me? Once you and I got married, I stopped meeting her. And ever since Mather's birth, I haven't had any communication with her whatsoever."

"Thank you for telling me," I whispered. I believed him. To have and to hold, for good times and bad, from this day forward until death do us part. He had said *I do* to me and good-bye to her. It fit into Crick's idea of mirthless duty. I touched my belly, the place that had once housed our son, thinking how both our lives could have been something so completely different. I started to open my mouth, not sure what words would come but knowing they'd be the right words, finally, the truth. *I tricked you*, I wanted to say. *I'm the one who should be sorry.* But Crick spoke before I could.

"I'll answer any questions you have when I get back to Jordan. But right now you need to tell me who took you to Petra."

"What are you talking about? *I* drove to Petra. I told you I've been driving. It was just me and Mather."

Crick lifted his palms to his face, rubbed his eyes so hard it looked painful, his wedding ring glinting. So he hasn't taken his wedding ring off, all these days and nights in Italy. That's something.

He put his hands down, stared straight into the camera. "OK. Bottom line, Mar, a man lost his job." He waited, let it sink in. Then he cut me deeper that I could ever cut him. "Whether you are having sex with him or not, the entire embassy thinks you are."

I could barely breathe. How had this gone from something he *had* done with Karen to something I *had not* done with Saleh? What had I done exactly? Thought about the intensity of Saleh's green eyes when I was falling asleep at night? Been unable to escape him when I tried? Did that add up to an embassy-wide crisis? "Why would you say that?"

He put his hands down. "I checked with the Regional Security Office. They confirm a guard's been fired."

And I forgot Saleh. I even forgot Karen. I wouldn't have cared if Crick told me Karen was sitting in the bed next to him right now. "Wait. An *embassy* guard? Are you talking about *Hassan?*"

"Mar, I need you to tell me the truth here. I know you're angry at me, and you have every right to be, but you and this guy, this Hassan, are you sleeping together?"

The light from his screen was making his face look bruised and distorted. But I could tell he was concentrating. I could tell he was listening in a way he had never listened before. For a moment I felt a perverse desire to see how much I could hurt him. For a moment I wanted to say *yes.*

"No." I said. "Never. He's a friend."

Crick continued to watch me closely, or as closely as you can watch someone through a computer screen. I couldn't tell what he believed.

"I wanted to help him get a visa, that's all." My voice was high-pitched, screeching; I couldn't control it. I knew it was too loud, Mather would soon be crying, but I couldn't do anything about it. "He showed me Jerash. He's my only friend besides Cassie. He's, I don't know, a grandfather. There's nothing . . . *dirty* between us."

He nodded. He looked so utterly unlike himself. "Mar, don't do anything. Let me handle it when I get back."

"You believe me, don't you?" I scraped my fingernails across my temples. "You have to get him his job back. You can't wait. Please, please call the embassy right now."

"Yeah, I believe you. I'll figure it out." He kept talking, moving so close to his laptop I couldn't get a good look at him, but I didn't care, it was almost like he was next to me. For a moment, I thought he could save me. Crick would find a way! A couple of phone calls and Crick could clear this up, of course! But that's what I've always believed and look where it's gotten me.

Crick was saying, ". . . maybe two weeks left, then I'll be home. I'll talk to the guard's supervisor and the RSO in person. Explain. Everything will be better, everything will be good between us, I promise."

"This can't wait," I heard myself gasp wetly. I thought of Hassan. He had just two years until retirement.

Crick spoke over me, his voice soft, pleading. I'd never heard him like this, so gentle. "—could come out here. I have a decent enough hotel, you've never been to Italy, right? I'll book a flight now, you can stay a week, hell, stay and we'll all return to Jordan together, a family. I fucked up, Mar, I should have come clean about Karen. I'm sorry."

I shook my head. "I have to fix this now."

I watched him lift his hand in front of the camera, move it across the screen, trying to get my attention, to call me back to him.

"Margaret, I love you," he whispered. I looked into his face. Did he? We were an illusion, he and I. We stood in front of a priest and neither of us had come clean about anything. Liars, both of us. We'd spent two years together, created a child, and suddenly I couldn't remember his ever saying he loved me before.

"I have to go," I said, my fingers moving toward the mouse, ready to click disconnect.

"Wait!"

I didn't meet his eyes, just ended the call, his image freezing, his face held inches from my own, his dark eyes reflecting the blue of the screen before it went blank.

Hassan won't pick up.

It's late now, the way it's always late when I write, as I toss and turn and hope Crick has it all wrong.

I could drive to Hassan's house tomorrow or the next. I'll be able to find it, I think, I still have the map he drew. I felt so superior that day. *Look at me, all you expats, watch me enter the real Jordan the rest of you only shyly orbit.*

I feel sick in a way I haven't felt in a very long time, that childhood powerlessness, your small life just a series of commands you have no choice but to follow. Useless, listening to your parents fight in the next room. This must have been how my mother felt after she was diagnosed. Her body allergic to itself, the very sun an enemy, losing her autonomy, *Do this, and this,* the doctors said, while Dad receded and then I did too, nothing on her horizon but two hoarded bottles of Demerol.

Mather. I have Mather. I have to think of him. I hope he grows up completely different from me, grows up like Crick. Fearless and strong and just enough of a jerk that everything doesn't hurt so much. Things stay in my mind and I can't get them out—the boys who wait at the corner of Hashimeyeen with their newspapers and smudged faces, the old man next to them with his cane and box of Chiclets, the bony cats mewing from every street with their starved, eye-infected kittens. Hassan in his small home, sitting at his cracked plastic table, no pension because he offered me kindness. I ruin everything.

Oh, Mather, I want him to wake up—then I could at least nurse him, do something to feel like I have meaning in the world.

I pick up my cell phone, check for missed calls from Hassan. Stupid, stupid me, forgetting to pack my phone charger as I threw everything in a bag, never bothering to buy a new one in Petra, thinking, why would I need it? There was no one I wanted to call. I probably could have borrowed a charger at the hotel but I wanted the silence, I wanted to be unreachable.

I see Cassie called. Thirteen times, but only the first day I was gone. Six minutes after her final call the day before yesterday, Mr. Robert Riding called me. Cassie never called again.

May 13, 2011

11:13 P.M.

❧

"Excuse me, please, isn't there someone who can tell me the condition of Margaret Brickshaw? This is her baby. I don't understand why no one will tell me where she is or how she is doing."

The female cashier seems nervous. She looks at Mather in my arms, then at the man, who has rolled out of earshot and is flirting with a nurse.

"You are very late," she says softly. I can't understand what she means. My vision blurs.

"Are visiting hours over?"

I watch the woman stroke the material of her head scarf as if it calms her. Margaret would appreciate this, I think, the way this woman smoothes her fingers over the material like it's hair.

"This is not about correct visiting hour," she says, and I get the sense her English is too unschooled to allow her the subtlety she wants. Once more I demand to talk to someone in charge, once more she nods and makes an ineffectual phone call, speaking rapid Arabic, and then tells me five more minutes and someone will be with me, *inshallah*.

I convince myself Margaret must be sleeping, yes, they don't want to disturb her. I tell the woman I can give blood, bone marrow, a kidney, whatever it is Margaret needs, and she blinks at me, uncomprehending. Fine. I will wait. I sit back down with the baby. But my eyes are leaking, and I keep having to dab them, knowing my hands are covered in germs; hospital waiting areas are the most infectious places in all the world. Mather is watching me so I smile. I bring him over to the bin of used toys in the corner of the room, first spraying it all with Margaret's purse-sized can of Lysol.

While he is busy dumping every last broken toy on the ground, I return to Margaret's journal.

Margaret was right. When she was away in Petra, I did stop calling her. Once I handed her over to Robert Riding, I was done with her. She'd obviously put two and two together when she called me, the night she got back, around midnight.

She was sobbing.

"Did you tell?" she asked hoarsely. "Cass, was it you?"

She could have been asking about anything but I knew exactly what she meant.

"Margaret, are you OK? Is the baby all right? Where have you been?"

There was a silence so long I thought she'd hung up.

"I went to Petra," she whispered, her voice so soft, so lost. "Mather and I had to get out of here for a couple days. I should have told you."

I should have told you. Hearing her say those words didn't feel nearly as satisfying as I thought it would. "Margaret, take a breath," I said. "Why are you so upset?"

"Cass, I've come back and everything's been mangled . . . It's all my fault. I shouldn't have woken you. I'm sorry we fought. I'll call you tomorrow." And she hung up.

Petra? Just her and a toddler? *If only I had agreed to take her,* I thought as my phone went dark in my palm. If only. And I have been thinking this ever since.

I glance around the waiting room now. Mather is keeping himself busy, the man and woman at the reception desk are not looking at me, I don't know where to turn. I find my phone in my purse and I text: PLEASE, DAN, COME HOME COME HOME COME HOME

May 9
EMBASSY

I woke too early and called Hassan at 7:34 a.m. No answer.

So I went to the embassy to see Robert Riding.

At the first gate, I tried to smile. I wished Crick hadn't said anything, wished I could've driven in innocently. Instead my hands were shaking at the wheel.

The young guard with hazel eyes and acne-scarred cheeks came to the window. Today, no hellos, no smile, wouldn't even look in my face, only peered at the ID around my throat, checked that the pass on my dashboard matched the numbers on my license plate. The other guard, waving a mirror at my Land Rover's undercarriage, also didn't look at me once.

"How are you today?" I asked Hazel Eyes. He nodded curtly, stepped away from the window. An older guard I didn't recognize lifted the gate to let me through. There were two bags of sesame cookies on my passenger seat, cookies from Petra, one for Hassan, the other for the men here, but I didn't offer them. I just tried to drive in a straight line.

I waited in the RSO office, remembering slides from Robert Riding's security brief: murdered diplomat Laurence Foley draped in a white sheet, damage done when a roadside IED went off on the Dead Sea Highway, wreckage from hotel bombings in downtown Amman, all of it trying to scare me into good behavior. I'd been amused. Doodling.

"Glad to see you, Mrs. Brickshaw." He didn't look glad to see me.

I touched my face. I hadn't showered. Had I brushed my hair? Teeth? He must have thought I was deranged. I told him I needed to speak with him about Hassan Mahmoud. That I had to clear up the "rumors." I felt my face get hot, that burn igniting across my neck and cheeks.

The words started spilling out of me: "Nothing happened. I mean, we're friends. He applied for a travel visa to the United States online and, well, have you seen it? It's impossible, it's hard enough for me as a native English speaker, he needed help—"

"Please, sit. You do know you're not allowed to fill out the paperwork for a visa applicant? It puts the embassy's consular officer in a very bad position, creates a conflict of interest. It's hard to fairly adjudicate a visa if a friend or colleague is lobbying for the applicant."

I sat down, tried to inhale. Had I said something that would get Hassan in even more trouble? Mather reached for the bowl of colorful, foil-wrapped mints at the edge of Mr. Riding's desk. I pushed them away, gave him my keys to play with.

Mr. Riding looked at his watch. "Unfortunately, this has now become a situation."

He lifted the top page of a yellow legal pad on his desk,

skimmed handwritten notes, let the page drop when I leaned forward to see what he was reading.

"I understand your husband is out of town."

"Yes. He's in Italy." I shifted the baby on my lap.

"And you know my office has been trying to contact you?"

I told him about Petra. For a moment the words still felt like magic. Like saying them aloud would induce him to say, *Ah, Petra, why, it's about time you went, of course, now I understand completely.*

Instead he held my eyes.

"You traveled more than three hours outside the Amman city limits, heedless of our current political climate, with a small child; told no one, including your spouse; and couldn't be reached for nearly three days?"

I bounced the baby on my knee and said that I was an American citizen, surely I could visit a tourist site whenever I wanted to.

He stared, the moment stretching. Mather shouted as if the silence made even him uncomfortable. "Mrs. Brickshaw, the American embassy in Amman is ultimately responsible for you, and as such we emphasize not traveling alone as a woman, to always let a friend at the embassy know where you are, and at the very least to have your cell phone with you at all times. You know the road from Amman to Petra was shut down earlier this month due to protests? While Jordan is very safe—"

"It has a crime rate much lower than America's."

He smiled for the first time. It was not a nice smile. "That's true. However, there are always exceptions to the rule. In September 2005, four militants were arrested for plotting assassinations of Americans in Jordan."

"In 1995, Timothy McVeigh killed one hundred sixty-eight Americans with a bomb at the Oklahoma Federal Building." I couldn't shut myself up, no, I had to make it worse. But if I stopped talking I knew I'd start weeping. Mather screamed for the mints again and I pulled the bowl within reach, let him take one in his fat fist and start gnawing on the wrapper.

"Mrs. Brickshaw. I agree that terrorism is not just a Middle Eastern issue. But my job here in Amman is to protect American citizens in Amman. In light of security concerns, regardless of how arbitrary you may find them, we ask that you maintain a high level of vigilance. You were missing for nearly seventy-two hours."

"Hassan had nothing to do with my trip to Petra. I apologize for not telling anyone I was going there. That was a mistake, *my* mistake, and my mistake alone."

"Well, yes, I see that—"

Mather lunged at the desk and managed to knock the bowl over, mints spilling across Mr. Riding's desk and floor like colored confetti. Mather shrieked with delight.

Mr. Riding waited for silence before continuing. "We learned you have been spending a considerable amount of time with Mr. Mahmoud. Our security guards are hired by a locally contracted company with entirely different rules than those of the United States embassy. When I could not reach you, and since Mr. Mahmoud was not currently on duty, embassy protocol required I inform Mr. Mahmoud's supervisor." He brushed a mint off the typed report and paged through it. "A missing American is not something a Jordanian company takes lightly. I see the guard company called the *mukhabarat*, or state security service, who sent a team to Jerash to question Mr. Mahmoud and search his home."

I pressed my hand to my mouth, imagining this unfolding. How Hassan must have stood on the porch under his frail grapevines, amazed and embarrassed, while strangers went inside, searching for me.

Mr. Riding continued. "It seems that Mr. Mahmoud's contract has a clause prohibiting fraternization between guards and embassy employees. I am sure it is there for security purposes, and it is up to the discretion of Mr. Mahmoud's supervisor where he wants to take this next. For the time being, Mr. Mahmoud has been suspended. There is nothing my office can do."

I sat there. Tears gathered in my eyes, a thickness building at the bridge of my nose. That's when I started to beg. *"Please, please, please . . ."*

"I'm sorry, Mrs. Brickshaw, this is now between Mr. Mahmoud and his employer."

I asked to talk to this supervisor. Said he must understand that Hassan was following Arab rules of hospitality. I started to explain how the most common greeting is *welcome, ahlanwasahlan*, as if Robert Riding was the ignorant one in the room.

"If you'll forgive me, I think you should wait for Major Brickshaw's return. He might have a better chance of arguing your case. He knows the language and has spent a lot of years in the Middle East, if I'm not mistaken."

I stood. My nose was running, my entire body red and feverish. I stepped on one of the mints. I knelt to pick them up and Robert Riding hurriedly walked around his desk to help.

"Allow me, Mrs. Brickshaw." His voice was gentle, but he wouldn't look at me.

I stood, clutching Mather as he yelled and grabbed at the shiny wrappers out of reach, and I fled.

I called Hassan all night. I must stop, I look like a stalker, surely a woman scorned. But it feels like penance, touching his name on my cell phone screen, listening to the ring, ring, ring, holding my breath and hoping, beyond hope, he'll answer so he can hear me say *I'm sorry.*

May 11
HOME

The cats. I was so glad when I thought of them, when I thought of something I could do that was easy, that would make both Mather and me happy.

Little Man was shaking the Tupperware bowl of cat food in the air like a tambourine.

I pushed the stroller out of the building quickly, not wanting to see Saleh, hiding behind my big sunglasses. At the Dumpster, Mather waited for the usual mad cat stampede. No sign.

The three bowls I kept behind the Dumpster were gone. We circled the area, walked down the block one way and down the other, the whole while Mather yelling, *Cat cat cat!*

Saleh came out of our building, no broom, no garbage, his hands empty. He crossed his arms over his chest, leaned against the low concrete wall around our building, and watched.

I tried to smile in his direction, lifted my arm in an uncertain wave. We could still be normal, I thought, civil. And maybe in a few months we could go back to being friends.

Saleh didn't wave back.

"We'll try again later," I said to Mather, kneeling in front of the stroller. The baby was still shaking the food, refusing to give up. He doesn't understand *later*, only *now*. When I started to push him toward our building he began to cry, shaking the Tupperware even harder.

"Saleh?" I said, my voice oddly cheerful even to my own ears. I drew close. He was staring off to his right. I was glad the baby was loud so I could lean over to quiet him and avoid looking directly at Saleh. "Have you seen the kittens?"

"Gone."

"Gone?" I lifted my face quickly. "What do you mean?"

"Landlord not like cats. Now cats gone."

"But where did they go?"

He turned toward me and his face was filled with such hatred I almost stumbled backward. I looked at my feet, at the sidewalk, at my son's small sneakers kicking from his stroller.

"Gone," Saleh repeated. And he laughed. He stayed out front as we walked inside the building. He didn't help me open the door. He didn't push the elevator button.

Gone. Maybe the landlord called an animal shelter. I've looked up animal shelters and couldn't find any, but maybe the landlord has better connections, knows the correct word in Arabic. There's no reason to think they've been killed. Every once in a while I see a dead cat; sometimes it's bloody, clearly hit by a car, and more than once I've seen an intact animal stretched out near a Dumpster. Mather and I'd walk by, waiting for it to twitch itself back to life. Poisoned. But Saleh wouldn't do that. They say the Prophet Muhammad, peace be upon him, loved cats, had one called Muezza, and when Muezza fell asleep on his sleeve, he cut off the sleeve rather than disturb her rest by moving her. They say striped cats are her descendants, the lines of their stripe marks left behind by the Prophet's fingertips. Didn't Muhammad tell a woman who starved a cat to death she'd go to hell?

I'm sure they're fine. Maybe someone adopted them and Saleh's just being cruel, setting terrible thoughts loose in my head.

Mather's playing with the shutters. I don't like the living room anymore; I can feel the eyes of those cherubs on the ceiling. Those sad eyes staring down out of their misshapen faces. I get goose bumps, the way they watch my every move. Even with the lights out, I can feel them, hovering, waiting for me to ruin something else. We keep to my bedroom, door closed, lights off. Mather at the window, tugging the shutters down. Up and down, up and down; the room fills with varying degrees of darkness.

Now he wants to play hide-and-seek; he goes to the bed, pulls off a pillow, swats me. *Play!* he shouts, but it comes out, *Pay, Mommy, pay!* I keep telling myself, *Don't cry, don't cry, don't cry.* I pull all the blankets and pillows down, make us a nest, a shelter. He dives in headfirst, my brave and beautiful boy. He doesn't understand grief, only knows I'm here, I'm picking up his soft bath toys and waving them in front of him, squeezing dying-animal sounds out of them to make him laugh.

I'm back where I started, in the dark, and there's comfort in sliding into something you know. Mom, for weeks deciding on pain rather than pain relief, saving all those pills, two bottles full. I must have known, deep down, from the moment I met Crick, that being a part of his life would mean no longer being a part of hers.

Pay, Mommy, pay!

Pay the piper.

The unpaid piper came back with his song and took everything. One hundred thirty children gone. That's how it comes around. All those sins wait to see if you'll pay your penance, and when you don't, they strike. Punishment comes out twisted, so much harsher than the original crime, hurting the innocent more than anyone else.

I need to fix things. Of all of my wrongs, I need to finally be able to make something right.

May 13, 2011

Mather has fallen asleep on the hospital floor. I quickly pick him up, appalled, wondering if this is a sign that I'd be a terrible mother. Or maybe it's just Margaret's voice inside my head, so much self-doubt. I sit down with Mather stretched out on the seats next to me, wedging him in with Margaret's huge purse.

I have to keep reminding myself that ultimately Margaret is right, this is her fault. She disappeared. So maybe I overreacted when I saw Hassan in her living room. But she should have let me know she was going to Petra. A text, a call, an e-mail.

I didn't want to get anyone fired. I just wanted someone with more sway to have a stern talk with Margaret. I wanted her to return to me, chastened and thankful for our trips to the Palestinian glass shop, the Swefieh bakery, the Syrian man with his scarves and tablecloths.

That's all I intended.

And yet.

If only I hadn't mentioned Hassan. Then the RSO would have had to speak directly to Margaret before setting all of this into motion. Then Margaret could have cleared this up on her own. Or at least there would have been no doubt where the blame would rest. With Margaret.

Not with me.

And yet.

I keep hearing the sound of Margaret crying on the phone, those soft and strangled noises.

Mather's pacifier drops from his mouth and onto the floor. MRSA, I think, but I retrieve the pacifier and put it in my pocket, unsure if I packed another. Can I spray it with Lysol? A nurse walks by; I hear sirens draw closer. Doctors go past. A teenage boy runs inside the waiting room, straight to the man with the wounded hand, and holds up a fat envelope. The man stands, mutters angrily under his breath, walks to the cashier, and slaps his newspaper-wrapped arm on the desk for attention.

I watch the boy count money out of the envelope carefully while the man speaks loud and quickly, motioning angrily at the clock on the wall, and the woman gesticulates at him, her voice impatient. You have to pay before getting medical attention here and the man must have sent his son out for cash. I wonder how long this hospital would have let him sit here without treatment. As the boy pushes the worn bills across the desk, I can see the man trying to fish his ID out of his wallet. His blood drips on the cashier's desk. *Margaret would have helped*, I think, and I almost stand to go to him. The cashier ignores the blood, prints out a page, puts her heavy stamp on it, slides it over to the man, and motions for him to return to his seat. He takes the receipt with the fingers of his bloody hand, leaving marks on the desk I can see.

Margaret. Certainly someone is tending to her right now, taking care of her?

Mistakes were made, Crick said.

Is it possible that I woke up just this morning in my own warm bed, the sun shining, the coffee hot? That I checked my e-mails and filed my nails and, when I had done everything else I needed to do, called Margaret? Was it really less than twelve hours ago?

"Hello?" she answered, her voice faint.

"Margaret, it's me. How are you?" I spoke with more enthusiasm than I felt.

There was a pause, as if she didn't know me.

"It's Cassie. Are you OK?"

"Hi." Her voice flat.

"Do you want to do something today?" I felt shy. "I was thinking we could go to Ajloun Castle—you haven't been there yet, have you?"

"No, thanks."

I continued. "How about the pottery shop? My order is in. Didn't you want to order a few things?" I moved the phone from ear to ear, waiting.

"I don't really feel like going out today."

I should have let her stay home, I should have hung up the phone. But I didn't want to be alone either.

"C'mon, it's gorgeous," I said. No reply. So I used the Mather card; I could always guilt her into submission by using Mather. "I bet the baby would love to get out in the sun. We can get lunch to-go at that café near the pottery store, then head to a park. I'll pack a blanket."

"Fine," she said, capitulating, exactly as I knew she would. "But can I drive?"

"Sure." If allowing her to drive was the price I had to pay, so be it. I was just glad she was speaking to me, was agreeing to see me. "I'll come to you. See you in an hour." I hung up and told myself everything would be fine.

When I arrived, Margaret was waiting outside, sort of wandering aimlessly behind the Dumpster as if searching for something. She held Mather in her arms, wearing big, bug-eyed sunglasses. Her hair was pulled back in a ponytail and her face was glossy with too much sunblock, but I could see that her nose was red and rubbed raw. She wore loose jeans and the pretty turquoise cardigan over a white blouse, Hassan's wife's sweater, I know now, which I thought was an odd choice but at least, finally, finally, she was listening to me and covering her offending elbows. I parked my car, got out, and tried to greet her with a kiss near her right cheekbone, but instead she turned her face away, hitting my lip with the edge of her sunglasses. I pressed my tongue against the side of my hurt mouth and followed her into the garage.

"Any news?" I asked as nonchalantly as possible as we got Mather strapped into her Land Rover.

"About Hassan?" She stopped everything and looked at me for a long time. "You heard about the suspension?"

I nodded. It was the buzz of the embassy, this new morality tale. I had gone to the embassy post office the day before and heard someone telling a woman who was paging through six-month-old mail-order magazines: *If you disappear for three days, tell your friends or someone will get fired . . .*

"Nothing has changed." Her voice was too loud, echoing off the low ceiling. "Not yet." She seemed to check herself, glancing around the garage as if she didn't want to be overheard, and resumed in a quieter voice. "The RSO won't help. Crick won't help. But I'm not giving up. I have a plan."

"Can't Crick do something when he gets back?" She was making me anxious. Something was off; she was twitchy in her skin. I didn't want to know about this plan. There had been a time when I'd longed to hear all of Margaret's mysteries, but now I wanted the safety of her vocabulary, the workings of Mather's bowels, even tales of her mother's illness.

"This is my responsibility." We got into her car. She maneuvered the rabbit-warren backstreets that led to the main road too quickly. She said she wanted Hassan to continue tutoring her in Arabic, but now she would pay him. I nodded as I directed her, left, right, straight, nodded while I thought to myself that her outlandish plan would never work. I was relieved when we arrived at the pottery shop.

We picked up my order. It was a large box and didn't quite fit in Margaret's trunk alongside the fold-up stroller, so I put it carefully in the backseat next to Mather.

She pulled out, too fast. She was quiet for a while, peeking at me from the side of her huge sunglasses.

"I know," she said finally. "I know you were the one who told Robert Riding."

I twisted in my seat. "Margaret? What—?"

She looked back at the road, her voice matter-of-fact, none of her questioning lilts, just a hollow straightforwardness I had never heard before. "You're the only one who saw Hassan in my apartment."

There was nothing I could say. I faced forward and took a deep breath. So this was it, I thought. We would have a fight, or not, but either way I would go home to my lonely apartment.

Then she said, "I forgive you."

I turned quickly to see if this was one of her new sarcastic remarks or if she meant it the way I hoped she might. She continued to stare straight ahead into traffic; I could see nothing but her sunglasses, her coldly shining face. Her voice was quiet. "You couldn't have known this would happen. I know you're a good person, Cass. You were genuinely worried about me."

I tried to think of something to say. I lifted my hand, wanting to put it over hers, wanting to prove I was her friend, that I would be a better friend in the future; I wanted to confess, I wanted her to know. But she was slowing at that yellow light at the intersection of Horreyya and Hashimeyeen, and a man was waving. Her flower man. I dropped my arm back into my lap. She had seen him, was already rolling down her window. And then, while Margaret was choosing from his wilted wares, we were hit.

The rocking heave of the car. The astonishment as we looked at each other and realized we were OK.

Margaret spun in her seat, checking on Mather, who had begun to yell. Her sunglasses had fallen off and she blinked nakedly, her eyes so swollen and pink it looked like she had violently ripped out all of her eyelashes. She turned toward the flower man, who was now at the median, three of his bouquets scattered on the asphalt at his feet.

"I'm calling Post One," I shouted, grabbing both my cell phone and camera from my purse.

Summoned by my call, the roaming patrol of embassy guards arrived within minutes. I climbed into the backseat and tried to keep the baby busy, shoving fruit snacks into his gaping mouth. One of the guards leaned into Margaret's window and told her she needed to wait for the police to ascertain who was at fault.

"*Fault?*" she asked.

"Man claim you stop at yellow light and reverse." The guard rubbed his forehead.

Margaret yelped, a poor imitation of her laugh, looking at me incredulously.

"He's lying," I chimed in. "Margaret was buying flowers, for goodness' sake."

The guard looked from me to Margaret to Mather. I wondered if he'd heard about Hassan's suspension. "Please stay in car," he said. Margaret leaned forward but he lifted his right hand palm upturned, pressed all five fingertips together, and said to her, "Shway, shway." *Wait*.

We glanced at each other helplessly, watching a local Jordanian police officer drive up on a motorcycle. We waited as the officer shook hands with the US embassy guards, and then the angry young man, and finally the flower man. He did not come over and shake Margaret's hand.

Finally the embassy guard returned. "The officer had decided you are the fault. You must go to the police station and fill out the paperwork."

Margaret hit the steering wheel with her fists.

The guard lifted his eyebrows. "Madam? Would you like to follow?"

"I'm not going to any police station!" Before my astonished eyes, Margaret began to fight with him, her voice rising, explaining she knew what she was doing and for once she was in no way at fault for *anything*.

The guard listened. When she paused to take an indignant breath, he said, "In these situations, it is usually the woman. There is your word, and the word of your passenger"—he nodded at me—"against the word of the man from the other car, and his witness."

"Witness?" Margaret said, looking back at the men.

"The man who is selling the fruit and the plants."

"My *flower man?*" Margaret gasped. She glanced at the damp white blossoms strewn across her dashboard and quickly gathered them up. Then she handed the haphazard mess to the guard, who held them away from his body, confused.

"Will you let us lead you to police station?" he asked.

Margaret refused to answer, refused to even look at him. She pushed her sunglasses up her nose, turned the car back on, and pulled out into traffic, the guard standing there with flowers dangling from one hand, his other lifted as if he was about to give her directions.

"Can I leave Mather with you?" she asked me. "I don't know how long this will take."

"Of course," I said, looking over my shoulders at the surprised guard before settling back into my seat. I almost smiled. It was so good to be needed again, to be the one who knew what to do. "Margaret, it's OK," I said. I thought to myself that this might be exactly what she needed to get her mind off the Hassan debacle. "This happens to everyone. You haven't really lived in Jordan until you've been in a car accident. And they always blame the American. The foreigner. Always."

Her mouth trembled into an ugly thing.

She kept her eyes ahead, her foot on the gas pedal, but a sob escaped her, a low, wet gasp, and from the way she clutched the steering wheel, I knew she was trying to keep her hands from shaking. I sat up straighter. It was as if I could see the pretty little bridges she had built, all those things she thought would connect her to the people of Jordan, the smiles and *salaam alaikums*, the Chiclets, the dinars handed over to widows weeping outside of mosques, all of it falling away.

I struggled to explain the Jordanian saying *My brother before my cousin, my cousin before my tribe, my tribe before my country, my country before any other.* But she shook her head as if she didn't want to listen, and no matter how I tried to reason with her I could see the damage had been done. Something frail inside of Margaret had begun to fracture.

What I didn't know is that something inside of Margaret had been fracturing all along.

Then we were back in her apartment. She left me in the kitchen and shut herself up in her dim room. I can only assume she nursed her baby and when he had fallen asleep, she managed to scribble out her final entry:

May 13
I MUST FIND HIM.
I MUST MAKE IT RIGHT.

Maybe Mather knocked her journal behind the bedside table, or perhaps Margaret herself knocked over all the records of her life here, wanting them out of her sight. She was not going to go to any police station. After everything that had happened, she still would not listen. Margaret had her own plan.

May 13, 2011

11:55 P.M.

The receptionist in the *hijab* hangs up the hospital phone and waves me over. "The woman from US embassy here. She talk."

I glance over my shoulder and see a woman in a tailored pant-suit emerging from the elevator. With a jolt, I recognize her. It's Deborah-rhymes-with-Gomorrah. The Cat Kicker. She nods at me. She's clutching a folder to her chest, her ruddy skin pale.

"It's Cassandra Hugo, right?" she said, offering me her hand. "We've met before. I'm Deborah Morgan, consular officer acting for American Citizen Services." She assesses me for a moment, nodding her head to herself as if I've somehow met her expectations, perhaps because I seem calm. "I really appreciate you coming out in the middle of the night." She glances at Mather but doesn't like the sight of him; her brown eyes quickly center back on my face. "We need to move on this as quickly as possible, and Major Brickshaw won't be here for at least another eight hours."

I nod, ready.

She opens up the file in her hand and continues. "Under Islamic law, we only have seventy-two hours to prepare the body—"

"Body?" It suddenly feels as if all the air conditioners have been turned on in the room; my skin is cold, my ears fill with white noise.

"Yes, we realize you're not the next of kin, but in her husband's absence, we need to get started."

She looks at me, perhaps noticing how the blood, and all understanding, is draining out of my face. I don't even get a chance to take a breath before she blinks and says, "Oh, no, I assumed you knew?"

I cover my face with my hands and count to ten, hoping I'll lift my head and find out that I'm still in my bed, that today hasn't even begun.

But today is already over.

"I'm so sorry!" she gasps. "I must have misunderstood Major Brickshaw, I mean, sit down, please, take a breath!"

"Are you sure?" I whisper, sliding awkwardly into the seat behind me.

She hesitates. "Do you have Mrs. Brickshaw's passport?"

I reach into Margaret's large bag, drawing the navy booklets from one of the interior pockets.

Deborah sits next to me and I find myself pulling back from touching any part of her. She examines the passports, glancing up at me as she looks at the photo in Margaret's, then slides them into her file. She squints into her cell phone and then puts it in her lap facedown. "I know this must be very difficult for you. Do you think you are capable of identifying an image on my phone? Let me know when you are ready, and, please, take your time."

I move my head, halfway between yes and no, and she hands me her cell phone.

"Please tell me if this is Margaret Brickshaw."

Someone is whimpering; I don't know if Mather has woken up and is making this noise or if I am.

In my mind, I see a sudden hundred images. Margaret in the sandbox with Mather as he pours a cup of sand over her head, Margaret reaching for the spinach in my teeth, Margaret lifting her glass of Chardonnay high into the light, Margaret floating in the Dead Sea, Margaret pressing her lips closed in an attempt to contain a wild burst of laughter.

The screen of the cell phone shows someone I do not know, someone broken and flimsy and gone, but somehow still Margaret, undeniably Margaret.

I nod my head *yes*.

Epilogue

So much hope, and so much failure. A year that seemed on the verge of freedom and greatness, devolving into so much crisis, displacement, blood. So much meddling that led to more death.

"Didn't you know that woman who died?" people still ask. "Didn't you know Margaret Brickshaw?" They have heard the rumors, the accusations; everyone at the embassy has. All these months that have passed, all these new people who arrive at the embassy, fresh from America, eager to learn this new place, and somehow they find me, ask me, as if this is the penance I will be doing for the rest of my life. "What happened?" over and over again.

I don't tell them that whenever I close my eyes, I see that final photo.

It was taken from Margaret's shoulders up, hair pushed back from her face, her eyes closed, her mouth slightly open as if she was inhaling gently in her sleep. But there was also blood, not great quantities, but blood, ruby ripe and fresh, pricks of it along her bared shoulders and the slender arc of her throat, at the side of her mouth and splintering through her bottom lip, bloody highlights stippled through her fair hair. I also remember the glass, uneven, yet oddly geometric, uncut diamonds, glinting everywhere. The glass made me think of the day at the Turkish baths, how she had been stretched out on a table then too, and naked, how her skin had been mottled and glistening, beaded with sweat and oil. Now I find the two images have become blurred and confused in my mind. Margaret beaten, exhausted, but retaining a fierce beauty.

Deborah stayed with me in the Medical Center and let me hold her phone until the screen went blank, and then she brought the image of Margaret up again and let me look at it some more. This was a kindness. I know the clock was ticking, there were things to be done, paperwork to be signed, but she sat on that cold hospital seat while I made choking noises deep in my throat, and she told me everything she knew about Margaret's final day.

At three o'clock the embassy guards left the scene of what was our minor accident at the intersection of Hashimeyeen and Horreyya. They waited for Margaret at the police station for more than an hour. Finally they shrugged, assumed Margaret was too upset to face the police—it was, after all, a man's work—so they called the embassy to report that the guilt fee had not been paid and they went back to their posts.

Meanwhile, Margaret was trying to pay a different sort of guilt fee.

Margaret had gone to Jerash.

She went to Hassan's little house.

Hassan opened his door. He had once told her, *You are like daughter to me*, but he must have felt fear at seeing Margaret on his doorstep. Didn't she know Jordan's state security service had come a few days ago and questioned him? It wasn't Margaret's fault, of course, that he had invited her to visit him before, but a small part of him must have wished she had never seen the Roman ruins, never sat down to eat with his family, never left behind that wallet-sized photo of her and her son. Hassan had put the photo in the middle of his small table to remember to give it to Margaret the next time he saw her, and that's where one of the inspectors found it, writing down ominous words in his small notepad.

Margaret, standing on his porch, had been oddly energetic, effusive even, talking too much, too quickly, claiming she needed to tell Hassan about a *plan*, a *terrific plan*. Couldn't Hassan be her Arabic tutor, full-time? Couldn't he come to her home every afternoon while Mather slept and fill her days with Modern Standard, or even better, Jordanian dialect and Levantine? She wanted to begin tomorrow! Yes, the sooner the better! She'd pay whatever salary he needed. And if that didn't work, she'd come to Jerash for lessons! Maybe Hassan's sister-in-law, Karida, could watch her baby. Didn't Hassan say Karida was good with children? Meanwhile Hassan could look for another job if he liked. She'd work around his schedule. Wouldn't that fix everything? Please?

She was talking too fast. Hassan tried to be friendly, but the only job he wanted was the one he had been suspended from at the Unites States embassy.

Margaret would have recognized that, despite his attempt at a smile, despite the way he nodded as if considering her offer,

Hassan was not in the least bit happy to see her. Margaret would have seen his anxiety and it would have frightened her, for this was the one face she had expected to understand.

Hassan looked around. This time he did not invite Margaret inside. He did not offer her tea. He did motion for her to sit on the white plastic chair beneath his grapevines. Margaret sat stiffly and Hassan pulled up a plastic chair next to her, but not too close. He wanted his neighbors to see the distance between them.

The more she tried to convince him of her plan, of his tutoring, the more uncomfortable Hassan grew, looking everywhere but at Margaret. He kept asking about Mather, about Crick, as if needing to remind Margaret of her role as wife and mother. *Um-Mather*, Mother of Mather, he called her gently, insistently. It was clear tutoring was not going to work out. And suddenly it dawned on her. It was over. The more she tried to mend things, the more they splintered apart. So she stood, reached to shake his hand. But Hassan hesitated, uncertain if he should let his neighbors see him touch her. Margaret was desperate for contact and she reached for his palm, tried to press it.

Hassan pulled his hand away.

With that, she turned and ran for her car. Hassan called out to stop her. He watched her drive away, a burst of gas pedal and brake. He wished he had offered her tea.

No one knows exactly what happened next. How could we? How could anyone really be sure of anything hidden in the mind of another? Hidden even in ourselves?

Witnesses at the scene say Margaret's Land Rover did not slow as it entered the traffic circle, not at all, and that there was a water truck coming around, too fast, from the northern side.

One witness claims Margaret seemed to accelerate toward this truck. Perhaps her foot slipped off the brake pedal. Perhaps she caught a glimpse of Hadrian's Arch and became distracted. Perhaps she remembered when I told her "Might is right," when I was wrong, so very wrong. Her Land Rover and the water truck collided. Margaret was not wearing a seat belt, which is common enough among local Jordanians. Nor did her airbag deploy. She was sent out the window, her long blond hair sparking with shattered glass.

Crick arrived in Amman the following day, at nearly three in the afternoon. He knocked on his own door and I opened it slowly, unsure of what he had heard, what he knew. There stood a rank slab of man, circles under his eyes, stubble on his face, stains on his clothing, nothing like the man I had known before. His thick hair had been cut very short, as if he had shaved his head in the hotel room with a razor, leaving just a shadow over his skull, a coating of ash, like fingerprints. He didn't say a word, looking at me with eyes that seemed nearly blind with rage, as if he had convinced himself the embassy had it wrong, that he would come home and find his wife holding his child. She would lift a cool, pale palm to his cheekbone and tell him all was well. The sight of me must have immediately told him the truth, my own eyes swollen and sore, and he came at me fast, as if I was the one who has done this, all of it, and he tore Mather out of my arms as if my touch was toxic.

He turned away, pressing his stubble into Mather's tender head and letting loose a wounded noise, as if something was ripping inside. Mather began to cry; he grabbed my sweater and held on. No baby had ever done that before, no child had ever preferred me to anyone else. But Crick refused to let him go.

"Let me, let me," I kept saying, but Crick clung to the baby until Mather gave up, gasping, and put his head on Crick's shoulder in utter exhaustion, finally releasing me. "Please let me help," I said, knowing it was too late now for me to help anyone.

When Crick stopped his awful noise, his body still shuddering, I could hear him hiccupping as he held his child.

I thought of Margaret, how she had loved that innocent sound. Crick needed to know all the ways she loved him.

"I'll get my things from the bedroom," I whispered. The baby's blue eyes, his mother's eyes, watched me as I walked down the hall and into Margaret's room. I found her dictionary where I had left it under her lamp and slipped it into my bag. Then I placed her journal in the center of the bed where Crick couldn't miss it. Where he couldn't do anything but pick it up and read and finally know everything.

Crick and Mather left Jordan within a week of Margaret's death. "Compassionate reassignment," they call it in the Army. I offered to help him pack but he didn't return my calls or e-mails, and Dan told me to "let it slide." Major Creighton Brickshaw is now a professor of military science in Georgetown's ROTC program. Shorter hours, a manageable schedule, a good position for a single father juggling a toddler in daycare. "PMS" is the acronym, which I can't imagine sitting well with Crick, but surely he is a changed man.

I have been back to Margaret's apartment building. I went looking for Saleh, to confront him, around the time Crick left.

Instead I found Deborah parking her car in the garage. She invited me to coffee. We now share the experience of Margaret's death, this unspeakable, indelible moment. Out of that horrible night, we've fashioned a friendship. She has no husband, no children, and she makes me grateful to have Dan.

Deborah says that Saleh is gone. A few days after Margaret's accident, she saw him in the hallway, his prettiness marred by a swelling around his left eye, a purplish tinge of bruise, a split lip. She never saw him again. The landlord hired a Pakistani man as *boab*, an older man who wears a gray *dishdasha* and a long beard, who keeps his entire family, a fully covered wife and three children, in that same small basement room.

Who bruised Saleh? Perhaps he had a dispute with the men at the construction site. Perhaps they too realized he got rid of the cats they all loved. And yes, it could have been Crick. Reading Margaret's journal, unstrung and desperate, tying up the ends of her unfinished life.

I don't need to know. It is enough that Saleh's cruelty came back to him, the way Margaret understood it always does. The way it will someday come back to all of us. The way it will someday come back to me.

I think of this, and I try to make amends.

What happened? people ask, as if there is one moment that can be studied, examined, interpreted.

I tell them what I can. I carry Margaret's dictionary with me, finally understanding her compulsion to pin down the meaning of a word. Life so rarely has discernible, exact meanings.

Fault, from the Middle English *faute*, for "*lack, failing,*" from the Old French, based on the Latin for "*deceive.*"

I admit that, yes, I called Robert Riding. I try not to make any excuses. I am working toward honesty. In the meantime, I have been carrying around my own Ziploc bag of cat food; I have been buying Chiclets, polyester socks, cheap hats, matches made in China that sizzle more than light. I even buy flowers from Margaret's flower man.

I'm sorry, I'm sorry, I'm sorry.

Words I never got to say to her. Words I will be thinking for the rest of my life.

Dan was waiting for me the same day Crick returned home from Italy. I walked into our apartment, smelling the hospital in my clothes, smelling death and every fetid thing I should have done differently, and saw him. He had come when I asked. He was there. "Of course," he whispered, catching me in his arms. "I couldn't let you deal with this alone." I told him everything: he listened, he believed. I told him about Margaret. And I told him I felt like he was blaming me for not having a baby, that I was afraid he had stopped loving me a long time ago. Perhaps I was wrong about Dan too. He accepted everything, he accepted me, the way he always has, though somehow I didn't see it.

And now we are packing, Dan and I. We are leaving. Dan's new assignment is at the Pentagon, and we have already researched fertility specialists, made appointments, are preparing ourselves for the next step. We do not know what the future will bring but we are willing to keep trying, together.

Dan keeps in touch with Crick. We'll soon be nearby, all of us living in Virginia, and my anticipation for seeing Mather balances out my dread of seeing Crick. I'll tell him the truth too, fill in the gaps of Margaret's story that he has not yet figured out. Maybe I can help soothe, or at least share, the guilt he must be carrying. Whatever Crick thinks of me, he must know I tried to be Margaret's friend, and that has value. I hope it's enough to allow me to spend time with his son.

When Mather is older, there is so much I plan to tell him. Most important, he needs to know that Hassan Mahmoud returned to his post. Crick always did do the right thing. He promised Margaret he would try to get him his job back and he did just that. Margaret was never sure, but I think Crick really loved her, in his flawed way.

As we pack, Dan and I are putting aside a box for Mather. There are the photos I took of Margaret. And of course there are Mather's left-behind toys, including the dinosaur. There is also a piece of pottery. It was inside the box Margaret and I picked up, in the backseat of Margaret's car. My name and address were written on it, and when Margaret's car and personal items were released, nearly five months after the accident, the box came back to me.

Everything inside was smashed into bits no larger than my thumb nail; you could hear it just picking the box up, the chime of broken things. I didn't want to touch it; I asked Dan to get it out of our apartment. He is the one who opened it, who carefully sifted through the shards, inspected the pierced bubble wrap, the shredded newspaper. He is the one who found something whole. This one perfect cup. Dan cleaned it off, checked for chips and cracks, but there were none. It made me think of Mather. It made me want to tell him that when everything else seemed ruined, his mother always kept him in her mind. Always. No matter how muddled she may have been that last day, how upset and irrational, he was her one shining hope.

It was everyone else who let her down.

There's only kindness, she said when I was teasing her for what

I thought was one of her trivial, useless acts. I had no idea what she was talking about.

But Margaret understood more than I ever thought she did. *Kindness*, a derivation of *kin*, Old English *cynn*, for *"one's relatives,"* or *cynde*, for *"natural."* She treated everyone as kin. She knew the line I drew between *us* and *them* might be crossed after all.

I had always assumed kindness was too fleeting, too weak and insubstantial to make a lasting difference, but, again, maybe I've been wrong.

It is not something I am good at, but from now on I will try Margaret's brand of kindness. I will see if acts so small can actually be enough. It is so easily destroyed, kindness, but isn't that what all of us are looking for, every moment of our sad and sorry lives?

It might have been the one thing that could have saved her.

ACKNOWLEDGMENTS

To KC, for continuing to bring me to places that inspire.

To Mom and Dad, Tierney and George, for always welcoming me home.

Many thanks to Helen Richard for patiently wresting a story out of an avalanche. To Lorin Rees for the good-hearted but repeated nudges that spurred a rewrite again and again and again. To Jenny Moore, Emily Jeanne Miller, and Oliver Boler for being honest readers of those many drafts.

To Ivan Held, who had faith, and all the incredible women at Putnam whose Blue Fairy editorial magic somehow takes a Pinocchio of ink and paper and makes it a real boy.

To Jordan and her people, who showed my family and I such beauty and generosity, thank you. To my readers, please go to Petra and Jerash, and if some kind soul comes out from his home, pulls a fig from a tree in his garden, and splits it open with his thumbs, eat it. It will be the most amazing fruit you have ever tasted.